PRAISE FOR ERIN KNIGHTLEY'S SEALED WITH A KISS SERIES

Flirting With Fortune

"A wonderful story of two real people . . . a fun summer read." —Romance Reader Girl

"An emotional and refreshingly original Regency tale." —*Kirkus Reviews*

"Charming, sensitive, and compassionate, this tale is Knightley at her best." —*RT Book Reviews*

A Taste for Scandal

"Very sweet and heartening. . . . The characters are likable and well written; the plot is delightful and . . . sigh worthy." —Smexy Books

"As satisfyingly sweet as one of the heroine's cakes, Knightley's delightful and charming romance is both tender and adorable." —*RT Book Reviews*

"With endearing characters, eloquent writing, and a spoonful of charm, you've got the perfect recipe for a perfect read!" —Under the Covers

continued . . .

More Than a Stranger

Also by Erin Knightley

More Than a Stranger
A Taste for Scandal
Flirting with Fortune
Miss Mistletoe (Penguin digital Special)

ERIN KNIGHTLEY

The Baron Next Door

A PRELUDE TO A KISS NOVEL

A SIGNET ECLIPSE BOOK

SIGNET ECLIPSE
Published by the Penguin Group
Penguin Group (USA) LLC, 375 Hudson Street,
New York, New York 10014

USA | Canada | UK | Ireland | Australia | New Zealand | India | South Africa | China
penguin.com
A Penguin Random House Company

First published by Signet Eclipse, an imprint of New American Library,
a division of Penguin Group (USA) LLC

First Printing, June 2014

Copyright © Erin Rieber, 2014

SIGNET ECLIPSE and logo are trademarks of Penguin Group (USA) LLC.

ISBN 978-0-451-46678-5

Printed in the United States of America
10　9　8　7　6　5　4　3　2　1

For my brother, Andy McLeroy, whose natural musical talent never ceases to amaze me. It's not every day a guy can say he was the inspiration for a heroine ;)

And for Kirk, even though you have terrible taste in music. Lucky for me, you're perfect in nearly every other way.

Acknowledgments

It's remarkable to me that four writers can gather around an ordinary kitchen table, makeup-less and uncoiffed, fueled by little more than coffee, chocolate, and exceptionally good cheese, and somehow manage to craft the bones of several great books in one epically awesome weekend. A big thank-you to Heather Snow, Anna Lee Huber, and Hanna Martine for helping me to plot not only this book, but the whole of the Prelude to a Kiss series. Your talent and wisdom are appreciated more than you can know.

Also, thank you to Catherine Gayle and Olivia Kelly for coming to my aid whenever I ask ... or beg, depending on how desperate I am!

As always, I am eternally grateful to my editor, Kerry Donovan, whose insights and guidance help to make my books the best they can be. Shout-out to Deidre Knight and the Knight Agency for their continued awesomeness.

This book is the first in a new series, Prelude to a Kiss, which all began when (spoiler alert for *A Taste for Scandal!*) Charity released Richard from their unofficial betrothal so that he could be free to marry Jane. Charity's character stuck with me—and readers, too, apparently!—and I knew she had to have her own happily ever after. Music is a huge part of who she is and, for the first time ever, I listened to songs while writing scenes. For a peek at the pieces that inspired me, head over to erinknightley.com and click on "Extras." Not surprisingly, you'll find each song was composed by my brother, Andy. For more of his music, check out his Web site at www.lineandlandscape.com.

Chapter One

Hell and damnation. Was he to have no peace at all? Hugh Danby, the new and exceedingly reluctant Baron Cadgwith, pressed the heels of his hands into his eye sockets, pushing back against the fresh pounding the godforsaken noise next door had reawakened.

"Go to Bath," his sister-in-law had said. "It's practically deserted in the summer. Think of the peace and quiet you'll have."

Bloody hogwash. This torture was about as far from peace as one could get. Not that he blamed Felicity; clearly the news of the first annual Summer Serenade in Somerset festival hadn't made it to their tiny little corner of England when she offered her seemingly useful suggestion. Still, he'd love to get his hands on the person who thought it was a good idea to organize the damn thing.

He tugged the pillow from the empty spot beside him and crammed it over his head, trying to muffle the jaunty pianoforte music filtering through the shared wall of his bedchamber. The notes were high and fast, like a foal prancing in a springtime meadow. Or, more aptly, a foal prancing on his eardrums.

There was no hope for it. There would be no more sleep for him now.

Tossing aside the useless pillow, he rolled to his side, bracing himself for the wave of nausea that always greeted him on mornings like this. *Ah, there it is.* He gritted his teeth until it passed, then dragged himself up into a sitting position and glanced about the room.

The curtains were closed tight, but the late-morning sunlight still forced its way around the edges, causing a white-hot seam that managed to burn straight through his retinas. He squinted and looked away, focusing instead on the dark burgundy-and-brown Aubusson rug on the floor. His clothes were still scattered in a trail leading to the bed, and several empty glasses lined his nightstand.

Ah, thank God—not *all* were empty.

He reached for the one still holding a good finger of liquid and brought it to his nose. *Brandy.* With a shrug, he drained the glass, squeezing his eyes against the burn.

Still the music, if one could call it that, continued. Must the blasted pianoforte player have such a love affair with the brain-cracking high notes? Though he'd yet to meet the neighbors who occupied the adjoining townhouse, he knew without question the musician was a female. No self-respecting male would have the time, inclination, or enthusiasm to play such musical drivel.

Setting the tumbler back down on the nightstand, he scrubbed both hands over his face, willing the alcohol to deaden the pounding in his brain. The notes grew louder and faster, rising to a crescendo that could surely be heard all the way back at his home in Cadgwith, some two hundred miles away.

And then . . . *blessed silence.*

He closed his eyes and breathed out a long breath. The hush settled over him like a balm, quieting the ache and lowering his blood pressure. Thank God. He'd rather walk barefoot through glass than—

The music roared back to life, pounding the nails back into his skull with the relentlessness of waves hitting the beach at high tide. *Damn it all to hell.* Grimacing, he tossed aside the counterpane and came to his feet, ignoring the violent protest of his head. Reaching for his clothes, he yanked them on with enough force to rip the seams, had they been of any lesser quality.

It was bloody well time he met his neighbors.

Freedom in D Minor.

Charity Effington grinned at the words she had scrawled at the top of the rumpled foolscap, above the torrent of hastily drawn notes that danced up and down the static five-lined staff.

The title could not be more perfect.

Sighing with contentment, she set down her pencil on the burled oak surface of her pianoforte and stretched. Whenever she had days like this, when the music seemed to pour from her soul like water from a upturned pitcher, her shoulders and back inevitably paid the price.

She unfurled her fingers, reaching toward the unlit chandelier that hung above her. The room was almost too warm, with sunlight pouring through the sheers that covered the wide windows facing the private gardens behind the house, but she didn't mind. She'd much rather be here in the stifling heat than up north with her parents and their stifling expectations.

And Grandmama couldn't have chosen a more perfect townhouse to rent. With soaring ceilings, airy rooms, and generous windows lining both the front and back—not to mention the gorgeous pianoforte she now sat at—it was a wonderful little musical retreat.

Exactly what Charity needed after the awfulness of the past Season.

Dropping her hands to the keys once more, she closed her eyes and purged all thoughts of that particular topic from her mind. It was never good for creativity to focus on stressful topics. Exhaling, she stretched her fingers over the cool ivory keys, finding her way by touch.

Bliss. The pianoforte was perfectly tuned, the notes floating through the air like wisps of steam curling from the Baths. Light and airy, the music reflected the joy filling her every pore. Here she had freedom.

Free from her mother and her relentless matchmaking. Free from the gossip that seemed to follow her like a fog. Free from all the strict rules every young lady must abide by during the Season.

The notes rose higher as her right hand swept up the scale, tapping the keys with the quickness of a flitting hummingbird. Her left hand provided counterbalance with low, smooth notes that anchored the song.

A sudden noise from the doorway startled her from her trance, abruptly stopping the flow of music and engulfing the room in an echoing silence. Jeffers, Grandmama's ancient butler, stood in the doorway, his stooped shoulders oddly rigid.

"I do beg your pardon, Miss Effington. Lady Effington requests your presence in the drawing room."

Now? Just when she was truly finding her stride? But Charity wasn't about to make the woman wait—not after she had singlehandedly saved Charity from a summer of tedium in Durham with her disgruntled parents. "Thank you, Jeffers," she said, coming to her feet.

She headed down the stairs, humming the beginning of her new creation. Her steps were in time with the music in her mind, which had her moving light and fast on her feet. The townhouse was medium sized, with more than enough room for the two of them and the handful of servants Grandmama had brought, so it took her only a minute to reach the spacious drawing room from the music room.

Breezing through the doorway with a ready smile on her face, Charity came up short when the person before her was most definitely *not* her four-foot-eleven, silver-haired grandmother.

Mercy!

She only just managed to contain her squeak of surprise at the sight of the tall, lanky man standing in the middle of the room, his dark, rumpled clothes in stark contrast to the cheery, soft blues and golds of the immaculate drawing room. She swallowed, working to keep her expression passive as her mind raced to figure out who on earth the man was.

Charity had never seen him before—of that she was absolutely sure. It would be impossible to forget the distinctive scars crisscrossing his left temple and disappearing into his dark blond hair. One of the puckered white lines cut through his eyebrow, dividing it neatly in half before ending perilously close to one of his vividly green— and terribly bloodshot—eyes.

He was watching her unflinchingly, accepting her inspection. Or perhaps he was simply indifferent to it. It was . . . disconcerting.

"There you are," Grandmama said, snapping Charity's attention away from the stranger. Sitting primly at her usual spot on the overstuffed sofa centered in the room, her grandmother offered Charity a soft smile. "Charity, Lord Cadgwith has kindly come over to introduce himself. He is to be our neighbor for the summer."

Kindly? Charity couldn't help her raised eyebrow. The

man had come over without invitation or introduction, and Grandmama had actually allowed it?

Correctly interpreting Charity's reaction, the older woman chuckled, clasping her hands over the black fabric of her skirts. "Yes, I realize we are not strictly adhering to the rules, but it is summer, is it not? Exceptions can be made, especially when the good baron overheard your playing and so wished to meet the musician." Her gray eyes sparkled as she smiled at their guest.

It was all Charity could do not to gape at the woman. Yes, no one was more proud of Charity's playing than her grandmother, but this was beyond the pale. Good gracious, if Mama and Papa knew how much Grandmama's formerly strict nature had been changed by her extended illness, they never would have allowed Charity to accompany her to Bath without them.

The baron bowed, the movement crisp despite his slightly disheveled appearance. "A pleasure to make your acquaintance, Miss Effington," he said, his voice low and a little raspy, like the low register of a flute.

Despite the perfectly proper greeting, something about him seemed a little untamed. Must be the scars, the origin of which she couldn't help but wonder about. War wounds? Carriage accident? A duel? Setting aside her curiosity, she arranged her lips in a polite smile. "And you as well, Lord Cadgwith. Are you here for the festival?"

"Please don't mumble my dear," Grandmama cut in, her whispered reprimand loud and clear. Charity cringed— the older woman insisted that her hearing was fine, and that any problem in understanding lay in the enunciation of those around her.

"Yes, ma'am," she responded in elevated, carefully pronounced tones. "Lord Cadgwith, are you here for the festival?" Heat stole up her cheeks, despite her effort to keep the blush at bay. She had never liked standing out—when away from her pianoforte, of course—and practically shouting in the presence of their neighbor was beyond awkward. One would think she'd have come to terms with the easy blushes her ginger hair and pale, freckled skin lent itself to, but no. Knowing her cheeks were warming only made her blush that much more violently.

It certainly didn't help that the man was by far the most attractive male to ever stand in her drawing room, scars or no. She swallowed against the unexpected rush of butterflies that flitted through her.

For his part, Lord Cadgwith did not look amused. "No, actually. I had no knowledge of the event until my arrival." He made the effort to speak in a way that Grandmama would hear, his dark, deep voice carrying easily through the room. A man used to being heard, she'd guess. A military man, perhaps?

"Well, what a happy surprise it must have been when you arrived," her grandmother said, smiling easily. "Charity is planning to sign up for the Musicale series later this afternoon. There are a limited number of slots, but I have no doubt our Charity will earn a place."

And . . . more blushing. Charity gritted her teeth as she smiled demurely at her grandmother. Music was the one thing for which Charity had no need for false modesty, but sharing her plans with the virtual stranger standing in their drawing room felt oddly invasive. "I'm sure Lord Cadgwith isn't interested in my playing, Grandmama."

"On the contrary," he said, his voice rough but carrying. "It is, after all, your music that prompted me to visit in the first place."

Her mouth fell open in a little "Oh" of surprise before

she got her wits about her and snapped it shut. Still, pleasure, warm and fizzy, poured through her. Her music had called this incredibly handsome man to her? Not her looks (such as they were), not her father's station, not curiosity from the gossip. No, he had sought her out because her playing touched him. Pride mingled with the pleasure, bringing an irrepressible grin to her lips.

Grandmama beamed, her shrewd gaze flitting back and forth between them. "Well, I do hope you'll stay for tea, my lord."

His smile was oddly sharp. "Unfortunately, I must be off. I just wanted to introduce myself after being serenaded this morning. Lady Effington, thank you for your indulgence of my whim."

She nodded regally, pleasure clear in the pink tinge of the normally papery white skin of her cheeks. He turned to face Charity, his green eyes meeting hers levelly. "Miss Effington," he said, lowering his voice to a much more intimate tone as he bent his head in acknowledgment. "Do please have a care for your captive audience in the adjoining townhouses, and keep the infernal racket to a minimum."

Lost as she was in the vivid dark green of his eyes, it took a moment before his words sank in. She blinked several times in quick succession, trying to make sense of his gentle tone and bitingly rude words. He couldn't possibly have just said . . . "I beg your pardon?"

"Pardon granted. Good day, Miss Effington."

And just like that, the baron turned on his heel and strode from the room. It was then that she caught the fleeting hint of spirits, faint but unmistakable, in his wake. A few seconds later, the sound of the front door opening and closing reached her burning ears. *Of all the insufferable, boorish, rude—*

"My goodness, but he was a delightful young man." Grandmama's sweet voice broke through Charity's fury, just before she was about to explode. The older woman looked so happy, so utterly pleased with the encounter, that Charity forced herself to bite her tongue. It wouldn't do to upset her—not after she was only just now recovering from her illness. The currish baron wasn't worth the strife it would cause.

Forcing a brittle smile to her lips, she nodded. "Mmhmm. And you know what? I think I'll go play an *extra*enthusiastic composition just for him."

With that, she marched from the room, directly back to her pianoforte bench. The baron could have been pleasant. He could have kindly asked her to play more quietly, or perhaps less frequently. But, no, he had chosen to go about it in the most uncivilized, humiliating way possible. It was his decision to throw down the gauntlet as though they were enemies instead of neighbors.

She plopped down on her bench with a complete lack of elegance and paused only long enough to lace her hands together and stretch out her muscles. Then she spread her fingers out over the keys and smiled.

This, Lord Cadgwith, means war.

Chapter Two

"**I**'m so sorry I'm late!"

It was perhaps the third time she'd said as much, but still Charity felt awful. When she'd declared war on Lord Cadgwith, she certainly hadn't anticipated that *she* would be the one to suffer the first loss. Now she had made both herself and her friend, Sophie Wembley, late to register for the festival recitals.

Charity was *never* late—punctual to a fault, in fact— but the one time she happened to get swept away in what she was doing and lose track of time, of course it would be before something important.

Sophie rolled her eyes and shot her an exasperated smile. "For the last time, it's all right. I'm always the one who's late to these sorts of things, so it's certainly nothing unusual. Oh, look," she exclaimed, gesturing to the island in the center of the Circus. "Flowers planted to look like music notes! How very clever."

There were so many carriages clogging the street, Charity caught only a few quick glimpses as they hurried along the pavement, but it was indeed beautiful. Each note was several feet long, and a dozen or so decorated the grass with brilliant pops of reds, yellows, and blues.

"Yes, lovely," Charity agreed, checking both ways before dashing across Bennett Street.

They ducked beneath the banner several workers were struggling to raise, and wended their way through the crowd. Street vendors dotted the pavement, their carts overflowing with flowers, fruits, roasting nuts, and bottles of Bath's famous waters.

"If I'd have known the pavement would be as crowded as the streets, I might have suggested the carriage," Charity said between pants. The sun beat down on them, wilting Sophie's dark curls and causing sweat to form on Charity's lower back.

"Nonsense—it's an adventure," Sophie insisted. Her brown eyes sparkled beneath the brim of her straw bonnet. "Just look at all there is to see. And think: We could be passing a famous opera singer or acclaimed composer as we speak. Well, if they decided to arrive early, and assuming they'd be out and about in this heat, and, well, I don't suppose they'd need to register for the Tuesday Musicale series with us amateurs—that's what the Monday, Thursday, and Saturday schedules are for. But still, they could be here."

Charity laughed despite herself. Sophie did have a way with words. They were close enough now that they could see the sprawling limestone building housing the Assembly Rooms. Dozens of people milled about outside, and heaven knew how many were inside. What time was it, anyway? They'd had less than ten minutes when they'd left Sophie's townhome, and it seemed to take forever to navigate their way through the clogged streets. She bit her lip; she just knew they weren't going to make it.

This was all *his* fault, of course. If she hadn't been so agitated from the baron's visit, she wouldn't have thrown herself so thoroughly into her music, and she wouldn't have lost track of time. After all, one must be fully committed to the passion of the moment if one is to annoy one's beastly neighbor to the fullest.

Sophie adjusted her hold on her sheet music and oboe case, slowing her pace a bit. "Look at all those people! Oh, I hope they don't turn us away."

Anxiety pingèd Charity's stomach. "Oh, please don't even say it. This is the first thing I've had to look forward to in months."

Sophie tossed a wry smile Charity's way. "You, too? I must say, this summer promises to be *so* much better than the Season."

Charity nodded emphatically. God willing, no one in Bath would be watching her over raised fans, whispering to yet another gossip lover. *Oh, look,* Charity imagined them saying, *there goes that Effington girl. The one who lost that earl to a common baker!* She clenched her jaw. They would never understand that Charity had gladly stepped away from the betrothal, and that she was delighted for Richard and his new wife. All they saw was scandal and the irresistible opportunity to bring Charity down a notch or two.

She firmly pushed back against the uncomfortable feelings that thought evoked. Sophie was right: This summer was Charity's chance to start anew, to find her own happiness, and she intended to do just that.

They ducked through the open doors of the entrance and hurried down the wide corridor leading to the Great Octagon, where the registration was to be held. Judging by the noise, a great many people had turned out to partake of the opportunity, and as they stepped into the room itself, Charity could see that that was exactly the case. The room was packed, with men and women seeming to fill every available nook and cranny. The conversation hovered at a low buzz as people indulged in the opportunity to speak with other music lovers.

"May I help you?"

Charity and Sophie turned to the harried voice of a man dressed all in brown and sitting behind a small table to their right. Sweat beaded at his temples as he peered at them above the gold rims of his spectacles. If he was meant to welcome them, he was miscast in the role; he looked as though he would rather be just about anywhere on earth other than in that room.

Sophie smiled brightly, apparently less intimidated by the situation. "I'm Miss Sophie Wembley, and this is Miss Charity Effington. We are here to register for the recital."

The man raised an eyebrow first at Sophie and then at Charity. "Is that so? Pity you didn't come sooner. After all, if you wished to register, you should have arrived on time."

For the second time that day, Charity was struck speechless by a man's insolent comment. Who did he think he was, speaking to them like that? Beside her, Sophie gaped at him, her normally cheery brown eyes round with astonishment. Rallying, she said, "Yes, of course. And we did try, Mr. . . . ?"

"Green," he answered flatly.

Sophie's smile took on a determined quality as she clasped her hands in front of her. "We did try, Mr. Green, but there was just so much traffic, as though the whole city was out, and the moment we arrived we rushed right here, even though it was *most* unladylike." As always, her words came out in a flurry, as though she were determined to say everything on her mind without being interrupted.

The man pressed his lips into a thin line before shaking his head. "I understand there was congestion." He leaned forward a few inches, as if about to impart a secret, and Charity and Sophie naturally followed suit. "Astonishing, isn't it, that all these people still managed to make it here on time? It's almost as though they anticipated the possibility of traffic and planned accordingly."

What a horrible, self-satisfied lout! Charity's blood roared through her veins as a retort came to her lips, but, as usual, she couldn't bring herself to say the cutting words that lay heavy on her tongue. Her heart pounded with both embarrassment and anger, but twenty years of a gentlewoman's raising could not be overthrown so easily.

As she stood there, stiff and miserable, she could *feel* every eye in the room boring into them. Her cheeks flared as hot as coals, making her humiliation complete.

Swallowing the useless words, she leveled pleading eyes on the man. "Please, sir, there must be something that can be done. We're both great music lovers and quite accomplished." She linked arms with Sophie in a show of solidarity. "It would mean the world to us if you could forgive our tardiness and allow us to register."

The man was completely unmoved, his colorless eyes showing remarkably little emotion—unless apathy was an emotion. "Believe it or not, this entire room is filled with music lovers. *Punctual* music lovers. Now, I would appreciate it if the two of you would refrain from making a scene and leave. Perhaps next year you will have more respect for the honor of participating."

Sophie looked absolutely stricken, her normally rosy cheeks fading to nearly white. "You're asking us to *leave*? Just like that? It is not as though we are a pair of beggars from the street. Surely there is someone else we can talk to. I *must* not miss this opportunity."

She actually looked close to tears. Charity knew *ex-*

actly how she felt. This was the opportunity she had been waiting for—to be a part of the musical community, not just the novelty entertainment after an evening dinner. But thanks to two completely unrelated men with a penchant for ruining her day, she was going to miss out. A rock settled in the pit of her stomach. *Why* had she allowed herself to get so carried away in retaliation against the baron?

He smiled placatingly, like a long-suffering uncle addressing a wayward child. "Have no fear, ladies. You can still participate."

Charity tilted her head, ready to grasp at any opportunity the man would extend to them, though still wary of his abrupt change in position. "We can?"

"Certainly. After all, an audience member is *almost* as important as the musician."

Sophie's expression mirrored Charity's emotions, going from hope to heartbreak in the space of a second. They exchanged glances, but it was clear there was nothing that either one of them could say to change the man's mind.

They started to turn, to leave this place and put as much distance between them and this humiliating experience as possible, but a stunning blond woman suddenly stood from her chair. "Wait," she said, her voice firm and authoritative in a way that Charity's would never be. She pinned her vivid blue eyes on the wretched man. "This is absolutely absurd. There is no reason you cannot accommodate these two."

Charity's jaw dropped right there in front of the whole room. Her cheeks flamed with the knowledge that everyone's attention was riveted on them, but she couldn't have looked away from the woman for anything. Beside her, Sophie's gasp of astonishment had yet to be followed by an exhale. It was just so . . . *bold*. So incredibly forward and just not *done*.

Their champion stood taller than most women, with a statuesque figure wrapped in the finest fabric Charity had ever seen. The lush, rich shimmer of the pink silk was enhanced by incredible gold embroidery that highlighted her enviable décolleté and adorned the entire hem of her dress. She looked as though she had just stepped from the most perfect of portraits or perhaps given life to one of the ancient Greek goddess statues.

Charity wasn't the only one struck mute. The clerk blinked rapidly, clearly unsettled by the challenge. His throat bobbed as he swallowed—the only noise in the suddenly silent hall. "Er, I, that is—" He paused as his fingers rustled nervously across the papers in front of him. Drawing a deep breath, he lifted his chin and said, "I'm sorry to say I cannot. Rules are rules. There are a limited number of openings, after all."

The woman stepped closer to him, and the sweat that had glistened from the man's temples a few minutes earlier now slipped freely down his face. She tilted her head, allowing disapproval to emit from her entire being. "And yet you seemed to have no problem allowing me to register when I myself was late. Is there some reason why you would not extend the same courtesy to these young women?"

The collective whoosh of a hundred heads turning to gauge the man's reaction was almost comical. His eyes, magnified behind his spectacles, made him look remarkably like a trapped rodent. "A mistake—a misjudgment I am determined not to repeat, Miss Bradford."

Sophie's fingers found Charity's arm and squeezed tight. Charity was too flabbergasted to move, but she did exchange wide-eyed glances with her friend. She was at once appalled and impressed; horrified to be the center of such a confrontation and delighted to have a front-row seat.

Lifting one gracefully arched brow, Miss Bradford said, "Let us not be melodramatic, Mr. Green. In a sea of musicians, there is surely room for two more."

At the "melodramatic" comment, Mr. Green's eyes narrowed and he gave his papers a sharp shuffle. "Certainly. If you wish to relinquish your spot, then I will happily pass it along to one of these newly arrived young ladies."

Charity's hopes sagged; the mulish flare of his nostrils was back. She bit her lip, wishing she could somehow gracefully extract herself from the scene. She hated the feeling of standing out in the crowd. The sole exception was when she was at her pianoforte, and that was precisely because everything around her simply disappeared.

Miss Bradford's hands went to her hips. "I should do just that. I was under the impression this was a program for the love of music, not petty rules and punctuality."

No—surely she wouldn't toss away her chances to make a point. Charity's hand stole up to squeeze Sophie's. It wasn't right. They couldn't let the poor girl suffer simply because she had stood up for them. But with the weight of everyone's stares boring into her chest, she couldn't bring herself to say anything.

Mr. Green snatched up his quill and held it threateningly over his ledger. "Very well. Which of you would like to take Miss Bradford's place?" He glared up at them expectantly, somehow taunting the woman without even looking at her.

"No, no, no," Sophie said, tugging her hand from Charity's arm and depositing it on her waist. "We'll not take this kind woman's place."

Charity swallowed and nodded. "Certainly we cannot. Not," she hastily added, cutting her gaze to Miss Bradford, "that we don't appreciate the gesture. But it is our own fault that we didn't arrive when we should have, and I won't have you suffering for our mistake." Cheeks flaming, Charity forced herself to stand tall.

Shaking her head, Miss Bradford showed no signs of giving up the fight. "Well, I will *not* take a spot that I haven't earned by the *rules*. And I don't believe I need to be involved with an organization that has so little heart." She stalked over and picked up a small stack of papers from her chair.

With her stomach in the vicinity of her knees, Charity drew in an unsteady breath. "Please don't leave. We could never forgive ourselves if you lose your opportunity because of us. We'll leave and you stay."

A small smile teased the corner of Miss Bradford's lips. "After taking a stand on the matter? Absolutely not. Besides, I am not so very attached to the idea. And, provided *he* shan't be there, I shall happily cheer you from the audience."

She took two grand steps toward the door, her head held high, before Sophie sprang forward to stop her. "I have an idea!" she said, her face suddenly alight. She whipped her head back to look at the clerk. "Mr. Green, you may indeed leave Miss Bradford's name right where it is. But do please add Miss Effington and me to her slot."

The man tilted his head like a confused spaniel. "I don't follow, Miss Wembley. Adding your names to the slot solves nothing."

Sophie smiled broadly before turning her attention first to Charity and then to Miss Bradford, mischief lifting her brow. "Of course it does, kind sir. How else is a trio to perform if not together?"

*   *   *

God, but he was a jackass.

Not that this was a new revelation; it was half the reason Hugh was here in the first place, really. But it was something he could see with uncomfortable clarity now that the fog of pain and exhaustion had lifted somewhat.

Sighing, Hugh pulled his shirt over his head and tucked the tails into his breeches. The fine lawn soaked up the remaining moisture from his skin as he pulled a comb through his still-damp hair. There—he was halfway human again.

As much as he disliked soaking in hot, murky water with a bunch of gouty septuagenarians, he had to admit that the Baths actually seemed to help. His body seemed looser, his mind somewhat clear. He tossed down the comb and regarded his clear-eyed reflection in the wall-mounted mirror of his private dressing room. Perhaps Felicity was right about the healing properties of the mineral-laced spring. And if what she said was true, then he fully intended to stay put for the next couple of weeks, at least—no matter how obnoxious the festival was. Or his neighbors, for that matter.

Which brought him back to being an ass.

Yes, the girl had prodded him beyond reason, but, to be fair, she had no idea of his condition this morning. Of course, to be fair to *him*, no neighbor should have to endure music of such volume and verve. God, the world would be a lot better off if debutantes were taught to be more than empty-headed twits focused on naught but ribbons, embroidery, and the damned pianoforte. Sure, they could be very pretty, with their auburn hair and blue-gray eyes, but the moment they opened their mouths or put fingers to keys, it was nothing but noise.

And noise had no place in his life right now. Not since

hitting the blood-soaked battlefield headfirst, when his mount was shot from beneath him four years earlier. The scars were ugly, but the chronic head and neck pain was far worse.

He bent to retrieve his waistcoat, and shrugged into it with quite a bit more ease than when he had shed the thing an hour earlier. It was amazing what an hour's soak in the healing waters could do for his neck. More than all the quackery he'd endured from the past four years combined. Pity he couldn't submerge for an hour or so and do his head the same service. Damn need to breathe.

After tying his cravat in a simple but serviceable knot—a skill any officer was able to do in a pinch—he exited the room and headed for home. Traffic was utterly ridiculous, and there were just as many people walking as were on the road. The place would be a bloody circus in no time. He avoided making eye contact with any of the dozens of people he passed on the pavement.

Once in his townhouse, he shrugged out of his jacket, dragged his shirtsleeve across his forehead to wipe away the fine sheen of sweat that had formed during his walk, and made his way to the study. Pulling out a fresh sheet of foolscap, he penned a quick note to the landlord, informing him of Hugh's intention to visit at the man's earliest convenience. God willing, Mr. Sanburne would have another property that Hugh could transfer to.

As he dashed some sand over the letter, his batman, Jacobson, appeared in the doorway, a bemused expression lifting the unscarred side of his face. "Do I even want to know what happened this morning?"

Hugh raised an eyebrow before shaking his head. "Probably not. I'm back to my normal delightful self now, however."

Jacobson approached the desk, his hands clasped behind his back as he shook his head. His willowy, slender frame was a far cry from the hardened soldier's physique he'd had while serving by Hugh's side in the army, but his posture was as straight and proud as ever. "As delightful as a summer peach, I'm sure," he said with a wry twist of his lips. "However, within minutes of your hasty departure this morning, I found myself enjoying the redoubled efforts of the pianoforte-playing lady next door. For *an hour*," he emphasized, his brow creasing above the black strap of his eye patch. "What the bloody hell did you say to the girl?"

Clearly not enough if she had taken it upon herself to torture his staff in his absence. Apparently, *cease and desist* meant "play all the more aggressively" to the chit. "What do you think? She might as well have moved the damn thing into my bedchambers, for all the noise abatement the walls provide. I told her to cease the racket."

Amusement flickered in Jacobson's eye. "Is that so? Imagine her defying such an order. After all, I'm certain you asked so nicely."

"Jacobson?"

"My lord?"

"Shut the hell up."

Just as he anticipated, his batman chuckled at the mildly spoken reprimand. "As you wish. What time would you like to change for the dinner with Lady Cadgwith's cousin?"

Hugh's spirits collapsed in a heap. *Damnation*. He had forgotten all about the promised evening with his sister-in-law's family. It was to be a quiet evening to welcome him to the area, now that he was settled. He would have turned down the invitation, but he knew it meant a lot to Felicity that he be friendly with them, and he had no doubt that her family was eager to hear all about the baby. He sighed, raking a hand through his hair. "Make it nine o'clock."

Jacobson offered a crisp nod before turning to leave.

"One more thing," Hugh said, stopping him in his tracks. He quickly folded and sealed the missive before holding it out. "Please see that this makes it to Mr. San-burne's office before it closes."

Accepting the note, the batman lifted his brow in question. "The estate agent?"

"The very one. If I've any luck at all, the man will have another house we can move to. Preferably as far away from this location as possible."

The good side of Jacobson's face lifted in a grin. "Very good, my lord."

Chapter Three

"I'm sorry. You play *what* instrument?"

Charity felt just as shocked as Sophie looked when she blurted the question to Miss Bradford. Thankfully, they were far from any prying eyes or ears, walking on a wooded footpath along the River Avon, just a few blocks from the Assembly Rooms.

Or at least they *had* been walking. Miss Bradford's answer to Charity's simple question of what instrument she played had caused an abrupt stop to their little victory promenade.

Miss Bradford took a few steps back to where they stood, her expression an odd mix of apologetic cringe and wry humor. "Perhaps I should have mentioned that *before* we made our grand exit?"

"Yes, perhaps," Sophie said. One dark eyebrow was raised as she delivered the quip, but her tone was lighthearted enough to elicit a smile of relief from Miss Bradford. "What the devil is a goo . . . chin, anyway? It sounds terribly exotic. Well, *terribly* as in 'exceedingly,' not 'terribly bad,' of course."

"Guzheng," she corrected, her blue eyes twinkling with amusement. "It is a Chinese zither. And I am still getting used to the fact that it is an unusual instrument to you English."

"'*You* English'?" Charity repeated, reassessing the fair, thoroughly English-rose-looking girl. She spoke the King's proper English, looked as though she had stepped out of one of Sir Frederick Tate's masterpieces, and was summering in Bath, for goodness' sake. "I must say, you are not very convincing as a foreigner."

"Would it help if I told you my Christian name is Mei-li?"

Sophie's jaw dropped open. "No! How extraordinary. My goodness, you must be the single most interesting person I have ever met. And we shall have the single most unique trio in all of England. Let us hope that what Mama has always said is correct."

"About?" Charity prompted, still stuck on the fact that this blonde before her clearly had more to her than met the eye.

"The more unique the instrument, the more memorable the musician." Sophie said the words as though reciting from a long-memorized book. "It is how I came to play the oboe, and my older sister the bassoon. My younger sisters play the recorder and the viola. You know, because the flute and violin are so dreadfully overrated." She rolled her eyes dramatically.

"The viola? But . . ." Charity trailed off, not wanting to offend Sophie by pointing out that the instrument, considerably larger than the violin, was much better suited to men.

But Sophie seemed to know exactly what she had been thinking. "Yes, I know. Pippa is quite stout, I'm afraid. Mama is convinced the large size of the viola will make her look more delicate.

"Ah, I see." It wasn't entirely flawed thinking, really.

Still, the poor girl. Charity did not envy her when she debuted in a few years. Deciding to change the subject, Charity turned her attention back to Miss Bradford. "Well, now that we are to be the most notorious trio ever to have lived, I find I must know how it is you came to be here in the first place with us English folk."

"The usual, I'm sure. Father works for the East India Company, daughter is raised in various places in the East before mother contracts exotic illness and dies. Father overreacts and sends furious daughter to live with stuffy aunt in a faraway land that she is suddenly supposed to call home. Aunt is intent on 'improving' her heathen niece and thus proceeds to make her life miserable. Luckily for niece, music is her one escape, so her new home becomes slightly less horrid." She shrugged with a breezy sort of negligence. "I'm certain you've heard the story before."

Charity couldn't help but be impressed with the plainness of her answer. She didn't seem to have even a moment's pause in revealing such details of her private life. It was rather liberating to think someone could be so frank. "And you almost relinquished your place for us?"

"Music is my passion, with or without an audience. My aunt has been nagging me to show some interest in the city, so this was my attempt. It turned out better than I could have hoped, thanks to you two." She paused, sliding a smile to Sophie. "Although I feel I must point out, you, Miss Wembley, are mad. Quite, quite mad."

Charity grinned at the joking comment. Sophie's solution had been completely inspired, but brazen and presumptuous as well. The three of them exchanged collusive glances before bursting out with laughter. The sound echoed gaily through the woods.

"Oh, Miss Bradford, you don't know the half of it," Sophie replied, winking good-naturedly. "I shall warn you now that you may not wish to befriend me, as I do tend to get myself in trouble. Mama claims my mouth always moves faster than my brain."

Brushing aside a low-hanging branch, Miss Bradford grinned. "I must say, despite the fact I have known you both for all of an hour, I think you have earned the right to call me May. And fear not: My father raised me to always align myself with the outspoken, for their thoughts are rarely hidden. It's the quiet ones that one must worry about."

"Hold on," Charity said, putting her hands to her hips. "Are you saying I am not to be trusted?"

May lifted a shoulder. "It does rather make you suspect. I recommend tossing aside any introversion while in our little trio."

It was such fun to tease with these women—it felt like honest friendship. While Charity was growing up, her father had disapproved of her mingling with those beneath their family's status. A rather inconvenient stance when he outranked everyone in a thirty-mile radius. She counted the Moore family as friends, but after ending the betrothal with Richard last year, it had felt a bit awkward to visit his sisters. They were wonderful, of course, but the broken engagement always felt like an invisible curtain between them and Charity.

She smiled easily at her new friend and nodded. "Very well. I hereby promise to chatter like a magpie when it is just the three of us."

"I'm not altogether certain it would be a good idea to have *two* magpies in the group," Sophie said, her tone wry. "Heaven knows no one would get a word in edgewise."

"Excellent point," Charity conceded. "A sparrow, then. And, May, what shall you be?"

"Why, a malkoha, of course."

"A mal-what?"

"My mother used to call me her little malkoha because my eyes are so blue." A flash of sadness passed over her features, but she quickly rallied. "They're funny little birds in the East Indies with bright chestnut breasts and blue-green wings. Mama simply overlooked the fact that the males were the ones with the blue eyes." She paused, tilting her head. "What?"

Charity exchanged glances with Sophie. "It's just so very . . . *foreign*. I thought I was quite adventurous to have traveled from Durham to Bath."

A delighted smile brightened May's entire face. "Oh, there is just so much to see beyond the borders of this soggy little island. I've spent almost my entire life in the warmth of the tropics. Brightly colored birds, lush tropical landscapes, and the heavy scent of spices define my idea of home. Being here in Bath is such a culture shock, I hardly know what to do with myself."

Sophie just shook her head. "I can't imagine how different it must be. I mean, what on earth does one do in the East Indies? Other than play the zither, of course. Are there as many dangerous animals there as I've read? And are the natives really as scantily dressed as I heard? Not that I blame them, if the rumors of the intensity of the sun there are to be believed."

If Charity had known Sophie was this outrageous, she would have made a better effort to befriend her during the Season. Charity never had the nerve to say such things, which made being around people who did that much more fun. Chuckling, she said, "Perhaps we should start with one question."

"One question is not nearly enough. Do please tell us *everything*, my dear."

May laughed with delight, clearly making no effort to temper her enthusiasm. "As you wish. But first I have one question for you."

Sophie cocked her head, allowing dappled sunlight to kiss her cheeks. "Yes?"

"What on earth will we play for the recital?"

An excellent question. Charity had almost forgotten their whole reason for being together. She didn't even attempt to search her brain for a composition tailored for a pianoforte, oboe, and zither trio; she was positive such a thing didn't exist. And for good reason. An odder pairing, she couldn't imagine.

She closed her eyes, heedless of what the others would think of her, and listened for the music that came to her when she was quiet. It had always been her gift. She composed because the music wanted her to write it, not because she wished to capture it. It couldn't be created, only heard—recognized and recorded as it came to her.

As she listened, soft strains teased the back of her mind, but nothing distinct enough to capture. It was like trying to look at a dim star. Sometimes one had to focus on something else before it would come clearly into view.

"I think Charity may have given up on us," Sophie teased in a stage whisper. "But I have no doubt something brilliant will come to us—or, rather, *her*. She's quite a marvelous composer."

Charity's eyes popped open. "You know?" Her compositions were little known to others. Mama believed it very ill-bred for her to think herself better than the masters. It was so frustrating because it had nothing to do with her feelings toward the masters, and everything to do with giving voice to the music inside her. So for years,

Charity pretended to play from the music books her mother supplied her, all the while playing her own creations. Fortunately for her, Mama couldn't read music, and Charity sprinkled in just enough of the boring songs to avoid suspicion.

Sophie put a hand to her hip. "Yes, of course. I'm a musician, after all. I may not play as masterfully as you, but I am exceedingly well educated in the art. I daresay I could recognize your pieces no matter who was performing them—you have a very developed personality, musically speaking."

"I think," May said, grinning broadly, "that I am very lucky to have fallen in with you two prodigies. I just know we shall come up with something inspired."

Charity wasn't nearly so confident. The thought of having the committee laugh at them was daunting indeed. Her music was the one thing for which she could always count on a positive response. She pursed her lips, weighing the need to do well with the desire to embrace the chance to truly befriend these women. "I certainly hope so."

"Just you wait," May said, her voice entirely confident. "We shall be absolutely brilliant. If for no other reason than to prove that dreadful clerk wrong for ever trying to repress the pair of you."

Charity straightened her spine, drawing on the strength of the women beside her. She was done with people trying to repress her. Be it the gossips, her parents, the clerk, or the awful Baron Cadgwith, this was her summer and she would *not* be talked down to.

She pursed her lips, once again distracted by the man that would be her neighbor for the next few months. He clearly thought himself above her. Men like that were little more than bullies. She looked at the other two women, with their confident smiles and clear ability to attract trouble. They would be the perfect allies this summer.

"Right you are, May," she said with a decisive nod. "And I'd be more than happy to offer up my house as a place to practice."

Promptly at ten, Hugh stood outside one of nearly two dozen identical white doors that dotted the curving row of homes on Lansdown Crescent. Surely he had the wrong address. He double-checked the brass numbers glinting in the flickering lamplight. It was definitely the address provided.

He glanced again to the brightly lit second-story windows, where the sounds of conversation and music could clearly be heard, and muttered a curse. Damn it all—this was no intimate gathering. Felicity's cousins had specifically assured him that it would be a small dinner with a handful of their close friends. Judging by the noise, there were likely twenty or more present.

He reached a hand up to massage the growing stiffness of his left shoulder, tilting his head away in order to stretch the tight muscles bunching at his neck. The familiar build of tension had him closing his eyes and exhaling deeply. The night air was unusually warm and humid, and he suddenly wished he could yank off his bloody cravat and the restrictive wool coat that Jacobson had insisted he wear.

This was ridiculous. He didn't need to subject himself to the pointless frivolity of a party he had not agreed to with people he didn't know or care about, all because his sister-in-law thought it would do him good to socialize.

Turning abruptly on his heel, he started toward the street when a carriage came to a stop just in front of him.

He stepped back several paces as the tiger quickly disembarked and pulled open the door. A rustle of fabric, a feminine murmur, and then one delicate silk and pearl slipper found the step outside the carriage door. A glimpse of a white stocking, and then billowing pale pink skirts were adjusted to obscure the wearer's trim ankle. He lifted a brow. *Very nice.*

The lady emerged into the lamplight, her face averted as she kept her gaze on the ground. She bent to clear the doorway, allowing him the perfect view of the tops of her breasts above her lace-trimmed bodice. *Very nice, indeed.* He may not be in the mood, but he sure as hell wasn't dead.

Once on the ground, she released the servant's hand, smoothed her skirts a moment, and finally raised her head. In an instant, all thoughts of appreciation for the woman's form evaporated to dust.

Bloody hell, he knew that face. Even in the golden light of the lamp, he could see the freckles dotting the bridge of her nose and the tops of her cheeks. Her hair was arranged in a waterfall of curls, mostly secured at the crown of her head before cascading down over one slender shoulder and resting against the pale skin at the hollow of her collarbone. In this light, it looked much darker than it had in the daylight, but the hint of red was unmistakable. Almost immediately, she seemed to sense his presence and her gaze flitted to where he stood a few paces back. Her eyes narrowed and her mouth thinned as all pleasure leached from her face.

"You." The word was curse on her lips.

He couldn't have put it better himself.

Chapter Four

And here Charity thought all the trials of this day were behind her.

The baron lifted his scarred eyebrow in condescension. "Very good, Miss Effington. Proper use of pronouns is always to be admired."

Saints above, but the man was insufferable! She cast about for a scathing rejoinder, something to wipe the superior expression from his smug, handsome face, but of course no words would come. As frustration billowed in her chest like a building storm cloud, she crossed her arms protectively and glared at him. "What are you doing here?"

"I don't see how that's any business of yours, but, as it happens, I was just leaving." He gave a mocking little bow, then turned, preparing to depart before she ever even formulated a proper retort. *Blast it all!*

"Lord Cadgwith! What a lovely surprise." Grandmama's booming voice startled them both, making Charity jump and stopping the baron where he stood. She had completely forgotten her grandmother was alighting behind her, thanks to the unwelcome distraction.

Blowing out a breath, Lord Cadgwith visibly worked to

turn his lips up into something vaguely resembling a smile as he faced the older woman. "Lady Effington, how nice to see you." He spoke loudly, his words carefully formed. Charity begrudgingly conceded that it was well done of him to remember to do so. *Not* that it was enough to make up for his rudeness of a moment ago, and it didn't even begin to offset his atrocious behavior of earlier.

"You must be here for the Potters' little soiree," Grandmama responded, her eyes sparkling with delight in the dancing lamplight. "How fortuitous that we should arrive together."

He cleared his throat, switching his weight from one foot to the other. "Actually, I was just leaving. But I do hope you and your granddaughter enjoy your evening."

"Oh, you must stay for a little while longer, my lord. We've only just arrived, and I would so love to learn more about you." Without waiting for him to offer— indeed, without even giving him a chance, Grandmama slipped her arm from beneath her light wrap and snaked it around his elbow. "There, now. Shall we?"

It was all Charity could do not to laugh out loud at the baron's stricken expression. Though she held her tongue, she freely grinned at him with absolute satisfaction, positively *daring* him to extract himself from the situation.

His narrowed gaze was as cold as the Thames in January.

Charity only smiled that much more broadly. Never mind that she'd rather be escorted by Napoleon himself than the baron; it was worth the discomfort to know he was miserable. "Why, yes, Grandmama. I think we shall."

Was that grinding teeth she heard? One could hope. She waited, smile in place, until at last he nodded.

"If you insist."

With shoulders stiff and jaw clenched, he led the way

to the front door. He may have had an early lead in the encounter, but she was definitely the victor. Now all she had to do was figure out how to avoid the man for the rest of the evening.

A prospect that proved much more difficult than she could have anticipated when Mrs. Potter imparted to her with whispered delight that Charity was to have the *honor* of sitting beside him at dinner. It was Charity's turn to grind her teeth as she attempted to smile gracefully at her hostess. In hindsight, she should have realized they would likely be seated together, with him being a baron and she the daughter of a viscount.

"Lord Cadgwith is family, Miss Effington," the older woman confided, pride beaming from her apple cheeks to her sweetly pursed lips. "My cousin was married to the old baron, God rest his soul." She glanced briefly heavenward before meeting Charity's gaze again, concern clouding her coffee-colored eyes. "Such a shame, that was. A terrible shock, to be sure." She shook her head gravely.

Despite herself, curiosity tugged at Charity like an insistent child. *What* had happened to the old baron? Clearly something tragic. Had the man been the new Lord Cadgwith's father? Brother? A cousin or uncle? She wasn't normally the overly curious type, but, for some reason, she couldn't suppress her interest. "Was the old baron's death recent?"

"Just over seven months past. Poor Felicity—Lady Cadgwith, that is—was in the family way. The whole estate was in limbo until the baby was born two months ago. Unfortunately for my cousin, the child was a girl, so the title and estate passed on to the new Lord Cadgwith."

The older woman smiled as if to reassure Charity, and patted her hand. "But the new baron will do beautifully, I haven't a doubt. Quite the catch now, he is. Young and handsome despite the, well, *you know*," she whispered, widening her eyes for emphasis.

Yes, Charity knew exactly. She nodded absently as her gaze flicked to where he stood talking with Mr. Potter and Sir Anthony Harrison. The scar through his eyebrow was like a stark road carved through an otherwise perfect wheat field. The ones down his temple were less distinct, but still visible even from half a room away. Did the scars have something to do with the tragic end to the old earl? No—they looked too old for that.

He nodded at whatever Sir Anthony was saying, but showed no real interest. His posture was stiff, and there wasn't a hint of a smile that she could see. Funny, he didn't look like a man overjoyed with his recent fortune in life. Of course, with his wet-rag personality, who was to say what his happy face looked like?

And besides, none of this was really her business. The less she knew about the man, the better. Resolutely she turned her attention back to her hostess. Her stomach sank when she saw Mrs. Potter's sly smile. Oh no— clearly the woman had the wrong idea about Charity's interest in the man.

She smiled tightly. "I'm sure there are those who may find him"—she cast about for an adjective that might describe him that was even remotely positive, and said at last—"interesting." Manners were manners, and the baron was family to this woman. Never let it be said that she hadn't learned from all the etiquette lessons her parents had invested so heavily in.

Mrs. Potter chuckled. "I imagine there are several young ladies here tonight who envy you your position." She winked as though she had just imparted the greatest of gifts upon Charity, and not the unwanted company of her self-important neighbor. "Well, I must go chat with your grandmother. It is so nice to see her looking so well. Do enjoy yourself, dear."

Charity nodded, holding her smile in place until Mrs. Potter walked away. Sure, she'd enjoy herself for the next half hour. But all bets would be off when dinner started.

Judging by the icy silence to his left, Miss Effington was about as happy to be sitting next to Hugh as he was to be sitting next to her. Which, in turn, was about as happy as he was to be there at all. He took another draft of his red wine, wishing it were something stronger.

To his right, Miss Remington, the overly perky blonde with an unfortunate tendency to nibble her food like a nervous rabbit, set down her fork and smiled. "Do tell us, Lord Cadgwith: How are you finding Bath?"

He was rusty on his societal manners, but even he knew it was best to avoid words like *tedious* when describing a person's city of residence. "Tolerable, Miss Remington." Hopefully, leaving the *barely* off his answer was concession enough.

She tittered nervously, her nose scrunching up as though she were about to sneeze. "Well, clearly our fair city has made little impression upon you, sir. But soon the music festival shall be in full swing, and you cannot help but be enchanted then."

A small, barely audible scoffing sound came from his left. He turned toward Miss Effington, whose frosty gray eyes rose to meet his gaze. "I beg your pardon, Miss Effington?"

"Pardon granted," she replied tartly, smiling mirthlessly before spearing another forkful of the cinnamon-glazed carrots.

Ah yes, his own words tossed back at him. Fair enough. He hadn't the desire to speak with her, anyhow. He stabbed a piece of lamb and lifted it to his lips. The sooner this cursed dinner was over, the sooner he could make his excuses. His temples felt as though his head was pressed within a vise, the pressure growing by the minute.

Why the devil had he allowed himself to be coerced by her grandmother, anyway? Yes, she reminded him of his own grandmother who had died years ago, but it wasn't as though he owed her anything. It mattered not whether she thought him rude. She was little more than a temporary neighbor—just like her granddaughter.

He glanced to the gold-rimmed plate to his left, where the granddaughter in question's long, tapered fingers precisely worked her utensils, cutting the meat into perfect little squares. She was uncomfortable. Served her right after the discomfort she had brought his staff today in her ill-conceived effort to punish him.

"I almost forgot," he said casually, slicing into his own meat. He waited for her to take the bait for several seconds. Nothing. Just as well—he shouldn't have engaged her in the first place.

"Yes?"

He nearly grinned. Her tone was exceedingly reluctant. She knew he had won by getting her to reply. He took a bite of lamb, taking his time chewing. Swallowing, he indulged in a leisurely sip of his wine before dabbing his lips and turning to face her. "My staff was so *very* impressed with your serenade today. Pity I wasn't home to hear it."

A blush stole up her chest, momentarily diverting his attention. "Indeed," she said making an obvious effort at nonchalance. "I'll have to make certain you are at home next time. Early morning ought to be a sure bet."

God, but she was a pest. He bit down on the unexpected humor that lifted one corner of his mouth. She looked sweet enough, but clearly she had spunk.

"So you *are* a music lover," Miss Remington broke in, her trilling voice overly bright. "I myself am as well. Indeed, I have played the harp for years. There should be *much* to entertain you this summer, I'm sure."

Hugh blinked, looking back to the blonde with a lifted brow. Was that innuendo he heard in this young miss's voice? Good God, he hoped not.

Miss Effington chuckled softly beside him, and, against his better judgment, he looked at her. She grinned innocently at him before leaning over to address the rabbit. "Fear not, Miss Remington. I'm absolutely certain he shall find himself with more entertainment than he knows what to do with."

Growing bolder, was she? Well, the threat was toothless, given his confidence the estate agent would be able to work something out in short order. If not, Hugh was quite prepared to bribe the man until he did. She wasn't a terrible person, but she was most definitely a terrible neighbor for him.

Some little bit of the devil came over him, and he found himself saying, "Such confidence, Miss Effington. It is a shame that Bath has provided precious little entertainment so far. In fact, this very morning I was awakened by the most awful of noise from the townhouse next door. I can only hope it wasn't a dying cat."

Miss Remington's knife screeched across her plate as she gaped at him. *Oh, for the love of God—* He'd already forgotten she was following their conversation. That's what he got for indulging the long-dormant desire to tease. He drew a deep breath before saying evenly. "An exaggeration, Miss Remington. I apologize for my poor humor."

Her gaze shifted slightly away from his as she gave an uncomfortable little giggle. "Yes, of course."

Well, he hadn't been looking to impress anyone this

evening, and he was succeeding spectacularly. He longed to rub his throbbing temples or, better yet, simply abandon the evening altogether and head home. Clearly he wasn't fit for mixed company.

"Do you often find yourself in poor humor?"

He turned his attention back to Miss Effington, who fluttered her eyelashes expectantly. She had such an incredibly innocent look about her, which irked him for some reason. She was probably eighteen or nineteen years old, with no real experiences and certainly nothing noteworthy about her. She was just one of a thousand empty-headed debutantes hoping to snag a husband. Undoubtedly, that was exactly the reason she played her dreadful pianoforte in the first place. God knew a proper English wife must have accomplishments.

He gave a careless shrug. "Depends on the company." Not exactly the truth. He found himself in black moods more often than he'd like to admit. It was none of her damned business, though. For her, life was little more than sitting around in her pretty gowns with her unblemished skin and undoubtedly petal-soft hands.

He gave himself a mental shake. Christ, he didn't used to be like this. It was hard to remember when he had readily laughed and flirted with young women, but it had happened. Back when he was young and naïve, and was whole in body and spirit. With the dull pounding in his head blossoming to sharp jabs, he lifted his goblet to his lips and drained the rest of his wine.

"Is that to say your humor is related to the quality of your company?" Miss Effington mused, oblivious to his maudlin turn of thought. "If so, then one must assume you find yourself in poor humor whenever you are alone."

Her comment caught him off guard, coming from her oh so innocent, angelic facade. She sat with proud, straight shoulders and steady eye contact even as a dull pink blush rose up her neck and suffused her cheeks. Without a doubt she irritated him, but he had to admire, however reluctantly, her nerve. After a moment, he tilted his head an inch or so. "*Touché*, Miss Effington. *Touché*."

Aha! Charity bit back a grin, ridiculously proud of herself. She never thought of those sorts of witty rejoinders until it was too late to say them. And if by chance she did think of it, she never had the nerve to speak it. But really, a *dying cat*?

He raised an eyebrow, stretching the silvery scars along his temple. "Regardless, I am most often in my own company, so my humor, poor or otherwise, is my own concern."

Somehow she wasn't surprised that he was little in the fellowship of others. "Pray, you needn't feel obliged to change that while here in Bath. Somehow we shall scrape along without you."

"And yet I am here now solely due to the efforts of Lady Effington and yourself."

They were speaking low now, quietly enough that their conversation wouldn't be overheard by those around them. She was close enough to smell the subtle spice of his shaving soap. It was oddly intimate in such a public setting, but she imagined he was no keener than she for their less than civilized exchange to be observed.

"I'll admit, it was rather amusing to see you bullied by my grandmother. It was almost worth being seated next to you now."

"Glad to know my suffering could be a source of amusement for you," he said without any real heat. "Although I suppose we established that this morning, did we not?"

"You must have a very thin skin, my lord, to be so easily wounded," she replied archly.

"My, my," Grandmama said from across the table. "What have the two of you got your heads together about?"

Charity cringed at the spectacularly loud statement, which drew the attention of nearly the entire table. With the weight of so many eyes on her, her blush heated two times over. "Nothing of note, ma'am."

Chuckling indulgently, the older woman looked to the baron. "I daresay it looked quite noteworthy from here. What say you, Mrs. Potter? Shall we scold them for their whispered conversation?"

Mrs. Potter's smile could not have been more delighted. "Oh no, Lady Effington. Allowances must be made for besotted young people, I think."

Besotted? Mortification filled every inch of Charity's body, making her stomach drop and her ears ring. She wanted to say something, anything, to deflect their attention, but all the proper words seem to flee her tongue.

"I assure you, ladies, 'tis nothing so exciting as that." Lord Cadgwith sounded completely composed, even slightly amused. "Miss Effington has confessed to a headache, so I was endeavoring to speak quietly so as not to offend."

Charity cut her eyes to the baron, who spoke the lie with perfect aplomb. Why had he said such a thing? Predictably, Grandmama turned distressed eyes toward Charity. "Oh, my. I had no idea. I thank you, my lord, for having such courtesy. Shall we depart after dinner, my dear girl?"

Well, Charity could scarcely say otherwise after such an excuse. Never mind that it provided the perfect escape from the baron's company and the other guests' scrutiny, including that of Miss Remington, whose bewildered expression still somehow held accusation; the man had no right to rope her into such a lie. He as good as secured her ejection from the party. And for this, Grandmama was *thanking* him?

Her gaze slipped to the baron, where he sat watching her with lifted brows. Daring her to deny his explanation, perhaps? There did seem to be a gleam of triumph in those green eyes of his. With a quiet huff of annoyance, she turned her attention back to her grandmother. "Yes, ma'am, I think it's probably best."

As the other guests returned to their conversations, Charity cut narrowed eyes to the baron. "You fiend. I can't believe you just got me kicked out of the party."

He shrugged. "Why? Seems fitting, if you ask me."

"Fitting? In what way?" He was maddeningly unperturbed by his part in this.

"If your intervention resulted in my forced attendance, it's apropos that mine should result in your forced departure."

"So you planned this, did you?"

He snorted, shaking his head. "If I had thought that far ahead, I would have said *I* was the one with the headache."

For the first time, she saw the hint of drollness in his expression. Could it be that the churlish Lord Cadgwith actually possessed a sense of humor? As Charity sat back and allowed the footman to set her dessert in front of her, she considered the possibility.

Perhaps there was more to the man than she originally thought.

Chapter Five

What, exactly, had they gotten themselves into?

Charity bit her lip as May's servant carefully laid the long wooden zither, with all the care one would expect for a newborn infant, upon the designated table. Set against the pale gold-and-white damask wallpaper and Queen Anne furniture of the townhouse's music room, it was almost absurdly out of place. At May's thanks, the footman left them, and Charity stepped closer in order to properly inspect the thing.

There were at least a dozen strings stretched across the instrument's nearly five-foot length, with several bridges fanning along the top. It had a rich rosewood border with a blond wooden inlay polished to a high shine. A watery painting adorned the top, depicting a stylized oriental garden and several Chinese symbols.

A piece of the Orient, right here in Bath.

"It truly is beautiful," Charity breathed, trying to keep the doubt from her voice. How on earth were they to marry three such disparate instruments? It'd be like drawing a carriage with a horse, an ox, and a zebra.

May's smile was as sunny as the day was dreary. "Yes, and foreign enough to give you the vapors, no?"

"Indeed," Sophie said, after swallowing her bite of apple puff. "In the very best possible way. I cannot wait to hear you play that thing. It's the closest I shall ever come to China. Or the East Indies. Or across the Channel, for that matter!"

"Is there a best possible way to have the vapors?" Charity asked, grinning as she spoke. Sophie did have a manner of speaking that could not help but amuse.

"Oh yes!" Sophie's dark curls bounced with her enthusiastic nod. "The best vapors are to be had when a very, *very* handsome gentleman asks you to dance, or you have a bite of the most divine cake ever, or you catch a glimpse of a rather spectacular nude statue that you were forbidden from seeing."

"Sophie!" she laughed, widening her eyes in teasing reproof. Charity wouldn't have thought the girl could ever be scandalous, but clearly she had a little devilment hiding behind those rosy cheeks and sparkly eyes. "It's a good thing my grandmother can't hear very well—you'll get us all in trouble."

"Not I," said May, looking very worldly with her knowing little smile. "The natives of the East Indies are more often than not half-naked. Most aren't much to look at, but every now and then . . ." She trailed off, grinning wickedly.

Sophie and Charity gaped at her for one shocked moment. Then all at once they all broke into gay laughter, the sound echoing beautifully around the high ceilings of the music room.

"Oh, my word," Charity said, wiping tears from the corners of her eyes. "You two shall be the death of me, I can already tell." After the odd dinner last night, it felt wonderful to laugh with people she actually liked.

May patted her arm: "No, darling—we shall be the *life*

of you. Anyone who blushes as easily as you has not had nearly enough adventure in her life."

Probably a more accurate statement than Charity would like to admit. "Yes. Well, let us start with hearing you play. That shall be adventure enough for the day, I think."

Sophie dragged a chair from the wall and plopped down directly in front of the zither. "I have thought of little else since we parted, and, yes, I do realize that makes me sound very boring. But in my defense, my mother is not yet settled and therefore doesn't wish for us to attend any functions just yet. So, you see, you and your zither are certainly the most excitement I have had in days. Perhaps weeks."

Taking a seat in front of the table, May fitted little black picks to the ends of her fingers. "In that case, I shan't delay a second longer. Are you ready, Charity?"

Settling on the comfortable butter yellow settee nearby, Charity nodded. May smiled, then closed her eyes and took a long, deep breath. She was the very picture of an English miss, dressed in shimmery white muslin with gorgeous emerald embroidery in place of a sash at her waist. Her blond hair was pulled up into a simple twisted knot, and a plain gold cross lay against her chest.

The soft patter of rain against the wide back windows was the only sound as May seemed to meditate a moment. Then, with the graceful descent of a landing bird, her fingers settled on the strings and she opened her eyes.

The first pluck filled the room with an almost harplike sound, full and resonant as the strings sang. But then she slid her fingertip down the chord and the difference was notable, apparent in the tinny, almost flat twang of the notes. Her fingers danced over the strings, playing a song that was as unfamiliar to Charity as the instrument itself.

Her passion was unmistakable, her focus complete as she plucked and strummed with masterful hands. The song flowed from her fingers like a kite dancing in the wind. It bounced and bobbed, swooped and slid, calling forth a different time and place. It wasn't just a song; it was an experience.

When the last note rang out, May looked up for the first time since beginning. Her smile was firmly in place, but it was different from her teasing grins before. She seemed almost wistful, with a hint of sadness touching her eyes. It was a look Charity recognized well. One that graced her own features whenever she was stuck in London, subject to the *ton*'s snide comments and belittling stares.

Homesickness.

"Oh, May," Sophie said, pressing her hands to her chest. "That was so very beautiful."

Plucking the picks from her fingertips, May offered a rueful smile. "If only I could play more freely in my own home. Aunt Victoria despises my guzheng. She believes that if God had intended an Englishwomen to play such an instrument, he would have given it a more palatable name."

Charity shook her head, trying not to laugh. "Yes, because the bassoon is such a dignified name. And the tuba. And the viola, for that matter."

Tapping her tiny musical case in her lap, Sophie said, "And *oboe* sounds more like the name of some tribe in Africa than an instrument."

At this May laughed, finally rallying. "To be honest, I am not altogether certain that any instrument was invented by an Englishman. They have always excelled at improving things, not discovering them."

"Next you'll be telling us that Sir Isaac Newton wasn't an Englishman," Charity teased, earning a laugh from both girls. "Although the Englishmen I have met in the past few days do not recommend their species."

"Ugh, that dreadful Mr. Green. I should so dearly love to see him put soundly in his place."

"The best way to have our revenge is to shock them all with our fabulous trio. I think the first thing we need to do is decide on a song. May, do you know any pieces we might be familiar with?"

"I do, actually. My mother felt it best that I have as round an education as possible, including the great European composers' work. How does a little Mozart sound?"

"Mozart?" Sophie squeaked. "Now, that I'd like to hear."

"As would I," Charity agreed. She considered herself to be extremely musical, able to hear things in her mind without ever having heard them played—handy when composing—but for the life of her, she couldn't imagine what such an unlikely song for the guzheng would sound like.

May nodded, placed her fingers over the strings, and dove into Mozart's Piano Sonata No. 11. Charity closed her eyes, listening to the familiar melody transformed into something subtly exotic. It was different, to be sure, but much more recognizable to her ear. Instead of the sliding runs she had done earlier, May plucked at the strings like a harpist or the way cello players occasionally do. The tinniness was still there, but the notes sounded almost normal. Better than normal, really.

By the time May reached the second movement, gooseflesh covered Charity's arms and her heart pounded with excitement. This was something she could work with. This was something she could make even better.

"Stop!"

May immediately broke off, blinking up at Charity as if emerging from a trance. "Is something the matter?"

"No," Charity said, coming to her feet. Both girls watched her as though she had quite lost her mind. "It's exactly the opposite. I'm sorry if I startled you, but can you start over? I want to try something."

At May's bewildered nod, Charity sat down at her pianoforte. The notes in her head were not the same ones that she was used to playing. They were altered a bit, intended to complement May's unusual interpretation. She listened for a minute to the song as it played out in her mind, then nodded. "Go ahead, May."

As soon as the strings began to sing, Charity closed her eyes and set her fingers in place. At the right moment, she started to play, letting the music flow from her without interference. It wasn't perfect, but it was exciting nonetheless. So different that she wiggled a little in her seat as the notes rose toward their crescendo. She always disliked playing other people's pieces, but this arrangement was something so unique, she felt as though the two of them were painting in the lines of an unfinished drawing.

When they finished, Sophie erupted into applause, popping to her feet in her enthusiasm. "Bravo, you two. That was brilliant! I cannot—"

She stopped midsentence when a succession of several loud bangs rang out from the wall. "What in blazes was that?"

Charity's jaw dropped as she realized what the sound had to be. For heaven's sake, they were civilized adults in one of the most prestigious areas of the city! Heat rose to her cheeks as she turned her mortified gaze to her guests. "That," she said, biting off the word as fury set in, "is the illustrious Baron Cadgwith. He's only just ascended to the title, and I am fairly certain he was raised with all the manners of a donkey."

"Do not tell me that a *baron* was just now banging the walls in protest," Sophie said, her eyes as round as doorknobs. "I cannot believe such a thing. Even my youngest sister wouldn't do such a thing, and she once put a frog in my bed while I was sleeping."

Charity chewed on the insides of her cheeks, fighting the need to march next door and tell the man exactly what she thought of his protest. She had genuinely thought they had reached a sort of truce yesterday. For him to revert to this level of rudeness was beyond the pale. Had she imagined his dry humor? His wry, understated wit?

Well, she had no intention of bowing to this sort of uncivilized, unspoken demand. She drew a calming breath and forced a smile. "Oh, I don't believe it was a protest. I imagine it was his ill-executed attempt to applaud us. It was my impression that he *adores* music."

May and Sophie exchanged dubious looks. Raising a blond brow, May said, "Somehow I doubt that."

Allowing her smile to transition to something a little more mischievous, Charity crossed her arms. "Nevertheless, I say we pretend it is true and play accordingly."

"You wish us to play it again?"

Charity glanced back at the wall, imagining the maddeningly rude man on the other side of it. He seemed to think her weak and submissive, a reed that should bend to his will. And, yes, she normally did whatever others wished of her. She believed it to be a good thing that she wanted to accommodate others.

But when it came to Lord Cadgwith, she had no intention of being biddable. She had no need to make him happy, and certainly not at her expense. And it was time he learned that rudeness would not triumph over her. *He* would not triumph.

She glanced back to the other women, who watched her uncertainly. "Yes," she said firmly. "And I wish for us to play it *louder*."

"There must be something, sir. I assure you I am willing to pay handsomely." Hugh raked a hand through his already disheveled hair, frustrated beyond bearing with the cagey old estate agent.

Mr. Sanburne's caterpillarlike white eyebrows slunk up his forehead. "Though I would be more than happy to help myself to more of your funds, my good man, I was quite serious when I said there isn't a set of rooms to be had in all of Bath just now. The festival is the best thing to happen to this town in years."

Of all the bloody rotten luck. "So you are saying," Hugh ground out, "that in one of the largest cities in England, there isn't a single other place to let? Every nook and cranny is occupied until the end of the summer?"

Was this to be a completely wasted trip? Hugh tugged at his cravat, wishing he could just yank the damn thing off. God, what he would give for the sea breezes of Cadgwith. Despite the cloudy day, Sanburne's office was already uncomfortably hot—as was the rest of the city. Hugh had yet to cool off after his visit to the Baths, and sweat dampened the fine lawn of his shirt, making it stick to the small of his back.

"It's possible there is an attic room I'm missing, but I rather doubt it." The man leaned back and stroked his pointed white beard, eyeing Hugh with interest. "I find the request rather extraordinary, my lord. I've met the Dowager Lady Effington. She is as fine a woman as I have ever seen."

The sparkle in his pale blue eyes wasn't exactly encouraging. Despite his age, Sanburne was a jovial, good-looking sort of man. Hugh could readily imagine him charming women of a certain age, like the viscountess. Clearly he thought much of the lady in question. Hugh rolled his shoulders, working at the tightness that temporarily had been assuaged during his soak but was now returning in spades. "Lady Effington is quite acceptable. It is her granddaughter's constant pianoforte playing that gives me issue. Impossible for a man to hear himself think with that sort of ever-present distraction."

He had almost liked the girl at the dinner party. Something about her spoke to a part of him that he had thought long dead. But it didn't matter. He simply couldn't be near her—especially now that the musical racket seemed to have multiplied.

He could admit now that banging on the wall like a lowborn ruffian hadn't been his finest hour. But at the time, his head had been so racked with pain, even the tiny bit of daylight seeping around the curtains had caused him extreme discomfort. The music had been utter torture, resulting in throbbing pain so fierce, he had ended up on his knees, casting up his accounts. The banging on the wall was born of a desperate need to stop the pain.

It had been wrong. It had been the result of his own damn weakness, but he couldn't undo it now.

There were a lot of things he couldn't undo now.

Mr. Sanburne, oblivious to Hugh's dark turn of thought, chuckled. He leaned forward over his neat-as-a-pin desk. "In my navy days, there wasn't a sailor out there that wouldn't have given his eyeteeth for that kind of distraction." The caterpillars wiggled in an if-you-know-what-I-mean sort of way.

They were getting nowhere. Hugh wasn't about to delve into the details of his personal situation and how much Miss Effington exasperated it. And now he was to be stuck with her all summer. He rose abruptly, anxious to be done with the interview. "If there is nothing that can be done, then I suppose this meeting is at an end."

The humor faded from the agent's eyes and he came to his feet as well. "I am sorry, my lord. I shall notify you immediately if I hear of anything becoming available."

"Yes, please do. Good day, sir."

Hugh let himself out of the office, his mood as forbidding as the heavy gray skies that threatened another round of showers. He had gotten less than three, maybe four, hours of sleep in the past few days, thanks in large part to Miss Effington. Nights were always the worst for him; it had been years since he'd had a proper night's sleep. His best chance for rest was the morning hours through the early afternoon.

Exactly when his neighbor held her rehearsals.

He had tried moving rooms, but short of sleeping in the kitchens or switching rooms with the servants, there was no escaping the noise. God, he needed a drink. It had never once occurred to him that there wouldn't be a single rental left in the entire blasted city. Were there really so many people in this country with nothing better to do with their summers than to attend some pointless music festival?

One look around him gave him the answer to that question. In the week since he had been in Bath, the traffic seemed to increase every day. It was why he had forgone his carriage and even his horse and was instead on foot. Turning down his street, he kept his gaze straight ahead and his pace brisk in order to avoid talking with anyone around him.

All he wanted to do at this point was get home, down a bottle of whiskey, and sleep for many, many hours. Dreamlessly, God willing.

As he neared the townhouse, the neighboring door swung open, and Miss Effington and two other young women spilled out onto the pavement. He stopped abruptly, one foot still in front of the other. Damn it all, was he to have *no* luck today? He'd bet his horse the short brunette and tall, willowy blonde were her fellow musicians from hell.

They were laughing at something, and he had the fleeting thought that he could simply turn around and walk away, when the dark-haired girl spotted him and gasped.

The other two followed her gaze, and Hugh found himself looking directly into the stormy gray eyes of his neighbor. Whatever delight she had taken in the conversation of a moment earlier was utterly gone now, replaced by wariness.

"Good afternoon, my lord."

"Miss Effington," he said, not wanting to engage her. He adjusted his stance to one less precarious, resorting to the officer pose he had perfected years ago: straight spine, lifted chin, hands behind his back. *Never show weakness to anyone.*

"Don't tell me," the brunette said, her dark eyes lighting with understanding. "This must be the infamous Lord Cadgwith. Oh, do introduce us, Charity."

Miss Effington flashed an unhappy glare at the impertinent girl before sighing and holding a hand out to her. "Miss Wembley, Miss Bradford, allow me to introduce you to Lord Cadgwith. Now, we should be on—"

"Lord Cadgwith," the blonde interrupted, obviously recognizing his name. "So good to meet you. I understand you are quite the music lover." Both her voice and carriage projected the easy confidence that those in possession of such fine features tended to have. *Not* that Hugh gave a damn what the girl looked like.

Music lover, indeed.

"I'm sorry, but you must have me confused with someone else." He lifted a brow at Miss Effington. What, exactly, had she told these girls?

She raised hers right back. "Forgive us, my lord. We assumed your wall thumping was an ironic form of applause."

And so it returned to bite him. God, how he wished Mr. Sanburne would have had better news for him. If the Baths weren't so blessedly effective, he'd have already packed his bags for Cadgwith by now. How interesting, really, that he should find both heaven and hell in the same place.

"I think you'll find, Miss Effington, that irony tends to elude me."

Chapter Six

Charity watched the baron as he made his abrupt departure, quickly disappearing through the door of his townhouse.

"Charming."

Charity glanced back to May, whose sarcastic lift of her brow matched the tone of the single word.

"Yes, isn't he just delightful?"

Her heart was still racing from the encounter. She just couldn't seem to get a handle on the man. For heaven's sake, her father would have her hide if he knew how their encounters had gone—especially since the man was a baron.

She had no excuse, none at all, other than he just seemed to bring out her somewhat less civilized side.

"He certainly is handsome," Sophie said, twisting a curl around her finger as she stared after the closed door through which the baron had escaped. "I mean, not handsome like Lord Radcliff or Lord Raleigh— Oh!" she exclaimed, turning horrified eyes on Charity. "I am *so* sorry! I cannot believe I brought him up. I wasn't thinking at all and it just popped out and, oh, I really need to learn to keep my tongue behind my teeth sometimes."

Charity smiled reassuringly at Sophie. "You mustn't worry yourself. Lord Raleigh is still a dear friend of the family." No one had been privy to the details of their split but them, yet she knew rumors were rampant. She had been fortunate that they had called it off at the end of her first Season, but the *ton* still had plenty to say about it. Walking into any ballroom in London had been positively miserable last Season. Fans would snap up to cover wagging tongues as everyone speculated about what she must have done to have lost the earl.

"Who's Lord Raleigh?" May asked, her curiosity clearly piqued. She looked back and forth between them, her brows raised and her blue eyes wide.

Charity sighed. She really hated that the whole ordeal wouldn't just blow over. She hardly could remember feeling as though the earl was her proper match. "Last year, the Earl of Raleigh and I had a brief courtship. We ended the courtship when it became apparent that another held his heart. Lady Raleigh is truly a lovely person, and I wish them nothing but the best." Her one true blessing was that their betrothal had not yet been announced when they broke it off. She shuddered to think of how much worse things would have been had the *ton* known.

Sophie's expression was dubious at best. Putting her hand to her hips, Charity said, "It's true! The decisions made were absolutely the right ones for all involved. And it is my greatest wish that I will someday find a man who will—" She paused, her nerve floundering.

"Who will . . . ?" May prompted.

Embarrassment skittered through her belly, but she did her best to ignore it. These were her friends. If she couldn't say what she wanted to them, then who could she say it to? The road was busy with carriage traffic, but there was no one on the pavement close enough to hear them. Charity straightened her spine. "Who will love me above all others, and whom I can love in return."

"You say that as if it's a *bad* thing." Amusement tilted up the corners of May's perfectly formed lips. "A love match is something to be admired."

"Tell that to my father," Charity murmured.

"And my mother," Sophie added wryly. "And to the *ton*, for that matter."

May shook her head as if they were being quite ridiculous. "Well, my father loved my mother tremendously, and she him. As far as I'm concerned, it's a love match or nothing for me."

"Nothing?" Sophie asked, her voice rising in surprise. "If you don't find a love match, you will not marry?"

She snorted. "I'll be lucky to marry even *with* a love match. There also has to be a meeting of minds, values, and philosophies for me to ever pledge myself to another."

"Goodness." Given Sophie's propensity to talk, the single word held a wealth of meaning.

"Do not you require the same from a future husband?" May's blue eyes held no reproach or censure, just honest curiosity.

Charity bit her lip. Did she? Before her first Season, all Charity had hoped for was a spouse who respected her and would allow her to play her music as much as she liked. But then . . . then she had seen the way a man in love looked at the woman who held his heart, and she had known right then and there, with absolute certainty that *that* was what she wanted from a husband. Love she could see, feel, breathe, and live. And for her, all those could be summed up in a single sensation.

She looked to the damp pavement, shyness suddenly

setting in. Her two friends already felt like confidantes after only a short while, but that didn't make it easy to confess the desires of one's heart. "All I ever truly hoped," she said, her voice quiet as she looked up and shrugged, "was for butterflies."

The other women exchanged looks, and all at once it struck Charity how absurd it was for them to be holding this very intimate conversation in the middle of the street. She laughed and said, "And with that, I must attend to my grandmother. But I do so look forward to tomorrow's rehearsal. By this time next week, we shall do smashingly well at the private session in front of the committee—I'm sure of it."

Sophie nodded emphatically, upsetting the dark curls spilling from beneath her bonnet. "We really are coming along quite wonderfully. Thanks to the parts you wrote for us, I think this shall be the best rendition of Mozart ever to be played. Well, aside from an actual performance by Mozart, which is, of course, quite impossible."

Shaking her head, May said, "Yes, quite. Now, come, let's be off. I am accustomed to the heat, but I'd prefer to be home before the next showers."

"Are you certain you don't wish to take the carriage? Grandmama would happily have it readied."

"For three blocks? I should think not. We are made of sterner stuff than that, aren't we, Sophie?"

Though Sophie readily agreed, her frizzing curls spoke another story. Charity gave them both an impromptu hug. "All right. I'll see you tomorrow, then."

After waving good-bye, she let herself back inside and headed to the drawing room. As expected, her grandmother was ensconced on her favorite sofa, a plate of biscuits on the table in front of her and her stockinged feet resting on the cushions. Lorgnette in hand, she was reading through the day's correspondence, with three unfolded letters littering her lap.

"Good afternoon, Grandmama. Did anyone write anything of interest?" She settled onto the closest chair and helped herself to a chocolate biscuit.

"Oh yes," she responded, a smile brightening her whole face. With her comely blue-and-white gown and gay expression, she looked particularly pretty today. "Your mother writes that the visit with the Burtons is going quite well. Mrs. Burton seems to be comforted by her presence." She put a hand to her cheek and sighed. "Oh, I do so hope it will be a boy."

Charity smiled and nodded. They were all hoping it would be a boy. To Papa's great regret, Charity was an only child and the viscountcy would therefore someday pass to Mr. Burton, who was Charity's second cousin. If he failed to produce an heir as Papa had, the title would pass on to a distant cousin who lived nearly at the Scottish border, and whom none of them had even met before. Mr. Burton wasn't ideal, but at least he was known to them, and, according to Father, he had a good head on his shoulders.

He and his heiress wife had always been distant at best, preferring to keep to themselves in their massive estate outside of Bromsgrove, a good two hundred miles from the rest of the family in Durham.

However, after twelve years of marriage without a single pregnancy, she had at last conceived, and for the first time they were reaching out to the family. Having no close female relatives of her own, Mrs. Burton had happily accepted Mama's offer to come stay with her during her lying-in.

"I'm so glad Mama could be there to visit. I know they have never been particularly close, but nothing brings a family together quite like a new baby." She was exceedingly grateful for it, too. Mama might have decided to join them in Bath otherwise, and Charity really, really needed to get away from her parents for a while.

At the end of August, when the festival was over, she and Grandmama would head north to visit the Burtons and their new baby; then Mama would join them on their journey back to Durham. In the next two months, however, Charity planned to enjoy her little getaway to the fullest.

She popped the rest of the biscuit in her mouth and sat back against the cushions. With the small exception of the dreadful baron next door, this was proving to be the most lovely holiday she could remember. Could not the man find it in himself to be more polite to her guests? Granted, he wasn't nearly as disagreeable as he could have been, but he certainly could have been nicer.

Of course, she could have tactfully refrained from bringing up the wall-knocking incident. She grimaced. She really didn't like that he seemed to bring out the worst in her.

"Indeed," Grandmama said, shuffling her letters together and setting them on the table. "Now, my dear, tell me all about your rehearsals. From what little I heard, you ladies are coming together nicely."

Charity's favorite topic. She smiled resolutely and firmly pushed away all thoughts of the baron. "Everything is going splendidly. With the changes we've made to the sonata, I think it is the perfect complement to our instruments."

"It is too bad you hadn't time to compose something original, though I am quite certain you'll have brought some great improvement to Mr. Mozart's work. I think the three of you shall take the festival by storm."

Her smile was so sweet and encouraging, Charity stood and gave her a doting kiss on the cheek. She was the only one who supported Charity's efforts at writing music. When Grandmama had bad days during her illness, Charity would sit beside her bed, quietly composing songs. On the good days, she insisted on coming to the music room in order to hear the fruits of Charity's labor. On those days, Grandmama would rest on the settee beside the pianoforte, her eyes closed and her toes wagging in time with the music. Charity smiled at the memory.

Truthfully, the illness had brought them so much closer. When Charity was younger, Grandmama had been tight-lipped and strict, offering little more than distant nods or formal greetings. Charity would never have wished her long suffering or illness on her, but she was grateful for the changes it had wrought.

"Thank you, Grandmama. We shall certainly do our best. And even if everyone hates it, at least I will have made two very lovely friends because of it." Odd that Charity could have been in the same circles with Sophie for two Seasons, and was only now just realizing what a delight she was.

"That's wonderful, my dear. Although," she said, her slender silver eyebrow arching, "it does look as though Miss Wembley and Miss Bradford are not the only friends you are making in this city."

Charity bent to pour herself some tea. The steam curling from the tip of the delicate pink-and-gold teapot was thin, but still present. "Yes, I have high hopes of a much more successful summer than my spring was. I enjoyed meeting some of the young ladies at the dinner the other night." She added two lumps of sugar and stirred.

"I wasn't speaking of the ladies."

Charity froze, teaspoon in hand, as her gaze darted to

meet her grandmother's. She sat there beaming, her skin crinkling at the corners of her eyes as she smiled with delight. Charity did *not* like where this was headed.

She set down her spoon with supreme care. "Oh? I'm afraid I don't know of whom you speak."

Grandmama chuckled. "There seems to be one gentleman in particular who has taken notice of you. The same gentleman, I should add, whom I spied chatting with you on the pavement just now, though you neglected to mention it. Unless I am very much mistaken, the two of you have a certain spark between you."

If Charity had taken a sip of her tea, it would be all over the table by now. A *spark*? Yes, it could be called that if one was referring to the unfortunate combination of a torch and a thatch roof. "Lord Cadgwith has no special attachment to me, nor I to him. He was walking past when I escorted the others to the door, and he politely" — *not* the word she wanted to use — "acknowledged us."

"Ah, to be young and naïve again," Grandmama said wistfully, setting a wrinkled hand to her chest. Thin blue veins snaked beneath her papery white skin, reminding Charity of how delicate she truly was. "You may not realize it, but that young man has quite a bit of interest in you. Mark my words."

Charity grimaced. An interest in tossing her into the street, perhaps. "No, truly, I'm not being naïve. He and I . . . have very little in common." Unless mutual dislike was considered a commonality.

"And yet you were quite cozy at the Potters' dinner, were you not? I wasn't the only one to notice, either." She sighed and leaned back against the cushions, her eyes taking on that faraway look of one deep in their memories. "My own marriage was arranged, but I was quite amenable to it. Your grandfather could make me blush with a single look. Your Lord Cadgwith reminds me of him, you know."

Superb. Grandmama was developing a soft spot for the one man in all of Bath whom Charity could happily do with never seeing again. "Is that so? I wonder why." She lifted the tea for a sip, anxious to move onto some other topic without sounding rude.

"The wounded heart."

Charity's gaze snapped up at the wholly unexpected words. "Wounded heart?" Yes, he was clearly scarred, but when it came to his heart, well, she assumed he simply hadn't one.

Nodding, her grandmother's eyes went to the ceiling, though Charity suspected she didn't see the fine plasterwork at all. "Raymond was orphaned at the age of ten, and he learned the hard way how many would happily take advantage of a young nobleman. By the time we were betrothed, he was nearly thirty and quite jaded." She shook her head, a small smile emerging from her memories. "Handsome as the devil, and twice as shrewd. But behind it all was a kindness just waiting to come out."

Nostalgia relaxed her features as she stared back into time. As intrigued as Charity was to hear about this side of her grandfather, she simply couldn't let her grandmother's imagination run away with her when it came to Lord Cadgwith.

"Grandmama, I know the baron was physically injured somewhere along the way, but I don't think he is as deep as you may think. After all, we hardly know him."

The older woman turned the full force of her gray gaze on Charity, just as the first raindrops pinged against the windowsill. In that moment, the clarity in her eyes was arresting. "That is what you think. But when one is my age, one learns a thing or two about reading people.

Trust me when I say there is something more to him than just handsome looks and reserved charm."

An odd feeling settled in Charity's stomach, like a carriage suddenly lurching forward. She didn't want to believe her grandmother's observations. It was easier to think he was just an unpleasant man. A wounded heart would mean sympathy, which she wasn't quite prepared to give.

No, Grandmama must be mistaken. Deciding to let the topic drop, she nodded and took a sip of her now-cold tea.

Unbidden, the purplish smudges beneath his tired green eyes flashed through her mind. A teeny, tiny, insignificant whisper of doubt ghosted through her.

She somehow didn't think she'd be able to write him off so easily from now on.

Chapter Seven

He had known it was too much to hope that the quiet from next door would last.

Three days, three blessed days of relative peace, of not having a single headache, and now the proverbial shoe had finally dropped. Doing his damnedest to block out the noise, Hugh lifted the crystal tumbler to his lips and drank deeply of the clear liquid it held. It might look like water, but it burned a wicked path to his gut. It was a sensation he had not only grown accustomed to in the past four years, but one that he looked forward to. More so, even, since his brother's death.

And especially so now that *she* was his neighbor.

He supposed he should be impressed that the music somehow managed to reach all the way to his study. Perhaps he should also consider himself fortunate that it was well into the afternoon, and he was fairly well rested. It was possible he should be grateful that she had given him three days' reprieve from the noise.

But he wasn't any of those things.

He was too damn frustrated to be. He'd been here two and a half weeks now, and the tantalizing taste of freedom kept dancing away from him. Every time he felt the immense relief of nothingness, the blessed lack of pain that sharpened his mind and softened his dried and hardened soul, hope would rush in, bringing with it the long-dormant dreams for a normal life. But the thing about hope was, the more one had, the harder one fell when it was dashed.

Like now, when he could feel the slow but inevitable build of tension at the base of his skull. It gave him ample warning of what was to come, but no method by which to thwart it. It was like standing in the middle of a battlefield with the enemy visible from miles away, but having no means with which to either fight or flee.

Dropping his chin to his chest, he abandoned the tumbler on the desk and massaged the back of his neck with his hand. He was *trying* to fight. He was here, was he not? He was doing everything in his power to climb out of the darkness that had descended upon him years ago on that hellacious day at Waterloo. The fact of his continual setbacks just made his efforts that much more arduous.

He glanced down to the letter on the desk in front of him, its looping script overflowing with his sister-in-law's enthusiasm. The baby was doing well, continuing to thrive under the overprotective watch of nearly the entire village. Felicity was eager to hear word of how the dinner with her cousin had gone, and if the waters were working their magic. She mentioned her brother would soon be in town, and unapologetically admitted that she had written to an old friend to inform him of Hugh's arrival, so he should expect another invitation, which she insisted he must accept. She had so much hope for his therapy and was delighted he was "moving forward in his recovery."

Instead of making him feel better, as he was certain his sister-in-law had intended, it just exasperated the feeling that he was a bloody failure. Or perhaps the proper term was *more* of a failure. She was so certain that if he could just trust in the waters, trust in the doctors and their know-it-all advice, that he'd be healed. Never mind that in the past four years he had seen at least a dozen doctors — quacks and sawbones alike — who had a dozen snake-oil remedies for what ailed him. She just couldn't accept that he might not get better.

The problem was, he very well might not.

After all, a broken clavicle could mend in time and wounds could fade to scars, but there wasn't a whole hell of a lot that could be done for a compressed spinal cord of the cervical spine, as the most respected of the doctors he had seen had called it. Hugh could very well suffer the effects for the rest of his life.

But he didn't blame Felicity for her optimism. Her well-being, and that of his niece, depended on him now. With Ian gone, Hugh could no longer get away with living on the outskirts of society. He had to pull himself together if he was to be any sort of leader at all.

He settled back against the butter-soft leather of his chair and exhaled. If anyone should know about leading, he should. He had commanded scores of men as a captain during the war, demanding respect and delivering strong, dependable leadership. Until the moment it mattered most — that day everything had changed.

He pressed his eyes closed, willing the thought from his brain. He was here now, and he intended to do everything in his power to do right by his brother's wife and daughter. He'd do just about anything to free himself from this prison of pain.

"Jacobson," he shouted, dropping his hands to the desk.

His bemused batman appeared in the doorway several moments later. "Sir?"

"Bring the foul swill that serves for water to me, please." It was something that he should be requesting of the footman, but he stayed away from the other servants as much as possible. He didn't want them being witness to his struggles.

Wry humor lifted the man's good brow. "The recommended five liters before breakfast not enough for you, my lord?"

"Just fetch the damn water," he grumbled without heat. Jacobson was as good a man as Hugh had ever known, but he had no trouble showing irreverence.

Probably why Hugh liked him so well.

Jacobson's retreating footsteps seemed to fall in time to the tinkling music, which also matched the throbbing that built in intensity with every passing moment. Tonight would be hell, but tomorrow was another day.

"I think we should add just a little more flavor of the Far East."

It wasn't a statement Charity would have expected to make even a few days ago, but now she said the words with confidence. She nodded for good measure as May glanced to her in surprise. "I must say, I thought the Eastern influence made you a bit nervous."

Charity set down her pencil on top of the sheet music she had been working on and swiveled around in order to face May fully. Sophie had returned home early in order to join her mother at a final fitting of her gown for tomorrow's opening ball, so they were on their own as they worked on a few minor changes to the recital selection.

A little too guilty of the charge to deny it, Charity offered a sheepish grin. "Yes, I know, but the more we practice, the more I really appreciate the beauty of the added exotic element. I love that we can take a completely traditional piece and turn it on its head."

It was absolutely invigorating, actually. So far from her normal range, it challenged her in a way she truly craved. It was unique and beautiful, and she was proud of that.

May strummed a few chords as she pursed her lips. The resulting twang was full of notes that shouldn't technically sound good together, but somehow came across as melodic. "I would love it, of course. But only if you are certain it won't make you worry even more about the selection committee performance."

Ah yes, the dreaded selection committee. Auspiciously, its function was to properly assign the registered musicians to the Tuesday best suited to their talents. Since the event was meant to encourage the participation of the *ton*, they didn't dare be so crass as to call it an audition, but Charity knew full well that's what it was. If, for whatever reason, a musician—or trio—didn't meet their standards, she had no doubt they would find a way to prevent them from playing. The knowledge added an uncertainty to the whole thing that Charity really didn't like. After all, music was supposed to be the one thing that she never had to worry about.

Pushing aside the lingering apprehension, she smiled. "Think nothing of them. We shall play our hearts out, and that will have to be enough."

May's wide grin plainly revealed her happiness. "Then I couldn't be more thrilled. It's comforting to know that the sounds of my home and those of this country can blend so nicely. It gives me hope that I won't always feel so dreadfully out of place."

It was hard to believe that someone so beautiful could feel out of place anywhere. But even with Sophie and

Charity as friends, it was clear that May still felt like a trumpet in an orchestra of woodwinds. "As far as I can see, you fit in beautifully. No one would know you were from a different part of the world altogether just by looking at you."

"I'm not sure that's a good thing," May said wryly. "I don't want to be incompatible with my English home, but I also don't want to lose any of the elements that made me who I am. I miss the heat and the shouting and the brilliant colors." She idly ran a finger across the polished wood of her zither, lingering over the painted design.

"Well, then," Charity replied, picking up her little pencil once more and tapping it on the sheet music. "Let's bring that to our piece. Play me the section from the beginning of the third movement, only a little more forte, and with an extra run of your own feeling."

May repositioned herself before diving back into the music, her fingers working quickly over the taut strings. Charity listened, closing her eyes as she soaked in the music. May seemed to know intuitively what would work, though as far as Charity could tell, she never played the same thing twice. May was by no means a precise musician, but she had an accomplished ear. When she was done, Charity smiled broadly. "Brilliant! Let me work on this a moment to see if I can translate it to paper."

She bent over the already cramped five-bar staff and went to work tweaking the arrangement. An added note here and there, and satisfaction was blooming in her chest as she teased the perfect arrangement from the chaos. Together, they were creating a story unique to them.

"Why do you always do that?"

Startled from her thoughts, Charity glanced up from her music, confusion creasing her brow. "What?" She'd almost forgotten May still sat beside her zither, quietly waiting for Charity to make the changes.

Pointing to Charity's neck, May said, "Rubbing your shoulders. Are we working you too hard?"

Ah. Self-consciously allowing her hands to drop to her lap, she shrugged. "*I'm* working me too hard. I can't help it—whenever I am excited about something, I'll work and work at it until it sounds exactly like the music in my head when I play it out loud. Luckily, my mother isn't here to chastise my dreadful posture."

And it really was awful—she was hunched over like a miser counting his coins. Belatedly she sat up straighter, just as Mama would expect of her. "I suppose that is the cost of being a musician."

Bemused, May crossed her arms. "What is? Bad posture?"

"No," she said, rolling her eyes. "Losing oneself so thoroughly in the music. Forgetting everything else in the world except the perfect rise and fall of notes, dancing to the tempo in one's mind."

May quirked a single brow, looking at her as though Charity had quite lost her mind. "I think that sort of experience is reserved for the virtuosos."

It was Charity's turn to be taken aback. May sounded so flippant. As though music was just a hobby for her. "But . . . you play so beautifully. With such passion. Surely you have experienced the singular high of playing the perfect piece."

"Thank you for the compliment. Yes, I do play for the enjoyment of it, but I certainly don't live and breathe music. I don't play until my neck and shoulders ache or my fingers bleed. I play to think of home, and to pass time in a most pleasant way."

Though May seemed unperturbed with her comment,

Charity was shocked. May had such passion behind her performances—Charity could read her ability as another might read a book. But one look at her relaxed features and Charity could plainly see she wasn't nearly as invested in her talent as she'd originally thought.

"Come, don't look at me as though I just admitted to possessing a third eye. I do thoroughly enjoy playing. I simply bow to your superior musical sensibilities. Of the three of us, you are by far the most naturally talented."

"Well, thank you. I guess."

"You're welcome," May said with a regal tip of her head. "And you really should take better care of yourself while slaving to your art. Every time I see you, you inevitably are rubbing at those poor, abused shoulders of yours."

Charity couldn't help but chuckle. "Yes, Mother."

"You'd better listen to me, or I may have to set Suyin on you."

She was clearly teasing, her blue eyes merry in the diffuse afternoon sunlight. Charity smiled back. "That sounds rather unpleasant. What is sue yin?"

"Not what, *who*. Suyin is my lady's maid, and she is a treasure. She has a special technique to relieve muscle tension that is highly effective, if somewhat intimidating."

Charity raised a dubious brow. "I'm not certain I want to find out what that means." She vaguely knew of the oddities of Eastern healings, though nothing specific. It seemed that some very odd ingredients were involved in their tinctures.

Her reaction amused May, who chuckled and shook her head. "I don't even want to know what it is you are imagining, based on your expression. *Tui na* is simply a form of therapy for the joints and muscles. Papa paid

Suyin an outrageous amount of money to come work for us, specifically because of her skills, when Mama grew ill. It was the only thing in the world that brought relief for the terrible head and body aches Mama suffered toward the end." She swallowed, visibly regrouping. "We are forever grateful to her, and Suyin's become part of the family since then."

A shadow of sadness passed over May's eyes, before she shook her head and resolutely smiled. "Truly, having her with me helps to keep me sane now, living here with Warden Stanwix."

Charity laughed out loud at the description. "I must admit, the more I hear about your aunt, the more terrified I am to meet her. Is she really the battle-ax you make her out to be?"

"You shall simply have to see for yourself. I would say more dragon than battle-ax, but for all I know, she could be a typical English matron."

Charity gave an overdramatic cringe. "They are rather terrifying. To be avoided at all costs at any and all social functions."

"Duly noted. I was so very, very relieved that she has agreed to let me attend the opening ball for the festival, I didn't even think of all the scary people I may meet."

Charity couldn't help but think of the past Season, and how thoroughly unpleasant it had been to endure. Yes, the *ton* loved nothing more than finding a juicy piece of gossip to worry like dogs with a bone. She was determined not to let them get to her during the festival, however. This was a different sort of ambience, after all. They were all there for the common love of music.

Right?

Nodding with more confidence than she felt, she came to her feet. "There is nothing to worry about, my dear.

You shall impress them all with your beauty and talent. Just smile and nod, and you'll do fine."

May wrinkled her perfect little nose. "I suppose time will tell."

Footsteps in the hall heralded the arrival of May's footman to transport her instrument home. Charity walked the few steps to her friend and linked arms with her. "You'll have them eating out of your hand in no time."

The slightest bit of jealousy tainted Charity's tone, despite her effort to smile. She actually envied May's ability to come into this festival with a clean slate. During Charity's first Season, she had been a triumph; the next, a failure. Now she couldn't help but wonder what tomorrow's huge ball would bring.

Chapter Eight

Stepping though the doors of the cavernous Ballroom, Charity paused to marvel at the transformation. The last time she had been at the Assembly Rooms, there had been a smattering of wooden chairs and potted plants, with no special touches to enliven the lovely but somewhat plain place.

Tonight, however, the entire space was bathed in glittering light from hundreds of candles adorning the five crystal chandeliers spanning the arched ceiling. Garlands made from what looked to be thousands of summer blooms, in all their colorful and fragrant glory, swooped along the walls. Close to a thousand people filled the space, all turned out in their finest dress in order to celebrate the official start of the festival. It looked like a scene from a fairy tale, complete with the most beautiful gowns anyone could imagine.

"My, my," Grandmama breathed, lifting her lorgnette in order to better inspect the grand space. "Reminds me of the way things used to be here in Bath, back when I was a young debutante. You should have seen the splendor." She shook her head, memories clouding her gaze as she lowered her eyepiece. "Back then, Bath had been the single most fashionable place to be in all of England—outside the Season, of course."

Charity smiled. "This really is something to see. I simply cannot wait to hear the orchestra. One imagines the committee went out of its way to find the best of the best for such an event." Instead of being tucked away in an alcove or an adjoining room, a small stage had been constructed at one end of the room, and the musicians were busily inspecting their instruments and sheet music. Excitement crowded out any apprehension she might have had about being in such a crush. There were too many people here, anyway, for her to be of any notice.

Speaking of too many people, she glanced around the room again, this time searching for her friends' faces. They really should have devised a meeting place. The veritable sea of people flowed through the entire room and spilled out into the corridor and adjoining rooms. Even the balcony was packed, with some glancing out over the crowd while others were absorbed in conversation.

"There does seem to be an alarming lack of unoccupied chairs," her grandmother said, diverting Charity's attention. She was right. Seating was available around the perimeter of the room, but every one she could see was taken.

"Shall I fetch a footman and have one brought out?"

"No, let us take a turn about the room and see what comes up."

Charity extended her elbow. "If you're certain." Her grandmother nodded and joined arms with her, and together they set off into the crush. It was something of a surprise to realize how many faces she didn't recognize. After seeing the same people at each of her two Seasons, it was rather refreshing to be surrounded by so many that were unknown to her. To think she wouldn't be judged for the failed courtship was enough to bring a smile to her lips.

They made slow progress, moving counterclockwise around the room. The first door they encountered revealed the Great Octagon, which was filled to the brim with revelers. Through the next doorway was the Card Room, where both players and observers crowed around any one of the dozens of round tables set up across the room.

Grandmama's eyes lit up. "Cards! Oh, I wonder if anyone is in need of a piquet partner."

Charity hid a grin. If there was, said partner was about to find out how ruthless of a player her grandmother could be. "Let me see if there is someone nearby who can help us."

In a few minutes' time, Grandmama was seated, cards in hand and an entirely too-innocent look on her face. Smiling, Charity slipped back into the ballroom, eager to find May and Sophie. The music would be starting any moment, and she wanted to be able to experience it with them.

"Miss Effington?"

Charity stopped and glanced to the young woman who had spoken to her. *Oh, what rotten luck.* She stretched her lips into a polite smile. "Miss Harmon, how lovely to see you."

And by lovely, she meant dreadful. As the youngest daughter of Viscount Wexley, Marianne was of similar rank and station to Charity. Marianne also excelled at the pianoforte, though her style was drastically different from Charity's. She meticulously played each note exactly as written, perfect from a technical standpoint, but sorely lacking from a creative one.

What made Marianne such a disagreeable companion was the fact that she seemed to always be in some sort of unspoken competition. She smiled now, allowing her gaze to sweep over Charity as though she had just begged for her opinion. Charity's defenses immediately went up. She quite liked her gown tonight. The pale peach patent net wasn't an obvious choice for a person with red hair, but Charity thought it was very flattering to her skin.

"My, don't you look . . . colorful?" Marianne scrunched her nose in an oddly delicate way, making it abundantly clear that her meaning was not what her honeyed tone would suggest.

"Why, thank you," Charity replied, her tone equally sweet. Because, honestly, she'd rather be colorful than disingenuous. "You're looking well." Unfortunately, it was the truth. Marianne's hair shone dark gold in the candlelight, a near-perfect match for her diaphanous gold gown. Her brown eyes almost looked bronze against her pale skin.

"Yes," she agreed, patting her perfectly coiffed curls. "The city does seem to agree with me. Which is a good thing, since we'll be here for the entire two months. My father is on the selection committee, after all."

That was *not* good news.

"How lovely for him to donate his time so generously." The fact that Marianne had always considered Charity her greatest competitor did not bode well. Lord Wexley was the type who would do whatever possible to give himself and his family the advantage in any situation.

"It is, isn't it? I must say, I am surprised to see you here this evening. I would have thought that if you were in town, you would have shown up for registration. A pity you decided not to participate in the recitals." Her sly smile said exactly how much of a pity she thought it was.

She leaned forward, the mock sincerity on her face instantly putting Charity on guard. "Though I can certainly understand your desire to keep a low profile, what with the Season you had."

Charity ground her teeth together. Would the woman ever get over her need to want to prove herself better than Charity? Lord knew she had positively delighted in the gossip surrounding the broken courtship. And now, pretending commiseration for the sole reason of bringing it up again . . .

No, Charity would not fall into her trap. Setting her lips in a determined smile, she said, "I was a tad late, but I did indeed register."

Marianne's brow wrinkled unbecomingly. "What? But I didn't see your name on the list."

Charity flipped open her fan in an effort to combat the increasingly warm temperatures. "It was there, I assure you. You may have overlooked it since it was attached to two other names as well."

"I don't understand. You're performing with other people?" So much incredulity laced the woman's words, one would think Charity had said she had joined a band of gypsies.

"Yes—a trio. I'm very excited about it."

"You? A trio?" Marianne's voice rose a notch or two, effectively conveying her opinion on the matter. "I suppose it makes sense if one is not capable of performing solo."

Charity's fan came to an abrupt halt even as heat rushed through her veins at the rudeness of the comment. The snide remark about her Season was one thing, but this was too much. She cast about for some sort of response, but nothing came to her. Who *says* such things to another?

"Oh, she's plenty capable."

Charity whipped around to find May standing cross-armed directly behind her, looking every bit as intimidating as a Viking maiden, with her hair in gorgeous braids encircling her crown and her back ramrod straight. With its simple cut, her icy blue silk gown was subtle but undeniably exquisite. "She's simply secure enough in her abilities to take on new challenges." Her glittering blue gaze flitted to Charity. "Something for which I should tell you, Charity, we are exceedingly grateful."

Marianne's nose scrunched up as though she smelled something rotten. "I beg your pardon? We have *not* been introduced, and I don't believe either of us was talking to you."

Snapped from her stupor, Charity linked arms with May. She may not have a ready retort in these situations, but she would not allow Marianne to intimidate her friend. With a determined smile in place, she said, "Miss Harmon, do please allow me to introduce you to Miss Bradford. She is new to Bath—new to England, in fact—and I am very pleased to have her not inconsiderable talents in our trio."

"Charmed," May said, her voice flat.

"Indeed," Marianne replied, conveying dislike impressively well in the single word. She flicked her gaze back to Charity. "Good luck with your trio. I do *so* look forward to seeing you attempt to perform."

Charity kept her lips pressed together in an expression that could have been mistaken for a smile to the casual observer, as Marianne disappeared into the crush like a snake into the reeds.

"Friend of yours?"

Letting out a pent-up breath on a slight chuckle, Charity shook her head. "Not the term I would use to describe her. Thank you, by the way. I never seem to be able to defend myself. I really must learn to think faster."

"I don't imagine it is thinking faster that you need to worry about. I think it's a matter of not being bothered if you offend someone. Frankly, I'm not sure I'd wish for you to change."

"You say that because you are always brilliant in these situations. I might as well be a statue."

May grinned and patted her hand. "At least you are a very becoming statue. I quite love that color on you. In fact I have a bolt of embroidered silk in this color that would look divine against your peaches-and-cream skin."

An opportunity to get her hands on some of May's amazing fabrics? Charity wasn't about to let such an opportunity go to waste. "Truly? I'd so love to see it. If for no other reason than to hear what other description Miss Harmon can come up with should she see me in it."

They exchanged collusive smiles. After an entire Season of unpleasant encounters just like this one, it was rather thrilling to have someone so thoroughly in her corner.

"There you are!"

Charity glanced up just as Sophie waved and ducked between the pair of older gentlemen who stood talking nearby. Her cheeks were flushed bright pink, and her eyes danced beneath the proliferation of black curls piled atop her head. "My goodness, I think half of England is here tonight—and then some. I must have heard four different languages as I tried to find you. And just look how pretty you both are tonight."

"Isn't this ball amazing?" May asked, her gaze sweeping across the crush. "It only took moments to lose my aunt. She is probably cursing me as we speak."

Charity laughed. "Well, we must make the most of our freedom, then. As this is your first event, May, what would you like to do?"

"It's past time I learn a bit about the people I shall be seeing for the next two months. Let us take a turn about the room before the orchestra starts, and you can fill me in on all the gossip."

"You know," Sophie said as they started forward, "I don't recognize nearly as many people as I would have thought. It's like my first Season all over again! Oh, look. There's Miss Paddington—she plays the violin quite well."

Charity lifted a hand in greeting as Miss Paddington looked their way and smiled. She was nearly as tall as May, but was quite a bit stockier. Tonight she looked very pretty in her Grecian-inspired gown. Beside her, a dark-haired man nodded, and Charity smiled back. "That's the Earl of Dennington. Surprising to see him here—he doesn't usually attend events. His brother is married to a great friend of mine." Evie would have been her sister-in-law, had Charity gone through with the marriage to Richard.

They continued on, pointing out some people from afar, speaking with others, and even offering a few introductions. The knot of anxiety that had surfaced after the encounter with Marianne had eased, and Charity was really enjoying herself.

A man with light brown hair and a ready smile a few yards away caught her eye. "Oh, let's go speak with Lord Ev—"

Sophie cut her off with an emphatic "No!" In one smooth motion she forcefully guided them in a neat half circle, effectively turning their backs to the man.

Charity gaped at her friend. "What was *that*?"

Cheeks flaming red-hot, Sophie sheepishly shook her head. "No, please don't ask. Not here, anyway."

Biting back a smile, May said, "Well, well—I do believe somebody here may have a *tendre*."

"I had no idea," Charity replied, grinning broadly at poor blushing Sophie. "Very well, we'll leave it for now. But be prepared to tell us everything at the next practice."

The sound of the conductor rapping his baton against the music stand rang out over the low roar of the crowd, and Sophie visibly wilted with relief. "Yes, fine," she agreed, and the topic was set aside as the musicians raised their instruments. The other attendees quickly ceased their conversations and turned toward the stage. Excitement seemed to radiate around the room as the man raised his arms, paused for one dramatic moment, then plunged into the opening piece. The first strains of Handel's *Water Music* rose to the vaulted ceiling, magnificent in its perfect execution.

She was in heaven.

Hours later, Charity floated upstairs to her music room, still reveling in the delights of the evening. The orchestra had been spectacular, setting the perfect tone for the official start of the festival. Even the food had been delicious, with both sweets and savories to complement the wide range of beverages. She *may* have even had a few sips too many of the Madeira, but it had been worth it. Between being serenaded by such talented musicians and having the opportunity to meet people who had yet to form any opinion about her, it had been one of the best evenings she could remember.

Humming beneath her breath, she slipped into the music room and carefully set down her candelabra atop the polished surface of the pianoforte. So much music filled her head, the silence of the room didn't even register. The evening was magical, even now. Especially now. She wanted to set fingers to keys before the notes got away from her.

The room was stifling compared to the cool night air she had just been in. Letting her shawl slip off her shoulders and pool on the bench, she walked around to the narrow glass doors and pulled them open. She shivered as the chilly air touched her warm skin. There was a hint of moisture in the air, though not enough to cause fog. The stars were visible from where she stood. They twinkled like a million tiny pieces of crystal as the moon shed white light over the narrow balcony.

Shadows at night—who would have thought?

One of the shadows moved, and she squeaked in surprise. With her heart racing, she leaned over the threshold, her eyes adjusting to the darkness as she peered toward the balcony next door. A figure emerged from the gloom as her vision improved.

"Lord Cadgwith?" She didn't hide her shock at finding him there—it was well past midnight! Why would he be sitting out here, alone in the dark?

"Good evening, Miss Effington." His voice was low and quiet in the stillness of the night. He sat in a simple wooden chair, his feet propped on the metal railing.

She froze, unsure of what to do. She hadn't seen him since the encounter out front almost a week earlier, when they had parted on less than cordial terms. But tonight he seemed subdued, docile even. He stayed where he was, not bothering to rise at her presence. She was glad for that; she didn't want him towering over her. He was less intimidating like this, especially with his unkempt hair and the first hints of a beard shadowing his jaw.

She drew in a startled breath as she realized his shirt collar was open and his neck cloth quite absent. The darkness between the split white panels of his shirt had to be his skin.

His *bare* skin.

Her mouth went dry. She shouldn't be out here. She certainly shouldn't be seeing him in any state of dishabille. "I, um, beg your pardon, my lord. Do excuse me."

Clumsy with nerves and bit too much drink, she turned, almost banging her elbow on the door casing in her haste.

"Wait," he said, his voice sharp.

She stopped. Did he, of all people, actually want to her to stay? Taking a tentative step onto the balcony, she said, "Yes?"

He sighed, dropping his feet to the floor and leaning forward to rest his elbows on his knees. Running a hand over the back of his neck, he said, "It occurs to me, Miss Effington, that I have not been the consummate gentleman where you are concerned."

She quirked an eyebrow. A bit of an understatement.

"Therefore," he continued, dropping his hand and looking directly at her, "I feel I must apologize."

Apologize? She gaped at him for a moment, at a loss of what to say. Was this the real Lord Cadgwith? Or was he going to confuse her again, acting as though they were enemies the next time they met?

She tilted her head, scrutinizing the words. He did seem quite earnest. There was absolutely no irony, no sarcasm, no ambiguity in his tone. Though she couldn't see his eyes clearly in the shadow of the moon, he actually sounded sincere. Tired—exhausted, even—but honest.

"Er . . . thank you?"

He chuckled quietly, a rusty sound from deep in his chest. "I must not be doing it right if you're questioning your response."

As her eyes adjusted further, she could see his ragged, almost haggard expression. Something within her softened. He looked beaten, as though he hadn't any fight left in him. It was so starkly different from the other times they had been together, she had no idea what to make of it. Where was the brusque manner she associated with him? Was this what Grandmama had sensed within him when she spoke of his wounded heart?

Charity stepped closer to the railing separating their balconies. The landlord had mentioned that the two townhouses had originally been one. Apparently, his solution to the single balcony was to have a waist-high decorative metal divider installed to split it in two. Since this was her first time to actually use it, it hadn't occurred to her before now how very unprivate it could be.

"Thank you," she said with more conviction. "And you're not the only one. I think the both of us could have a lesson in manners, when it comes to the other."

"Indeed." He settled back in the chair, letting his head fall against the high back. "My brother's widow, Felicity, has quite given up on her quest to civilize me. You see how in vain her efforts have been thus far." He gave a tired, self-deprecating half smile that somehow made her belly give a little flip.

"It would seem that they are starting to have an effect. Her efforts, I mean." She curled her fingers over the cool metal railing. Her training, on the other hand, seemed to have abandoned her completely. She couldn't seem to force her gaze away from his open collar.

"Something like that."

Belatedly the implication of his words occurred to her: his brother's widow. A piece of the mystery that was the Baron Cadgwith clicked into place. "So, was it your brother, then? Was he the one from whom you inherited the title?" It was too bold a question by half, but the lingering effect of the Madeira made her brave. Or was it nosy?

He sighed heavily and nodded. "Yes."

A wealth of sadness resided in the word. Regret? Pain? His grief pulled at her, softening her heart further. "I'm so very sorry."

"No one is sorrier than I." He gave a quiet, humorless laugh. "In more ways than one."

She knew some men who would consider it a boon to inherit a title from a brother's untimely demise, but clearly that couldn't be further from the truth in this case. She had never had a sibling, but she had dearly wanted one. It was a relationship she envied, and she felt his loss keenly. It was in the rasp of his voice, the slope of his shoulders, the tightening of his jaw.

His meaning sank in then, that he himself was a sorry person. She shook her head. "As much as I might have agreed with you yesterday, I think there is some goodness in you yet, my lord."

He tilted his held up, searching her expression. Did he expect sarcasm? Irony? She allowed his inspection, allowed him to see the truth in it.

The silence stretched for a few moments until at last he let his head rest back against his chair again. "How was the ball?"

She blinked at his sudden change in subject. *The ball?* What did that have to do with anything? "One of the finest I have ever been to. It is a pity you did not attend."

"As I said before, I am no music lover. For me, there is no more pleasing music than silence."

Loosening her grip on the railing, she tucked her hands beneath her arms and leaned a shoulder against the exterior wall. "I find you are an enigma. Why come to a city in the midst of a music festival if not to enjoy the music? It's not as though you're here for the waters," she said, wry humor lifting her brow.

"No, indeed," he said, so softly she almost missed it.

Blowing out a breath, he unfolded himself from the chair. His shirt, unrestricted by waistcoat or jacket, billowed loosely where it tucked into his pants. The wanness of his countenance struck her again. Was he unwell? Something he ate, perhaps?

"If you'll excuse me, Miss Effington, I believe I will retire."

"Yes, of course," she said quickly, straightening her posture and dropping her hands to her sides. "Good night, my lord."

He nodded before disappearing inside. The air stirred as he closed the door, and she detected the slight hint of spice and spirits. Could that be the cause of his subdued mood and quiet reflection? Could spirits be responsible for softening his normally sharp temperament?

As she slipped back inside, she realized that the music in her head had left her, and was replaced by the low, dark tones of a piece utterly foreign to her. She shook her head—the wine must be playing tricks on her.

The baron desired silence, did he? Well, tonight, just this once, she would grant his wish. It was the least she could do for the pain she had seen deep within him tonight. Clicking the door closed, she retrieved her candelabra and padded back to the corridor. For now, she was content to let the music within her remain where it was.

Tomorrow they might go back to disliking each other, or at the very least avoiding each other, but as she glided up the stairs, her hips swaying in time with her internal music, she decided that in that exact moment, she might actually like the baron next door.

Not bothering to light a candle, Hugh pulled his shirt over his head and tossed it onto the end of the bed. God, but he was weary to his very marrow. Today's attack had lasted upward of six hours, the pain throbbing in his head like waves pounding a shipwrecked vessel. He had already been torn apart, but still it hadn't stopped.

He undid the fastenings of his pants and let them drop to the floor before climbing into the tall, imposing master bed. As exhausted as he was, he was so damn grateful to feel no pain, no lingering pressure or residual throbbing.

Few people realized how freeing such a state was. To be able to move and see and speak like a normal person. Although he couldn't say how normal he had been with Miss Effington just then. She had looked gorgeous, fresh and sweet and alive with the joy of her evening. For once, he had wanted to talk with her. To exchange civil words while his mind was relatively unclouded and her claws were retracted.

He was glad for the encounter, no matter how unorthodox. Even though she had scoffed at the idea of someone like him needing the medicinal waters. Few people ever looked at him and suspected he would need such a thing. They looked at someone like Jacobson or any of the thousands of other gravely wounded soldiers and saw that they may require such treatment. But him? Besides a few old scars, he looked perfectly hale and hearty. Normal. The extent of his injury would be unfathomable to most.

And yet it was there.

He was an infirm, whether he wished to admit it or not. And though his attacks had been less frequent since his arrival, they were by no means gone. The idea of going home and being able to take up the full mantle of his responsibilities still seemed almost laughable.

He slid beneath the cool sheets and lay back against the fluffy goose-down pillow. What would Miss Effington think of him if she knew what sort of man he really was? Would she think even less of him than she already did? Was that possible? After the way their encounters had gone, it was hard to say.

Only tonight, he had glimpsed something different in her moonlit eyes. Compassion? Understanding? Pity? He wasn't sure, but he felt whatever it was, she had seen him in a whole different light tonight.

She'd caught him at a moment when his defenses were weak, his body exhausted, and, because of that, she'd seen a glimpse through the door he usually kept locked tight. How much of the real Hugh had she seen? He shifted uncomfortably beneath the covers, disliking the sudden surge of vulnerability.

The less she saw, the better.

Chapter Nine

"Good afternoon, my lady. How do you do?" Careful to adhere to proper etiquette, Charity greeted May's aunt with a solemn curtsy. Lady Stanwix could not have been in starker contrast to her niece. Everything about the woman demanded propriety and perfect manners.

The older woman peered up at her from beneath the lace of her generous mob cap. "I am well, Miss Effington, as I hope you are. How fares your grandmother in this dreadful heat?"

Charity wisely refrained from pointing out that the lady was wearing easily twice the amount of fabric necessary by today's fashion standards. No doubt she was of the opinion that modern gowns were dreadfully revealing and sorely lacking in the sort of voluminous skirts she clearly favored.

"She is well. Thank you for asking. I shall pass along your kind concern for her health." It was odd to discover that the two women knew each other. Though Grandmama had declined to elaborate, apparently Lady Stanwix had caused quite the uproar in her day by ensnaring the old earl some thirty years ago. Looking at her now, with her exceedingly modest style of dress and wisps of gray hair framing her somber face, it was impossible to believe she ever been anything but a stern matron. "And thank you for allowing us to rehearse in your lovely home."

The former countess pinched her lips together and glanced toward the door. "I daresay it will be a welcome change to hear good, respectable music in this house again."

Charity bit her lip against responding to such an underhanded insult to May's unusual but beautiful music. Better to fight with kindness—and deliberate obtuseness. "Yes, you must be so pleased to have such a talented musician staying with you now. My grandmother has said frequently how glad she is to hear song in her home once more."

Lady Stanwix's mouth flattened into a thin line, clearly displeased with Charity's response.

"Good afternoon, Charity!" May's greeting preceded her into the drawing room, her soft pink skirts swishing as she hurried in. She wore a pink sari-style sash across her chest, with golden flowers and deep green leaves embroidered along both edges. It was a much more exotic choice than usual. Perhaps it was because they were meeting here today, and she likely wouldn't be leaving the house.

It was a shame, if that was the case. May looked like a golden-haired goddess of the Far East—a perfect mix of two normally disparate worlds. Fitting, since that was exactly what she was.

"Good afternoon! You are looking quite lovely today." Did she imagine the soft, disagreeable sound from Lady Stanwix's direction? Charity smiled broadly to her friend. "Are you ready to rehearse? I'm eager to begin."

"Certainly. Hargrove," she said, turning her attention

to the loitering butler, "do please see Miss Wembley to the music room when she arrives." At the man's silent nod, May led the way to the small music room tucked at the back of the townhouse.

For such an enlightened purpose, the room was decidedly drab. The quality of the fabrics and furniture was obviously superior, but a less inspiring color palette, Charity could scarce imagine. Olive green and dark brown were the exact wrong choice for the dark wood of the pianoforte and trim. Even the antique brass frames and sconces seemed dull.

Closing the door, May offered an apologetic cringe. "So sorry about that. I don't know why Hargrove took you to the drawing room instead of straight here, where I was practicing. Was she very awful to you?"

"Not so bad," she said running a finger over the yellowed keys of the pianoforte. "Has this been used in the past decade? It's so fine, I hate to think of it sitting here unplayed."

"Only a half decade, I think," she said with a laugh. "My cousin Elizabeth married five or so years ago, and as far as I know, she was the last one to use it."

Charity played a few scales. "Remarkably in tune. This shall do beautifully."

"My aunt is very particular about all things in this house. She wants everything just so—including for me to set aside my dreadful ways and act like a *proper Englishwoman*." The last was said in a fair impersonation of Lady Stanwix's clipped nasal tones. May rolled her eyes. "If she is how a proper Englishwoman should behave, I think I'd rather stow away on the nearest ship.

"Oh," she said, brightening, "speaking of ships, that reminds me." She hurried to a credenza pressed against one olive-toned wall. She lifted one of the two bolts of fabric from its surface and turned to present it like an offering to the gods. "For you, madam."

Charity stepped forward, her hand coming to her mouth. It was exquisite. "Oh, May," she breathed, running a reverent hand over the shimmery peach satin. "It's gorgeous!"

Elegant cream, blush, and peach embroidered blossoms unfurled across the length of it, the vines swooping and curving like a living thing. Ivory-colored birds with hints of teal and purple on their chests nestled among the foliage. Crystals had been sewn in place of eyes, giving a hint of sparkle as the fabric moved. "You cannot give such a thing away—you must keep it for yourself."

"Not at all. I prefer the more dramatic colors to accentuate the embroidery. And at the time I bought it, I was still bronzed from the tropical sun. Now I'm as pale as a fish belly and would look dreadfully washed-out in it. You, on the other hand," she said, holding the bolt just beneath Charity's chin, "with your auburn hair, will look like an irresistible confection. Perfection."

Charity moved to the brass-framed mirror hanging between the room's two windows. It really was glorious. Sumptuous, rich, and perfectly suited to her unusual hair and lightly freckled skin. Marianne would eat her words if she ever saw Charity wear it. Out of nowhere, she wondered what the baron would think of her in something like this. A thrill raced through her veins, spreading through her whole body. She did her best to ignore the sensation—it shouldn't matter what the man thought of her.

Yet last night she had seen him in an entirely different way. A small part of her wanted to see more of *that* Lord Cadgwith.

"What do you think?" May asked, snapping Charity from her wandering thoughts.

She smiled at May's reflection. "I think you are much too kind for offering such a thing. I also think that I am much too selfish to refuse."

May grinned, her white teeth flashing brightly. "Thank God."

The door opened then, and they both turned just as the butler let Sophie in. Instead of her usual palette of yellows and whites, she wore a pretty pale blue dress with a matching ribbon threaded through her hair. Even without the cheery color, her smile was as sunny as ever.

"So sorry I'm late. Mama snagged me as I walked out the door, to discuss our plans for this evening. Not that she couldn't have done so during any of the previous five hours in which I was awake and unoccupied. Anyway, are either of you attending Lord Derington's dinner tomorrow? Please say that you are. I would rather not spend the entire evening attempting not to make a ninny of myself in front of a bunch of strangers. Though I do wonder how many will be strangers. It could be all the same people we always see in London, for all I know."

May shook her head. "Unfortunately, I shall be right here. I don't think my aunt is keen to foist me on society again just yet. I think she's holding out hope of civilizing me between now and the recital." Her tone was dry, though exasperation lurked behind it. "Thank goodness she let me attend the ball last night, though she is still upset with me for striking out on my own."

"Well, I certainly hope you resist her efforts to tame you," Charity said wryly, setting down the fabric before reaching out to give her fingers a squeeze. "I think anyone would find you interesting and intriguing, as evidenced by how brilliantly you did last night. And speaking of the ball . . ." She trailed off, raising her eyebrows expectantly.

"Oh *yes*," May said, grinning devilishly. "The *ball*."

They both turned to Sophie, who cringed, her cheeks brightening all over again. "You didn't forget that, I see." She sighed dramatically, then plopped down onto the nearest chair. "I may or may not have made a complete fool of myself the last time I spoke to Lord Evansleigh, and I wasn't expecting to see him there at all, so when I spotted him I more or less panicked. Not terribly sophisticated of me, to say the least."

Charity sat in the opposite chair and patted her friend's knee. "Oh, you didn't make yourself look the fool. And besides, the earl is always so nice, he'd hardly hold it against you if you did." He was one of the few people who had neither avoided her nor gossiped about her after she and Richard parted ways. In fact, Lord Evansleigh was the first to ask her to dance at her first ball of the past Season.

Sophie pressed her palms to her cheeks and shook her head. "I know, I know, I should just forget it. But you know me and my mouth; sometimes it has a mind of its own. The last time I saw him, I asked him how his *father* was."

"Ah," Charity said, cringing a bit on her behalf. The old earl had been dead for years. "Well, I'm sure he's probably already forgotten about it. I wouldn't worry with it overmuch."

"Says the woman who always gives her words due thought," Sophie grumbled good-naturedly. "Of course I know you're right. Maybe someday I'll be able to face him again. In the meantime, I shall simply have to hope he won't be at Lord Derington's party. I'm quite looking forward to it and would hate to have to spend the evening hiding in the retiring room." She gave a teasing wink. "Which brings me back to my original question. Will you be attending, Charity?"

Nodding, Charity said, "Grandmama and I shall be there. Lord Derington is well-known to my family. His father, the earl, is a longtime friend of my father's."

This was a dinner that she was actually looking forward to. Derington had always been an admirer of Charity's playing. He was tall and broad enough to almost be intimidating, but his jovial disposition made him infinitely approachable.

"Oh, thank goodness. Though we shall miss you, May. Oh!" she exclaimed, noticing the fabric for the first time. "How beautiful is that?"

Charity couldn't help but laugh at Sophie's quick change of topics. Her mind moved as fast as a runaway carriage at times. "Isn't it, though? May very generously gave it to me just now, though I must think of a way to repay her."

"Not at all. And, Sophie, I have one for you as well." She returned to the credenza and presented a bolt of creamy butter yellow silk. Both gold and silver thread twined to create a brilliant metallic design that gleamed in the afternoon light.

Sophie couldn't have been more thrilled. After much exclamation and admiration, draping the fabric this way and that over her own gown, she looked up with wide eyes. "I know! Why don't we have special gowns made just for the recital? We can choose a common design, and each use our own special fabric. We could let May consult with the modiste so we all look properly exotic. What do you think?"

"I think," May said with a grin, "that is a perfect idea."

"Seconded," Charity added. She could hardly wait to have a gown made of her peach satin, and the recital would be the perfect place to wear it. "However, if we are to be ready for the recital, we must get to rehearsing!"

They quickly took their places at their respective instruments. Charity rolled her shoulders and tilted her
neck back and forth to stretch the muscles. Between
their practices and the work she had done preparing the
pieces, her muscles seemed to protest every time she sat
down at the bench. But she wasn't about to allow a little
pain to get in the way of her music.

She did a few more scales, feeling out the new instrument. "We won't be bothering anyone, will we?"

May looked up from tuning her strings, her brow lifted.
"Lord Cad has made an impression on you, hasn't he?"

Lord *Cad*?

Her knowing look somehow made Charity blush, and
she rushed to fill the silence. "No! Well, I mean, yes, in
the sense that I am more mindful of those around me.
But that is the only thing he has impressed upon me."

Her mind leaped straight to the image of him draped
across his chair in the darkness, his feet propped against
the railing. None of his insolence or arrogance had been
apparent. Up until yesterday she would have said Lord
Cad was the perfect term for him. But now . . . well, it
just did not seem so fitting anymore. She absently rubbed
at the back of her neck, easing the tightness even as she
remembered him doing the exact same thing last night.

May's hands went straight to her waist. "Charity Effington, your cheeks are bright as hot coals. I thought
you thoroughly disliked the man. Have there been any
developments we should know about?"

Both her friends stared at her with great interest, making the blush that much worse. There had been developments, but for some reason, she wasn't quite prepared to
share the intimacy of the late-night visit. "I'm blushing
because you are both looking at me. Nothing out of the
ordinary with the baron. He's still our neighbor, and I

don't see how that will change between now and the end of the summer."

Sophie exchanged a wide-eyed glance with May. "I must say, that sounds quite a bit less disagreeable to you than it had a week ago. Was he at the ball last night? Drat it all, I will never forgive my mother for delaying our arrival so long. I just knew I would miss all the best parts of the evening."

That was the good thing about Sophie: her comments were generally so meandering, one could choose which question one wished to respond to. "He was not in attendance last night, and you really weren't that late—only a few minutes behind May and me."

"You're still blushing," May pointed out, a bemused smile lifting her lips.

"I am ginger-haired and fair-skinned—I'm *always* blushing. Now, do leave me be, and let's begin our practice." She lifted her chin in her best no-nonsense impression, and May relented with a chuckle.

"Very well, have it your way. Sophie and I will simply have to fill in any details with our exceedingly overactive imaginations."

Well, wasn't this just mortifying? Especially since she wasn't even sure what she thought of the man. He was still the same person who had barged rudely into her own home to insult her, not to mention pounding on the wall and hating her music.

"You may do as you please. I shall apply my imagination to our rehearsals."

But as they finally ceased their teasing and began to play, she realized what she had said wasn't entirely true. Even as she poured herself into the music, some small part of her lingered on the baron and their exchange the previous evening. His vulnerability, that small part of him that he hid beneath his normally brusque manner, called to her. It evoked a strange tenderness toward him that she wasn't quite sure what to do with. She pictured his haunted eyes and silvery scars as they had looked in the moonlight, and her heart twisted a bit.

There was much more to the man than she had ever imagined, a depth she wouldn't have guessed before last night. As she closed her eyes and listened to the music he so disliked filling the air around her, she didn't feel any of the resentment toward him she had in the past. Instead, she felt a measure of sympathy. And curiosity.

Desire, even.

And above it all, a passion to know more about the man she had glimpsed last night.

Chapter Ten

"Well, I'll be damned. Is that you, Danby, old boy?" Hugh smiled as Lord Derington pounded him soundly on the shoulder with one meaty hand. "Indeed it is, old friend. It's been too long."

"So it has, so it has. Cambridge was a long way off. Lifetime, really." Dering waved for Hugh to take a chair in the masculine den that served as his study.

"Perhaps two," Hugh agreed. He chose one of the dark leather club chairs grouped around a marble-topped round table. All the furniture seemed slightly oversized, but given Dering's six-foot-three height and impressively broad frame, it certainly made sense.

At the sideboard the viscount splashed some liquid from a stout crystal decanter into two glasses. "A drink for old times," he said, handing one to Hugh before settling into the opposite chair. It creaked ominously beneath his weight, though Dering seemed unconcerned. Despite his elegant dress and neatly combed black hair, the man was an ox, and he was probably used to such things. "Glad to see you returned to Britain's bosom alive and intact—for the most part, eh? I imagine women find that rakish scar quite appealing."

Alive? Yes. Intact? Hugh almost laughed. If only that were the case. But at that exact moment, he was feeling remarkably well, so he just smiled and nodded. "Of course. Can't get a moment's peace, what with all the attention." Eager to move on from the topic, he said, "How is your father? I still think the army could have used a shot like him, earl or not."

Dering chuckled good-naturedly. "Yes, he always was the bane of birds everywhere. Pheasants and grouse alike quiver when they see him coming their way. I'm happy to report that he is quite well, summering in Wales at the moment. Speaking of family, damn shame about your brother, old man. Never met him, but anyone good enough for Felicity must be worth his salt."

"He was. And thank you. I miss him greatly."

It had been a relief to discover Hugh actually knew the friend Felicity had written in order to procure an invitation. Not that he was surprised. He doubted the man had ever met a stranger in his life. Dering knew half of England in one way or another. When the viscount's letter arrived, Hugh actually found himself looking forward to the dinner. He had lost contact with the man, along with most of his other acquaintances, after the war. Retreating to his tiny seaside home at the very tip of England hadn't been conducive to entertaining. Nor had his injury.

Dering leaned back and propped his ankle on his knee. "I'm glad for the baby. New life in the face of death makes all the difference." His normally booming voice was quiet for once, and Hugh wondered exactly how well he related to such a statement. But Dering quickly recovered, offering a broad smile. "I really must remember to call you Cadgwith now."

The name still didn't quite feel right, despite how he tried to embrace it. It was like an ill-fitting shirt, uncomfortable no matter how one tugged and pulled. "Doesn't exactly roll off the tongue, does it?" he replied as lightly as he could manage.

"Lord Cadgwith suits you, really. You've always been the in-control, exacting type. I'm sure it served you well as a captain, and it will do so beautifully as a baron. Now, then," he said, sitting forward and lifting his glass. "Let us finish our brandy before the others arrive. We may need it to sustain us through the party tonight."

Hugh smiled and nodded, happy to do just that. It had been years since he had partaken of spirits for enjoyment and not to deaden the pain. He had slept remarkably well last night and had found perfect relaxation at the Baths that morning. The water still tasted like horse piss, but at least now he was convinced it was starting to help. The limberness of his neck was encouraging, and his normal pain at the base of his skull was actually mild enough as to be ignored.

A half hour later, he was still enjoying the warmth the brandy had brought when the first wave of guests arrived. The dark-haired girl from his neighbor's trio was one of the first to walk in the door. His hopes for remaining detached were dashed when she made a beeline for him after greeting their host.

"Why, Lord Cadgwith, how lovely to see you," she said, her warm smile reaching her dark eyes. "Allow me to introduce my mother, Mrs. Wembley. Mama, Baron Cadgwith is Miss Effington's neighbor for the summer."

The older woman was as short as her daughter but quite a bit rounder. Her eyes immediately lit up at the word *baron*. So, she was one of *those* mothers.

"How do you do?" he asked politely, careful not to show too much enthusiasm.

"Oh, quite well, my lord, as I hope you are. My, Sophie," she said, linking elbows with the girl, "I don't know how you could have failed to mention your introduction to Lord Cadgwith. Such a *notable* acquaintance."

And that, exactly, was one of the reasons he had dreaded inheriting the damn title. He wondered if she had actually noted his face, or only saw the word *baron* written across his forehead. Actually, she had probably already memorized his every feature—the better to recognize him later.

The girl seemed unperturbed at her mother's admonishment. "Oh, it had happened so fast. He was walking by while Miss Bradford and I were leaving, and, goodness, was it hot that day. We hadn't spoken for a moment when we all parted ways before the rain started again."

It was remarkable how many words she could fit into such a short amount of time. When she looked at him expectantly, he cleared his throat.

"Yes, it was a brief encounter," he murmured, glancing across the room for some form of escape. At that exact moment, Miss Effington entered the room, her grandmother at her side. He stood a little straighter, watching as his young neighbor greeted Dering warmly. Very warmly. Did the two have an acquaintanceship?

She looked around as her grandmother said something to their host. Charity's gaze caught on his, and whatever he had been thinking abruptly fell from his mind. Even from the distance separating them, he could see the subtle rise of her chest as she drew in a lungful of air. Licking her lips, she gave him a tiny nod of acknowledgment before looking away.

He pressed his own lips together, not sure what to make of the moment of awareness between them. It was the second instance he had felt such a connection between them, brief though each time was.

"Well," Mrs. Wembley said, drawing his attention back to her. "We shall have to remedy that, won't we? We have all the time we wish to get to know each other. Is this your first visit to Bath?"

All the time they wished? The woman knew how to stake a claim. "Yes," he said, trying to keep the impatience from his voice. Well, not *all* of it. He didn't want her to feel encouraged to keep him pinned down for the duration.

"How nice. Do tell us all about your plans for the summer. How are you tolerating this unusual hot weather?"

He concentrated on his peripheral vision, keeping Charity just in view. "Er, nothing overly exciting. The heat is tolerable enough. I wonder, would you excuse me for a moment? I see Lady Effington has arrived, and I have something I need to ask her before I forget." He smiled and gave a brief nod. "Pleasure to meet you, Mrs. Wembley, and to see you again, Miss Wembley."

Sophie broke out into a rather delighted grin, while her mother looked momentarily confused. He took advantage of her hesitation and dashed toward the front of the room.

It appeared that Charity's attention had returned to the conversation, her gloved hand resting upon Dering's forearm in a very familiar gesture. Hugh clenched his jaw—he didn't give a damn if they were lovers, so long as they would rescue him from more conversation with the matchmaking mama. He didn't pause to analyze the pang in his gut at the thought of Dering laying a finger on her. What the hell was it to him?

His gaze shifted to her face as she laughed at something the viscount said. It was open and joyful—not a look he had seen aimed in his direction. At least not in the light of day or glow of a candle. Her simple white

gown had some sort of gold netting atop it that comple-
mented her coloring. Her glossy curls, the color of fresh
cinnamon, were pinned at the crown of her head. Several
soft ringlets framed her face, bringing attention to her
wide gray eyes. Eyes that he hadn't given much thought
to before. They were quite pretty.

She glanced over to him as he approached. Her smile
didn't diminish, but it did somehow soften a little. So
their stolen evening on the balcony had made a lasting
impression after all. Every other time they had met had
started out with uncertainty, wariness, or downright ani-
mosity. He felt her welcome all the way to his fingertips,
which he fisted at his side.

"Good evening, Lady Effington, Miss Effington," he
said, nodding to them both. "If I had known you were
coming, I would have offered you a ride in my carriage."

Miss Effington's brows lifted in either surprise or disbelief. He'd bet the latter. Based on how he had treated
her in the past, she might assume he'd as soon leave
them stranded than offer a carriage ride.

His words were meant to be polite greeting, but
damned if he didn't actually mean them.

Lady Effington beamed at him. "Such a kind thing to
say—a missed opportunity for us, to be sure. Isn't that so,
Charity?"

"You are too kind, my lord," Charity murmured,
watching him as one watched a magician. Wanting to believe, but looking for the trick.

He dipped his head in response, not at all certain how
to feel about her. Last night had been odd, strangely relaxed and natural. He always thought of her as a silly
debutante, but she had shown herself in a different light.
Perhaps it was the moonlight playing tricks on him or
the exhaustion coloring how he viewed her, but what-

ever it was, for the first time he had really taken notice of her as a person.

As a woman.

That made a man feel uncomfortably vulnerable. He bloody hated vulnerability. He had scarcely been without it since the day he'd gone from a man to a near invalid in the space of a second.

"So, then, you're already acquainted, I see," Dering said, grinning as he looked back and forth between them.

"Oh yes," Lady Effington replied, the feather atop her lavender turban swaying as she nodded. "We're neighbors. Upon hearing our Charity's playing, Lord Cadgwith came over straight away to introduce himself. Unorthodox, but understandable."

Dering winked at Charity, the familiarity of the gesture not lost on Hugh. "Completely understandable. And do you know it has been far too long since I've had the pleasure of listening to you play? Would I be able to convince you to do so now? I can think of no better way to begin a party during the Summer Serenade in Somerset."

Her eyes darted to Hugh's for a moment before giving her head a little shake. "How kind you are, Dering, but I couldn't impose."

Unease weakened Hugh's polite smile. He had done so well this week, but the thought of having an attack now, with all these people around, made his chest tighten uncomfortably.

"Nonsense," the viscount returned, his deep voice brooking no argument. "It would be an imposition only if you refused. If the best pianoforte player in England is in my drawing room, I have no intention of depriving myself of her talents."

"Really, my lord—"

Dering held up one large hand. "No, I'll hear no false modesty." He gestured toward the adjoining room. "Come, let us put my poor, neglected pianoforte to good use. Either that or break my heart—the choice is yours."

A grin tugged the very corners of her pretty lips. "Very well, if you absolutely insist upon it."

Damn it all. Hugh already knew that Charity's playing seemed to trigger whatever it was that brought on his headaches. And in those instances, it seemed to come on quicker and more fiercely than usual. First his vision would dim, narrowing to a tunnel before going out completely in his left eye. He'd have five, maybe ten minutes before pain would consume him, thrumming and throbbing at the base of his spine so powerfully, it was a wonder his skull didn't crack beneath the onslaught. He'd be helpless as an infant, sometimes reduced to vomiting and vertigo.

As Dering led Charity to the pianoforte in the next room, Hugh remained rooted in place. There was a chance he'd be fine. It had been a good week, after all. He could stand back like he was and hope that the distance and low buzz of conversation would temper any reaction.

His palms started to sweat, and he rubbed them on his breeches. Or he could withdraw. Slip away for a few minutes, and return when she was done. Yes, that's what he would do. There was no reason to tempt fate when he knew of a perfectly good bottle of brandy right down the corridor in Dering's study.

He stayed a moment longer, watching as Charity laughed at another of Dering's quips before taking a seat at the instrument. The joy was back in her countenance. She was delighted, basking in Dering's attention. As she should.

Bloody hell.

Turning on his heel, Hugh stalked from the room. He didn't look back. He didn't need to. He already knew there was nothing for him there.

He had left her.

As Charity smiled and curtsied in response to the other guests' applause, her gaze raked the room, looking for a certain sandy-haired baron. She had seen the look on his face when Dering had invited her to play. She had even tried to avoid doing so in deference to him, but she couldn't be rude to her host.

Clearly Cadgwith had no such reservations. He had to have known he was meant to join them, to stand with the viscount and Grandmama while Charity played.

But he was gone. She gritted her teeth, irrational anger flaring suddenly. Was he so opposed to her music that he couldn't even be bothered to stay for a five-minute song? Was her music really that repulsive to him?

Hurt chipped away at her enjoyment of the evening. Had he even attempted to stay? Perhaps without the distortion of the walls between them, he might actually like what he heard. Had he ever considered that? Obviously not.

And here she thought they had turned a corner.

It was almost as if the man was *trying* to be an enigma. Charity gave her head a little shake, confused and frustrated. They'd had a connection there for a moment, she was sure of it. When she had caught his eye across the room when she'd first arrived, it was as though everything around them had faded. Even the distance between them seemed to disappear as his eyes locked on hers.

She drew a deep breath. Even just thinking about the moment made her heart do a little somersault. There had definitely been something charged between them, just as there had been last night. Why did he keep denying it? Not verbally, but rather emotionally and physically. Just when she began to think she was getting a handle on him, he up and withdrew.

Just like now.

"Absolute perfection, just as I knew it would be," the viscount said, patting her gloved hand. "It's been far too long between performances. We shall have to visit more often."

She smiled, despite her lips' reluctance to do so. "I should like that very much."

"As would I," Grandmama said. "My son's lands have become far too thick with grouse in your father's absence. You and he should join us this fall to remedy that."

As Dering and Grandmama chatted about his father, Charity chewed the inside of her cheek, wondering where her blasted neighbor had disappeared to. Assuming he didn't leave altogether, there weren't a lot of places he could have gotten off to. Coming to a decision, she turned back to the others. "Oh, look—Sophie and her mother are here. Will you excuse me?"

At their nods, she hastened across the long, narrow room, smiling and nodding at the two dozen or so other guests who offered her appreciative grins. She recognized about half the attendees, but she made no move to engage any of them. Not yet.

Sophie caught sight of her and waved. She waited until Charity was within arm's reach before saying, "Well done! And how pretty you look tonight! Have you—"

"Sophie, I was just on my way to the ladies' withdrawing room. Would you like to join me?"

Her mouth opened in a little *o* of surprise at Charity's abrupt interruption, but quickly recovered. "Oh yes, please.

I do believe the ribbon in my hair is coming loose. Mama, will you excuse us?"

The older woman looked up from her conversation with Lady Upton. "Hmm? Oh yes, whatever you wish," she said, waving a dismissive hand. Lucky timing on Sophie's part; Mrs. Wembley did always seem to be happiest when talking to someone of rank.

Not wasting a moment, Charity grabbed Sophie's hand and towed her toward the well-lit corridor that clearly marked the rooms available to the guests.

"I'm so glad you found me," Sophie said as they let themselves into the designated room. "I simply must know what Lord Cad said to you. You wouldn't believe the look on his face when he saw you come in—"

"I saw the look on his face." Charity broke in, her cheeks heating at the memory of that moment between them.

"You did? My goodness, I must be missing something. First he watches you with all that intensity, then he quite abruptly abandons us in favor of you, and then the next thing I know, he is rushing away. Did you tell him he had bad breath or something?"

At least Charity wasn't the only one confused by the man's behavior. It was validating to know she wasn't being overly sensitive. "I didn't tell him anything. One moment we were conversing quite nicely, and the next his smile is gone, his shoulders are stiff, and he is practically knocking over the other guests in his haste to get away from us."

"Where did he go, exactly?"

"I'm not exactly certain. Which is why I needed you."

Chapter Eleven

Holed up in Dering's study, Hugh sat in the same chair he had availed himself of earlier, without the benefit of the brandy. He didn't need a drink. He needed a moment's peace.

Late-evening light filtered through the sheers, providing enough illumination to bypass lighting a candle. He settled back and rubbed a hand to the nape of his neck. It was such an ingrained gesture, it didn't even matter that there was no pain there.

He was a bloody coward. For good reason—he sure as hell didn't want to end up an ashen shell of a man in front of dozens of witnesses—but still.

This was why it wouldn't do for him to be making doe eyes at a female. What would become of it? Until he was free from his attacks, he was fit to be with no one. Yes, he eventually needed to produce an heir, but at eight-and-twenty, he was in absolutely no hurry to address the issue.

Getting better—that was the only thing he needed to worry about. It needed to be his sole purpose. Hadn't he always believed that if a man could just try hard enough, work hard enough, or had a strong enough force of will, he could accomplish anything? The fact that his own damn body was out of his control or ability to change was difficult to swallow.

A noise at the door made him glance that way, his brow knitted with displeasure. Couldn't a man get away for two minutes without being bothered? Yes, it was a party, and he had chosen to attend, but he was not in the mood for talking to anyone at that moment.

The door opened and Charity poked her head in. His stomach dropped at the sight of her. The moment she spotted him, her eyes narrowed and she pushed the door wide enough to slip inside. Had she come looking for him? Surely she knew better than to shut them in a room alone together, but that is exactly what she did. As she quietly clicked the door closed, she met his disapproving gaze full-on.

"I think you owe me an apology. *Again*," she added, crossing her arms.

He wasn't in the mood for this. Purposely not standing, he shook his head. "I beg to differ. I was rude to neither you nor your grandmother."

Marching across the room, she parked herself in the chair Dering had occupied earlier. The large scale of the piece dwarfed her, but in no way made her look vulnerable. Not with the exasperation that was rolling off her in waves.

"You could at least be consistent, you know. I have never met a more maddening human being. The very moment Dering mentioned my playing, your whole countenance changed; you practically turned to stone before my eyes. And then to disappear when you knew full well Dering wished for you to hear me ..." She shook her head. "Did nothing change after the conversation we shared on the balcony?"

He pushed away the image of her bathed in pale moonlight, leaning against the narrow railing that separated their balconies. He had allowed the moment to become too personal, too unguarded, and now he was paying for it. "It was a perfectly pleasant conversation, just as our greeting was earlier. My stepping away from the party has little bearing on you. I am not sure what it is, exactly, that you are expecting from me."

What did she expect from him? "I thought we were beginning to forge a friendship of sorts. Setting aside our differences."

It was a forward statement, but her frustration was wearing on her normal reserve. He was sitting in his chair like some sort of monarch, well above all the little subjects at his feet. It was absolutely nothing like the way he had looked at her last night—or even a quarter of an hour ago! "I don't care whether you like or hate me, but at least choose one and stay with it."

He tilted his head, studying her for a moment. "Did you truly risk your reputation to come find me, *alone*, and tell me that you don't care what I think of you?"

She bit down on her cheek, willing away the embarrassment that threatened to cause her to blush. "A woman wants to know where things stand, same as any man."

"What 'things'? We are neighbors, which will lead to inevitable interaction. I think perhaps you're assigning far too much importance to our encounters. I should think my cordialness would be welcome."

"It is," she ground out, wishing this discussion was more in her control. "But it is beyond frustrating when you . . . you *look* at me one way and treat me another."

He sighed, coming to his feet. "I really don't know what you mean. I smiled when I saw you. I interacted cordially with you, your grandmother, and Lord Derington until we went our separate ways. Where, exactly, did I cause such harm that you felt you needed to chase me down?"

He made her sound like some sort of overreacting twit. Was he really going to act as though they hadn't shared such a charged look? As though he hadn't changed from welcoming to closed off in the space of a few seconds? "You disappoint me, my lord."

He scoffed softly, shaking his head. "Get in line, Miss Effington." The sharpness was notably absent from his voice.

She blinked, trying to figure out what to make of such a statement. Did he regularly disappoint people? Did he even care if he did? "If you wished to have a shorter line, perhaps you should try being nice for more than five minutes in a row."

"I am not here to make friends. It matters not what others think of me." He spoke imperiously, as though he were above anything as trivial as the need for forming bonds in life.

Sometimes he just seemed so blasted superior, she wanted to shake him. "If you are not here to make friends, nor for the music, why *are* you here? It is a question you handily avoided last night."

His green eyes dulled as he met her gaze. "I don't believe my reasons are any business of yours."

If he were as good at an instrument as he was at building walls around himself, he'd be a master musician by now. She dropped her arms, allowing them to fall to her sides. "You're right. It's not." Gathering her dignity, she swiveled around and stalked for the door. A sound from the corridor caused her to hesitate. *What was that?*

Before she knew what was even happening, strong

hands encircled her arms and swung her around to just behind the door. What was the man doing? Heat scorched her skin where his fingers wrapped around her arms. She jerked her gaze to his in time to see him place an urgent finger to his lips before stepping back.

Seconds later the knob rattled and the door swung open. From her vantage point pressed against the wall on the other side of the door, she watched, heart pounding, as the baron stepped back as if startled.

"Dering! I was just coming out to rejoin you." He sounded completely at ease, as though he wasn't hiding an unmarried female in plain sight not four feet away. She pressed her hand to her mouth in an effort to quiet her breathing—dear God, she couldn't be caught in here with him!

With Sophie waiting for her in the retiring room, she had her alibi all ready to go upon returning to the party, but all of that would be for naught if Dering took two steps in and caught sight of her. Her hammering heart seemed loud enough to wake the dead.

The viscount's deep chuckle rumbled through the room. "I'll bet you were. Something tells me you'd spend the whole evening in here if given the chance. Unfortunately for you, I promised Felicity I would force you to socialize, whether you liked it or not."

Force him to socialize? Why would Dering promise the baron's sister-in-law such a thing? Was it simply because he was antisocial in general, or was something else going on? Something to do with his brother's death? The scars on his face? The exhaustion that seemed to hang about him like an aura?

The sound of his advancing footsteps nearly stopped her heart cold, and all thoughts of the mystery fled in the face of discovery. Cadgwith sprang forward, his eyes betraying none of the panic she knew he must be feeling. "Well, then, best get back to it."

It didn't stop Dering, though. As far as Charity could tell, his footsteps didn't even slow. With horror tightening her throat, she watched as his broad back came into her field of vision as he headed for his desk. If he turned even a little, there was no way he could miss the girl in the golden gown pressed against the wall.

Good God, she didn't even want to imagine what would happen if he discovered she'd been there, alone with the baron behind closed doors.

Cadgwith quickly stepped between them, locking eyes with her for a moment before grabbing the door and swinging it open wider, effectively blocking her from view. "Needed a proper drink, did you?" he asked, his voice remarkably lighthearted.

"No, I need to pass along a bit of correspondence to Sir Anthony while he's here."

Breathing carefully through her nose, Charity listened to the scrape of the desk drawer being opened and closed. A rustle of paper, then Dering's heavy footfalls approaching again. Fear prickled her every pore and formed a lead ball in the pit of her stomach.

"After you, my friend," the baron said, and Charity could just imagine him sweeping his hand out.

The sound of retreating footsteps was the sweetest thing she had ever heard. The door swung closed, and for a second she just stood there, alone and stunned. Lord have mercy, that had been entirely too close. She leaned back against the wall, pressing a hand to her middle. Now that the danger was past, her knees barely had the strength to hold her upright.

Yes, Dering was a friend of the family, but would he have kept his tongue if he had found her? Impossible to say. She could have very easily found herself betrothed to the baron, just like that.

He had reacted perfectly. She wouldn't have been able to be so casual if her life depended on it—and, in a way, it would have. Wherever had that poise come from? He had seemed so calm and in control, as though nothing in the world was amiss.

She thought again of the viscount's strange comment. What was it that had happened to her neighbor? The more she thought about it, the more certain she became that, one way or another, he was hiding something.

The doorknob suddenly turned and Charity jerked back upright. The door eased open a few inches, and a soft voice whispered, "Charity?"

Sophie! Charity exhaled as relief cascaded through her whole body. She hurried around to greet her friend. "I have never been so happy to see anyone in my whole life."

"*I've* never been so happy to see someone hiding!" Sophie exclaimed, grabbing Charity's hands and squeezing. "I nearly died when I saw Lord Derington stride down the corridor and head straight for the study. Before I could so much as blink he was at the door, and then inside, and then I was *sure* he would find you. But then only he and Lord Cadgwith emerged, and, as they walked by, the baron spotted me and nodded toward the door, so here I am, come to rescue you."

The baron had sent Sophie to her? Charity smiled gratefully at her friend. "Well, do let's get back to the party. I don't believe my nerves could handle much more excitement for the night."

"Really?" Sophie said, her whispered voice rife with scandal. Charity could only imagine what sorts of scenarios were running through her friend's head.

A touch? A kiss? Something even more scandalous? She shivered, not daring to even think on such things, most especially not with Lord Cad. Even so, the memory of the baron's strong hands wrapping around her arms as though she belonged to him, as though he had every right and intention of pulling her into his arms, flashed through her mind. She swallowed before rolling her eyes for Sophie's benefit. "Nothing like *that*."

As they hurried down the corridor to rejoin the others, a small, traitorous thought emerged from beneath all the sensible ones of never allowing such a thing to happen again.

What would it feel like, exactly, to be wrapped in her neighbor's embrace for real? She didn't even want to consider what she would give to find out.

He had no idea what his food tasted like.

Nor what his dinner companion was talking about. Hugh couldn't even be bothered to remember what course they were on. All he knew was, Charity Effington had the softest skin he could ever remember touching.

And if she ever put them in a situation like that again, he would happily turn her over his knee. What in God's name had she been thinking? Why was it so blasted important to her to speak with him right then and there?

Jesus, he was just now able to breathe normally again. If Dering had realized she was in the room, well, Hugh didn't even know what would have happened next. Could they force him to marry the girl for something like that? What if he refused?

He didn't dislike her—unfortunately for him, the opposite was true—but he sure as hell didn't want to marry her. Having her witness to his every move, to the reality of his life, wasn't something he wanted to contemplate.

Had she learned her lesson? Her gray eyes had certainly been expressive enough—he could practically feel the terror radiating from her when the door opened. Served her right, trapping him alone like that. Although at least it was clear that it was not her intention to be discovered.

Lifting another forkful of mushroom fricassee to his lips, Hugh glanced down the table to where Charity sat. Even in the golden candlelight, her face was still a bit pale and her expression reserved. Why had she even felt it worth the risk to seek him out? She should save her energy and efforts for someone who would appreciate them. Tomorrow, he would finish the conversation they had started. If she had any doubts whatsoever about where they stood with each other, he planned to remedy that. They were neighbors and nothing more.

More important, they never could be anything more . . . no matter how soft her skin may be.

Chapter Twelve

"Lord Cadgwith, didn't expect I'd see you here."

Hugh grimaced, hesitating for a moment before stepping into the murky greenish waters of the bath. "Mr. Sanburne," he said cordially, nodding.

The estate agent waded toward him, ignoring Hugh's reserved greeting. "Been coming here for years myself. Bad leg from my days aboard His Majesty's finest. You take one bit of shrapnel to the knee, and damned if it doesn't hurt like the dickens every time it rains for the rest of your life." He grinned slyly. "Bit of a problem in jolly ole England, eh?"

Offering a shallow nod, Hugh lowered himself into the steaming waters. It wasn't the most encouraging thing in the world to have someone complain of his decades-old injury still bothering him. Why must these injures linger so, making life miserable in the process?

Sighing, he moved his arms back and forth slowly, savoring the warmth of the water. The fabric of his shirt billowed with each pass like a translucent white jellyfish in a changing tide. This place would be just about perfect if he could visit alone and shed the annoying clothes altogether. He wished now he would have stuck to his normal hours, instead of coming earlier. After another good night of sleep, he had actually felt invigorated and ready to start the day soon after the sun came up.

Sanburne walked slowly back and forth, presumably working his knee. "But I wouldn't live anywhere else, God's truth. I've seen some beautiful places in this world, but none of them is home quite like this little island. Know what I mean?"

Clearly the man had no intention of leaving him be. He wasn't bad company—just unwanted. Hugh allowed himself to sink deeper, until only his head remained above the water in the cool morning air. "I do. I've not traveled extensively—the army is generally closer to home than the navy—but it was enough."

Sanburne nodded but kept his peace this time, silently continuing his little circuit. Allowing himself to relax, Hugh closed his eyes and breathed in the sulfur scent of the water. He'd hated it when he'd first arrived—who liked the smell of rotten eggs?—but with the healing came acceptance, and now an odd comfort.

"So, this is why you chose to visit Bath, eh?"

Hugh's eyes popped open and he glanced to his uninvited companion. The man's eyes were good-natured but shrewd as he slowly paced by. Hugh didn't answer. It seemed to be the question on everyone's lips, but his reasons for being here were no one's business but his own.

Sanburne wasn't discouraged. "I was wondering, what with the way you spoke of your neighbor's musical talents. Anyone that vehemently opposed to the sound of music surely isn't here for the festival."

Was he expecting Hugh to divulge the nature of his medical need just to satiate his curiosity? He'd be disappointed, if that were the case. Hugh ignored the unspoken question and settled onto the submerged stone ledge along the water's edge before leaning against the wall. With a shrug, he said, "It was made clear to me that the Baths were not to be missed."

It was a completely true statement, not that he owed anyone even that much. Sanburne paused, considering him for a moment before coming to sit beside him. "They say the waters get their healing properties from the necromantic powers of the fabled Prince Bladud. Poppycock, of course," he said, stroking his damp white beard. "There have been theories of angel's tears, underground volcanoes, or water from the center of the earth.

"I, however," he said, extending his leg and rubbing at his knee, "think it is probably more simple than that. People needed a place to go to give them hope, and God gave them one."

Lifting his brow, Hugh gave the old man a sideways glance, trying to gauge what he was really saying. As lighthearted as his conversation tended to be, he seemed to hold serious stock in his words. "Is that so?"

"Not sure if it needs to be, if that's what it is in execution." Winking, he came to his feet and waded toward the edge. "These springs may run more or less consistently, but it is hope that springs eternal."

Hugh watched the older man as he climbed from the water and accepted a towel from a servant. After patting down his dripping clothes, Sanburne draped the linen over his neck and half-smiled to Hugh.

"You know, the ole sawbones on board wanted to take my leg. He said I'd never walk again, anyway. It took a few years, but I'm happy to prove him wrong every day." Without another word, he turned, retrieved his walking stick from the waiting servant, and headed inside.

Hugh stared back at him, not sure what to make of the man. What a singularly odd exchange. There was more to the man than Hugh would have imagined, but he wasn't entirely sure Sanburne was operating with a full deck. Whatever his meaning or purpose behind his theory of the Baths had little bearing on Hugh. All Hugh needed to know was that he was sleeping better than he had in years, and if soaking in foul water and drinking gallons of the stuff were responsible, he intended to continue until he no longer remembered what an attack even felt like.

He closed his eyes again and relaxed, ignoring the occasional splashes and odd conversation of the other bathers as they came and went. What would he do when he could live like a normal person again? Ah, to ride again. Not just pleasant walks in the park, but full-speed tears across the countryside. He'd been a cavalryman, for God's sake. He had learned to ride before he could even walk. Feeling the wind through his hair and exhilaration in his heart again would be incredible.

He'd ride, and sit through dreadful musicales, and be talked into attending the fireworks display that they organized every spring to kick off the flower festival in Cadgwith.

God, he sounded like a bloody poet. A dreamer, which he most assuredly was not. He was a realist. He understood limitation, expectations, and disappointments.

Still, as his body relaxed in the weightlessness of the warm water, his heart seemed to buoy as well. Sanburne's slight limp may seem a pity to others, but after what he had told Hugh, it looked a hell of a lot like inspiration to him.

"I have the most delicious gossip." Sophie grinned as she flipped open the case for her oboe, her eyes full of mischief.

May looked up from her sheet music, her brows raised in expectation. "Oh? Although, as new to town as I am, it may very well be lost on me."

"Oh, you know the subject of this gossip very well." Sophie looked pointedly to Charity.

Sophie had lasted all of three minutes—longer than Charity would have expected. Not that she would spread gossip to others, but this was May, and Charity had already planned on sharing all the embarrassing details. "I was going to tell her," she insisted, even as she felt the inevitable spread of heat in her cheeks.

May's eyes widened with interest. "My word, this promises to be very good indeed. I can only assume this has to do with the dinner on Saturday night. What have you done, little Miss Rule Follower?"

"Rule follower?" Charity laughed. "Is that a bad thing?" She hoped not, because with the minor exception of composing against her mother's wishes, the description fit quite well. Actually . . . come to think of it, the description *used* to fit quite well. But rule followers didn't converse with a man under the cover of darkness, or confront him alone in a study.

She was becoming quite the rule breaker, it would seem. Never a description she would have applied to herself in London during her previous two Seasons. Here, she was Charity the rebel.

May gave her a wink. "It is if you want to have any fun in life. Now, do tell what has those delightfully freckled cheeks of yours turning all pink."

Sitting down on her pianoforte bench, Charity gave an innocent shrug. "I may or may not have decided to give Lord Cadgwith a piece of my mind."

"What?" May said, pulling a chair up to sit beside her.

"What did he do? And where were you? Ugh—why couldn't my aunt have trusted me enough to allow me to attend?"

Sophie curled on the nearby settee, tucking her feet beneath her white skirts. "I wish you would have been there as well. You would not believe the way Lord Cad looked at her when she arrived at Lord Derington's party. I nearly swooned—and I wasn't even the recipient!"

"All right, now I'm confused." The smooth skin of May's forehead puckered as she scrunched her brow. "What, exactly, was this look?"

Charity bit her lip as fresh heat tinged her cheeks. "It was . . . intense. We locked eyes, and for a fleeting moment, there was something exciting and quite unexpected between us. I don't even know how to describe it, other than to say in that moment, I doubted either of us could have told you a thing about what else was going on in the room."

"So, you gave him a piece of your mind to chastise him?" Confusion still clouded May's blue eyes.

"No. I chastised him for showing such interest one moment, and then practically giving us the cut direct the next." Charity shook her head, the frustration still as keen as it was two nights ago. "I just wanted to know where I stand with him. One minute he hates me; the next he's offering me his carriage. It's infuriating that I can't get a handle on it."

She recounted the entire story, leaving out only the shocking feel of the baron's hands against her arms. When she was finished, May's expression was smugly knowing. "What?" Charity asked cautiously.

"Oh, it is exceedingly clear that the man is interested in you."

"Interested? Yes, half the time. The rest of the time he's driving me mad. Don't forget, we're *just neighbors*," she said, quoting his stony words.

May shook her head, looking very worldly all of the sudden. "I would bet a thousand guineas that he is interested, even though he may not wish to be. I think it is plain from Lord Derington's words that there is something more to the baron's presence than meets the eye. So," she said, flashing a wide grin, "we must figure it out."

Charity pursed her lips, considering her friend's words. She had come to the same conclusion, but was at a loss for how she was to go about doing such a thing. "Easier said than done, I think."

"You are a woman," May said, her voice firm. "Use your wiles."

"My *wiles*?" Charity squeaked, then couldn't help but laugh. "Oh, May, if only I had such a thing. I am far too shy to ever possess any wiles."

Sophie snorted. "Says the woman who cornered a baron in a closed room with more than two dozen potential witnesses in the next room."

Charity grinned. Shy rebels existed, didn't they?

"Then it's settled," May said, clapping her hands. "You shall work on the baron, and we shall look forward to your next report with great interest."

"I don't know why I even care to go through the trouble. It's not as though I have any true interest in the man. He just vexes me so very much."

"Mmhmm," May murmured, coming to her feet and dragging the chair back to her guzheng. "Men do tend to excel at that. Think of it as a summer project so that your poor, sequestered friend Mei-li can have something through which to live vicariously."

"Well, when you put it that way," Charity responded,

offering a wag of her brows before spinning around on her bench to face her pianoforte. She surreptitiously glanced to the shared wall, wondering if he was on the other side. On the days that they rehearsed in her home, she made certain it was midafternoon, so as not to cause any undue bother. Hopefully he wouldn't be sleeping, but what if he was listening? Would he ever stop hating her music so much?

She let her fingers work over the keys in a few mindless scales, wondering how one went about using one's wiles. All of her confidence tended to rest in her music ability, so she wasn't sure how to proceed without it.

The evening on the balcony came to mind, and she considered the encounter. He must be a nighthawk, since clearly mornings were not his favorite. That's when she should meet him next. How would she draw him out, though? She focused on the familiar black and white keys, considering her fingers as they tapped away.

Music, of course. What better way to ensure a reaction than by playing for him? Grandmama slept like the dead, and the servants knew better than to interrupt her when she was playing.

She licked her lips, reveling in the thrill of anticipation that snaked through her belly. They were to spend the evening in tonight, so by ten or so her grandmother would retire. Charity would give her time to be well and truly settled before slipping into the music room to play.

Still doing her warm-up, she glanced to the clock perched above the mantel. Midnight should be perfect. She breathed in a deep breath, surprised by the flutter of nerves that assailed her.

It was time to find out what the baron was all about.

Chapter Thirteen

Shedding his jacket, cravat, and waistcoat, Hugh stretched his arms high above him. Damn, it felt good to be able to do that. His shoulder was much looser than it had been in years, and he felt little in the way of discomfort.

Another relatively pain-free day. The only concession he made was to leave the house when the trio showed up next door. He was feeling better and better, and for once was actually well rested, but still. Between Charity's preference for high notes and that squeaky woodwind one of the other girls played, it was best not to tempt fate.

Instead he spent the afternoon walking. First the streets around the house, then farther, past the Baths, over the bridge, and finally along the River Avon. What he'd failed to notice since his arrival was that the city was actually quite attractive, with a proliferation of handsome cream-colored limestone used in nearly every building. The cobblestone streets were well maintained, and sturdy black metal railings added pleasant contrast. There were a surprising amount of flowers in the city itself—in the grassy areas, in window boxes, and even in hanging planters lining the walkways.

He had ended up taking a long walk at the waterfront.

It was pleasant and he enjoyed himself, but the soft sound of rushing water was nothing when compared to the low, ever-present roar of waves crashing off the beaches lining the side of his estate. It was one of the only noises that actually seemed to soothe him.

The village of Cadgwith lived and breathed thanks to the ocean. Fishing boats bobbed on the horizon year round as the fisherman trolled for their daily catches. He missed the smell of salt water, the roughness of the wind, and the taste of freshly caught seafood.

He missed home.

Sighing, he dropped his hands to his sides and walked to the window, peering up to the night sky. No moon tonight, not with the heavy layer of clouds that had gathered shortly after he returned for supper and had stayed ever since.

As he sat on the edge of the nearest chair to pull his boots off, a sound from next door had him cocking his head. Surely that wasn't . . . no. She was playing? *Now?* It was close to midnight, for God's sake.

Sure enough, the unmistakable sound of the pianoforte drifted through the wall. It was softer than usual, probably in deference to her own sleeping household, but it was still upbeat in tempo. He grimaced as the notes climbed the scale, tinkling like his mother's old wind chimes that seemed to never quiet as they whipped in the sea air when he was growing up.

He shook his head in disbelief. Was she *trying* to make a nuisance of herself?

Leaving his boots on, he stalked to the balcony door and yanked it open. Warm night air flooded past him as he stepped outside and leaned forward over the railing until the glowing interior of her music room came into view. The music was actually quieter out here. Of course it would be his luck that the walls would be thinner than the bloody windowpanes. He crossed his arms over his chest and stewed, debating what to do next.

He could leave her be, but Lord knew that was a hell of a precedent to set. He'd rather nip it in the bud now, when he was only mildly annoyed, as opposed to if he were in the grips of one of his attacks. Or, worse, if she should wake him from sleep after one of his attacks.

He looked around for something with which he could get her attention, but the balcony was empty of any pebbles or the like. He slipped back inside, retrieved a few loose coins, then returned to the darkness of the night. Throwing coins at her window wasn't exactly the most dignified thing in the world, but it was a step up from pounding the wall.

He chose a halfpenny, aimed, and tossed it. It pinged off the sash and fell to the stone floor. He tried another, but even though it hit the glass this time, it had a similarly unimpressive noise—certainly nothing that would be heard over her playing. Fishing around for a heavier piece, he chose a half sovereign, lined it up, and let it fly. This time, it connected with a loud, cringe-inducing clunk. The music stopped almost at once. Success! He counted to three before the sheers were pulled aside and Charity tugged open the door.

She squinted as she peered into the inky black night, her hands akimbo at her hips. Her eyes came to rest on him, then dropped to the stone floor beneath the window. "If you wish to make a request," she said drily, retrieving the half sovereign from the ground, "I assure you there is no need to pay for the privilege."

"Consider it payment for your silence," he returned, crossing his arms again and leaning back against the railing.

Instead of the anger or outrage that he might have expected from such a comment, she simply bent to retrieve the other two coins, slipped the lot of them into some hidden fold of her skirts, and nodded. "As you wish."

He almost laughed. "Truly? Is that all it takes?" He pushed away from the railing and approached the divider in between their respective sides. "Here, then," he said, holding out the remaining money, palm up. "Consider this payment in advance for the next few nights."

She stepped forward, and the light of the room behind her would have obscured her smile completely if it wasn't for the flash of her white teeth. "Is it really as bad as all that to you? Music is supposed to be a balm to the soul, you know."

She was close enough now that he could see her features more clearly. Her eyes, usually a light bluish gray, were dark pools set against her pale face. Even in this light, he could see the smattering of freckles over her nose and cheeks. Her gown, which had been a pale yellow in the candlelight, was now a ghostly white.

He lifted an eyebrow and gave the palmful of coins a rattle. "Silence is golden. And I am quite willing to purchase it with sterling."

"You, sir, are *très* unsophisticated. Lucky for you, I am not above bribery."

With an arch look, she plucked the coins from his palm one by one. Her fingers were surprisingly chilly for the warm night, and he had the fleeting desire to close his hand over hers to warm them. Instead, he dropped his arm the moment his palm was empty. "Thank goodness for small favors."

She held up the sixpence, turning it back and forth.

"Have you always disliked music?" The question was casual, almost offhand. She couldn't have known how personal it truly was.

It wasn't wise to stand out here and converse with her, but, for some reason, he was reluctant to return to the emptiness of his chambers. It had been a good day, and, to be completely honest, he wasn't sorry for her company.

He should be, but he wasn't.

"A sixpence for your thoughts," she said, holding the coin out to him. Her tone was light and teasing, inviting him to relax a bit. "It's only fair that if you can buy my silence, I should be able to purchase your answers."

A small grin curled the corners of his lips, and he reached out and tugged the coin from her grasp. She didn't recoil when his fingers brushed hers, and he had to make himself break the contact. Clearing his throat softly, he said, "I've never been a music lover, if that is what you mean. But, no, I don't suppose I've always hated it." He recrossed his arms and backed up until his hip was perched against the cool metal of the railing. There—a proper distance. Perhaps now his brain would work right.

A light wind picked up the loose wisps of hair around her face, and she tucked one side behind her ear. The scent of lavender reached his nose, and he found himself inhaling the soothing fragrance. He wouldn't have thought it would be a match to her personality, but somehow it fit.

So much for his attempt to recapture his right mind.

"What changed, then?" She seemed genuinely curious, as though unable to fathom such a thing. Actually, he doubted she *could* fathom such a thing.

This was the point in a conversation when he would usually change the subject or walk away, but he didn't want to leave just yet. There was something . . . less judgmental about conversations in the dark like this. There seemed less scrutiny, less prying. He couldn't see the pity in another's gaze, and they wouldn't see the pain in his. Shrugging his shoulders, he said, "A lot of things change when men go to war. That just happened to be one of them for me."

"You were in the war?" The words were softly spoken, but he could hear the surprise in her voice. Did she understand how truly horrific war could be? He certainly hoped not. But he did detect a certain amount of respect in her tone, which was reassuring.

"Three years. Captain Hugh Danby at your service. *Former* Captain, I should say." It'd been years since he'd claimed that title. His commission was sold shortly after he was injured, since it was abundantly clear that he could never serve in any true capacity again. It had been a very, very dark time.

"I can't believe I didn't know that about you. A war hero, right next door."

"I'm no hero," he said gruffly, the old pang of regret thumping him in the ribs. If he were a true hero, half of the men beneath his command wouldn't have died on the battlefield. Ten of them, to be precise. Each of their names were seared in his brain, reminders of how he had failed them. Yes, he'd been given a bloody medal and hailed a hero, but that meant damned little when his men were left behind to be buried on the field that day.

She pressed her lips together before giving a small nod. "I'm sorry. I presume too much." She'd taken it as a reprimand.

"No, I'm just being rude again." He struggled to smile, to pull himself away from the yawning pit that such thoughts threatened to topple him into. "I only mention the war since that is the last time I remember dancing. The music in Belgium was quite pleasing at the time, if memory serves."

Charity grasped the change of direction like a lifeline. "Really? I've heard a few traveling orchestras, but none with the skill of the one that played at the Assembly Rooms last week. I'd love to travel someday, to visit the major cities of Europe and soak in their distinct musical offerings."

It wasn't that she wasn't ravenously curious to know more about the war and how it changed his life. On the contrary, she was nearly drowning in her curiosity. But she'd sensed the hesitation in him, an odd darkness that dulled his voice and tightened his shoulders. Even though his pose was one of relaxation, he'd become as tense as an overtightened harp string. Yes, she did want to travel, but the point of her answer had been to soothe him. To offer him a safe subject about which they could freely converse.

"I think that is a noble and attainable goal," he said, nodding slightly. A gust of wind tugged at his overlong hair, whipping it in front of his eyes. He raked a hand through it, tugging it straight back. Her eyes were drawn momentarily to the white slash through his eyebrow, the only one of his scars visible in this light. The same wind that tugged at his hair pressed the fabric of his shirt against his chest, turning it to second skin.

Charity's heart kicked up, running at double speed. He was lean, with long limbs, naturally broad shoulders and a slim waist that tapered into his narrow hips. It was a pleasing figure, to say the least.

With a purposeful straightening of her spine, Charity dragged her attention back to the conversation. "I'll just bet you do. I know your true motive, my lord." She had meant the words to be teasing, but they came out slightly breathless.

He paused, watching her in the darkness. "Oh?"

"Yes. You're saying that only because it would result in me being as far from you as possible." She grinned, grateful for the lack of light. Her tendency to blush was the bane of her existence, and she'd rather him not know the direction of her thoughts only moments ago.

"Ah, how little you know me, Miss Effington." He sighed, the first sign of weariness she had seen all night. "It isn't that I'd wish you anywhere else; it's that I'd wish myself back in Cadgwith."

The burn of curiosity sprang to life within her all over again. This was what she had wanted to discover in the first place. Why was he here? He clearly wished himself elsewhere, so why stay? "What keeps you here?" she asked softly, unable to keep the question in.

He tilted his head to the side, watching her. Was he judging her? Questioning whether she was worthy of his trust? After a moment, he pushed away from the railing and came to his full height. "We all have duties. I'm doing my best to fulfill mine. Now, then," he said, clearly shutting the door to that particular topic. "I do believe you have your sixpence worth. Good night, Miss Effington."

Disappointment weighed on her heart. She wasn't ready to lose this—they had actually had a real, honest conversation. She liked that, liked knowing she was beginning to unlock a bit of the mystery that surrounded him. But it was clear there was to be no more between them tonight.

Her smile wasn't entirely sincere, but she doubted he could tell in the darkness. "Indeed. But you have paid for several nights of silence. I wonder," she said, gathering her courage to ask the next question. "What will I do with myself tomorrow night?"

The baron held himself very still for a moment, and Charity found herself holding her breath. "I'm sure I don't know," he finally replied, and, despite herself, she let out the air from her lungs on a whoosh.

She had put herself out there boldly, and he had rejected her.

Instead of retreating as she expected him to do, he lingered, looking out over the dark shapes in the garden below. At last his eyes flicked back to her, meeting her questioning gaze straight on. "However," he said slowly, as if coming to a decision, "the next night, I find myself with a free evening. The night air truly is pleasant, is it not?"

Her smile was one of pure satisfaction. "Indeed."

Hugh turned the coin over in his hand, studying the stamped design in the dreary gray afternoon light. Fat raindrops pounded the windowpanes even as wind rattled their casing. It was a miserable day to go calling, but the moment he'd received the note that morning that Thomas was in town, he hadn't even hesitated. Now, damp but in good spirits, he waited patiently in the Potters' overly ostentatious drawing room.

It had been two days since he'd talked with Charity on the balcony. He had contemplated the conversation a dozen times over, wondering why he had spoken with her, of all people, so freely. He didn't regret it; it had been unplanned, after all. Just a spontaneous happenstance that had evolved into something . . . intimate. Enjoyable.

But would he regret doing so again tonight? He was breaking his own rules, encouraging a relationship when there should be none.

The sound of footsteps approached, and he turned

away from the window and pocketed the coin. Moments later Thomas appeared, his smile broad and his arm outstretched. "Hugh! What an unexpected pleasure. Felicity led me to believe that I'd have to drag you out of your house by your ear if I wished to see you."

Grinning, Hugh accepted the younger man's quick embrace, pounding his back in return. "Your sister always was a bit prone to hyperbole. Besides, it wouldn't do to keep a man of God waiting."

"And best you don't forget it," Thomas said, nodding for emphasis. "I must say, you're looking good. A damn sight better than the last time I saw you."

Unfortunately, it was no exaggeration. Thomas's last visit to the estate had been three years earlier. He was a frequent visitor to Cadgwith when he was younger, but once he entered university, his ability to come see them in the outer reaches of British soil had drastically declined. That was squarely in the middle of Hugh's darkest time, when pain, anger, regret, and guilt had seemed as inescapable as even the most fortified dungeon. He had not been fit company during that year.

"Thank you, Thomas. Your sister may have actually been right about this place."

He smiled, his stark black clothes in no way diminishing his devilish grin. "The devil you say. Well, don't you dare tell her that. It's sure to go straight to her head." He gestured toward two fussy chintz chairs and they both took a seat.

"Too right. Wait a second," Hugh said, quirking an eyebrow, "I'm fairly certain that, as a vicar, you're not supposed to be cursing anymore."

Thomas laughed out loud. "Yes. Bloody annoying, that. I do manage to keep it under control when around my flock."

It was almost impossible to imagine the man leading anyone, let alone a congregation. He was all of twenty-three years old now, and with his white blond hair and pale green eyes, he looked even younger. As far as Hugh could tell, he had yet to even have the hints of a proper beard. Chuckling, Hugh shook his head. "Your poor, poor sheep. Do they know yet that they've been fleeced by you?"

"Hey, now," Thomas protested, more teasing than heat, "I know the Bible as well as the next vicar. I even live by it, on occasion."

Hugh merely sat back against his chair and laughed. "I'm sure your bishop sleeps well at night knowing that."

"I'm nothing if not obliging. Speaking of which, I'm grateful he agreed to cover my sermons this month. It feels great to be back in the city. Lucky the Potters had an extra room. I don't recall there ever being so many people here."

Groaning, Hugh said, "You can thank the blasted festival for that. It's as busy as London at the height of the Season, I swear."

"And that's a bad thing? Sweet Jesus, man, just think of all the women!"

Laughter, full and hearty, erupted from deep in Hugh's belly. God, but the man was a walking contradiction. The outrageous second son of the proper Earl of Landowne, living life as a respectable holy man. Hugh shook his head, wiping tears from the corner of his eyes. He hadn't laughed like that in years. The sort of laugh that rumbled deep within, called forth by unfettered joy.

Lightheartedness.

Thomas grinned unapologetically, completely unrepentant. "What? There's nothing that says a man can't admire an attractive woman."

"There is, actually," Hugh said wryly. "It's called the tenth commandment."

Waving a hand, Thomas said, "Semantics. Don't covet thy neighbor's wife, maidservant, et cetera, et cetera. I don't recall 'Thou shalt not covet a gorgeous woman.'"

"You are definitely missing the point," Hugh replied. "But that aside, I'm more concerned with the noise, crowds, and traffic."

"Come now. You're still a man. Look past the inconveniences and see the possibilities. I, for one, have every intention of finding an accomplished young lady with whom I can be entertained this month. Not like that," he said, holding up a staying hand at Hugh's lifted brow. "The company of an entertaining woman is one of God's greatest gifts to man, as far as I'm concerned. Now that I am away from my own congregation, I see no harm in a bit of innocent flirting."

Being around Thomas, Hugh could almost recall what it was like to be a young, carefree pup. Though it seemed like a thousand years ago, he had spent many a night carousing with his friends while at university. "Well, you can leave me out of such pursuits."

The disbelief on Thomas's face was priceless. "Do you mean to tell me that you have been here for almost a month, and you haven't yet taken advantage of anything this city has to offer?"

"Of course not. I've taken the waters every blasted day since I've been here. Bathed at least a dozen times, on top of that."

"My, what excitement," Thomas replied drily. "But no parties? No trysts? No stolen moments alone with a blushing young maiden?"

Hugh almost smiled. Thomas couldn't have better stated how things were between Hugh and Charity if he'd tried. She did tend to blush quite a bit, thanks to her coloring. And their time spent together both in the study and on the balcony had very much been stolen.

Leaning back, Thomas crossed his arms and grinned. "There's something behind that guarded expression of yours, I'm sure of it. You devil, you—you've been holding out on me."

With a completely straight face, he said, "Your career choice doesn't do that fantastical imagination of yours justice." He had no intention of divulging the nature of his relationship to the man—especially when Hugh wasn't even sure of it himself.

Thomas waved an exasperated hand. "Fine, fine— keep your secrets. I've time to discover them yet. In the meantime," he said, propping an ankle on his opposite knee, "I plan to head to my old club tonight. Care to join me? We need to have a proper toast in honor of your brother. He was a damn fine man."

Hugh thought of his plans to meet Charity on the balcony tonight. His *ill-conceived* plans. It hadn't been implicit; merely implied. Granted, overtly implied, but there had been no clear stating of intent. It was damn hard to walk away once they were together, as had been proved in their previous two encounters.

But if he never allowed it to happen in the first place, he could stamp out the growing . . . trust? Friendship? He didn't know what to call it, but he knew for certain that it couldn't end well. If he couldn't turn her away in person, this had to be the next best thing.

"A toast sounds like a great idea. Shall I meet you here or there?"

As they worked out the details of the meeting, he tamped down the self-reproach he already felt about Charity. He was a cowardly bastard to walk away from their plans without warning, although he couldn't very well send her a note canceling their assignation. Still, she would be furious, and probably a little hurt.

But contrary to the saying, as far as he was concerned, it was much worse to have cared and lost, than never to have cared at all.

Chapter Fourteen

This was clearly not going to be Charity's day.

She couldn't be more out of sorts if she tried.

As the three of them approached the Assembly Rooms, the knot of anxiety in her stomach tightened more and more. Ostensibly, the purpose of this session was to give the committee an idea of the musicians' abilities and style so they could decide which grouping in which to place them. In order to make the event palatable for the *ton* to participate, there was no audition or competition. However, they all knew that if a musician or musicians weren't up to the committee's standards, a way would be found to keep them from performing.

"You're looking a tad green," Sophie observed as she slipped her arm through Charity's and gave a reassuring squeeze. "I hope you aren't nervous about the audition. Although I suppose we should be, seeing how utterly unusual we shall be, but that is a good thing, is it not?"

She was all sunshine and happiness, wearing one of her signature yellow gowns and smiling gaily as they neared the understated entrance to the limestone building. Charity doubted Sophie had ever known a moment's nervousness. Excitement, yes, but she was far too outgoing to ever have fear of people paying attention to her.

And she had hit on the exact reason doubt was creeping up on Charity—the sheer unusualness of their trio. What if the judges laughed them out of the room? Or turned their noses up at them?

And, of course, that didn't even take into consideration the rejection she had endured last night. She had not told the others about it. As much as she trusted them, she hated to admit to anyone that she had foolishly waited for the blasted baron for so long.

She was positively stewing over waiting in vain for Hugh last night. And by now he was Hugh—she no longer thought of him as the detached Lord Cadgwith. They had shared too much between them for that.

So why, then, had he not met her? No note, no warning—just a dark, empty balcony on which she waited for nearly an hour for naught. And what wretched timing, too. Now not only was she hurt and more than a little angry about that, but she had to perform for the very first time in public with their little trio.

Crowds made her uneasy. Being the center of attention made her uncomfortable. And in an area in which she generally had absolute confidence, there was simply no way to know how the selection committee would react to their unconventional sound.

May, tall and elegant in another of her seemingly endless supply of glorious silk gowns, nodded with a confidence Charity envied. "Never, ever be afraid to be different. It is only when we distinguish ourselves from the expected that we make an impression."

"Oh, I like that," Sophie said. "Although it's dangerously close to one of my mother's idioms. I suppose she can be right some of the time, no?"

They had a point, of course. If she could set aside her lingering disappointment over last night, she likely was overreacting. All of their practices had gone quite well, with the one this morning proving that they were more than ready for this. Even Sophie, who had initially struggled with her part, had mastered it by their last rehearsal. The piece was superior, the musicians well matched. Their only danger now lay in how open-minded the committee would be about being presented with an altered classic work. She liked to think it was improved, but it was possible they could feel it had been bastardized.

Especially with Marianne's father sitting on the committee.

They reached the entrance, and Charity paused to draw a calming breath. "All right," she said, straightening both her spine and her resolve. "Let us do well, ladies. If we are to make an impression, I very much hope it is a *good* one."

As they entered the building, Mr. Green looked up from his little desk situated beside the door. "Ah, the trio." Sarcasm rounded the *o* at the end of his sentence.

"Yes, the *trio*," May echoed, her chin tipped up in pride. "Present and on time, as I'm sure you have noted."

He looked over the rims of his spectacles at her. "You are early, actually. The committee will call for you on the hour, as promised. Do feel free to avail yourselves of a seat in the meantime." He nodded to the room at large, then turned his attention back to his work.

Ugh, he was such a disagreeable man. Charity turned to the room, the knot still present and accounted for in her stomach. She really did not wish to sit in one of the straight-backed wooden chairs for the next ten minutes—she was entirely too anxious to sit still. Already her companions were moving toward the seating. "If it's all the same to you, I'm going to step outside for a moment to enjoy the fresh air. I'll stay close to the door."

Sophie's brow pinched. "Oh. Well, we'll come with you." She started to retrieve the shawl and packet of music she had just set down, but Charity held up her hand.

"Don't be silly—I'll be right outside the door. You two make yourselves comfortable."

"If you're sure. Don't go running off and leaving us a duet, however. We shall never forgive you if abandon us." She winked, her dimples bracketing both sides of her mouth.

"Don't give me any ideas," Charity teased, happy for the levity. "However, I promise not to escape." *She* at least could be counted on to follow up with her commitments.

Ignoring Mr. Green's raised eyebrow, she stepped back outside onto the pavement and exhaled. This was ridiculous. She had not been so nervous since her first ball, but at least then she had had the presence of Richard and his family to calm any uneasiness. Truly, in the earl's presence, it was almost impossible to feel insecure.

She breathed deeply of the warm air, happy for the moment of peace. The rain the day before had brought in some welcome cooler weather, with blue skies above and bright sunshine lying across her shoulders.

The area was significantly quieter than it had been the first time she had been here. The street beyond was still quite busy, but the pavement was nearly empty, thanks to the lull between morning bathers and afternoon festivalgoers. According to Grandmama, who had availed herself of the Baths several times since her arrival, the infirm had generally come and gone by ten or so, in accordance with the doctors' insistence that the greatest benefit from the waters was to be had first thing in the morning.

A person approached from the east, a solitary gentleman who appeared to be in no hurry at all. His figure was tall and lean, with narrow hips and long legs encased in buff-colored breeches that disappeared into the tops of his polished black Hessians. For a moment, all thoughts of the committee fled as she admired the man's unexpectedly fine form. He drew closer, and though his eyes were blocked by the brim of his hat, she saw the scars feathering down the side of his face and disappearing under his cravat.

Lord Cadgwith. *Hugh*.

Her jaw immediately clenched as the knot of anxiety yanked tight within her. She was angry enough that she wanted to confront him, to demand to know why he had left her out in the dark when clearly there had been an understanding between them. But, a small, rational part of her resisted. This was the city center at midday; she most certainly did not need to air her grievances in such a public place.

He continued toward her, and she retreated farther into the small, covered recess at the Assembly Room door, willing him not to see her. What was he doing out this early, anyway? Didn't he prefer to sleep the mornings away? And where would he be going with his hair wet like that? She tilted her head, squinting as a thought occurred to her. He wasn't going somewhere—he was headed in the direction of home. But where would he . . .

All at once, realization washed over her. Had he been at the *Baths*?

Old people and the infirm made use of the waters— not the young and well. He lifted his head then, and his expression made her blink in surprise. He looked . . . content. More relaxed than she had ever seen him— especially in the full light of day. So much so that he was almost unrecognizable. She'd seen him quiet, she'd seen him exhausted, she'd even seen him somewhat teasing. But she had certainly never seen him completely at ease.

His lips were curled up with a sort of effortlessness, as if such a state was natural. For once, his shoulders were without any tension. She shook her head—she just couldn't believe it was the same man.

It was a transformation that made his countenance so much more appealing, her heart actually fluttered a few beats. She swallowed; she really needed to get a grip on herself. He may be handsome, but he was still Lord Cadgwith. And she was still furious with him.

Even so, she took advantage of the moment, studying his features. His damp hair looked like bottled honey, a rich, dark golden blond that shone in the sunlight, with the overlong strands curling past the crisp white fabric of his cravat. The smudges beneath his eyes didn't seem as dark as usual. It could be the bright day, but she didn't think so.

Her gaze shifted to his bisected eyebrow. She contemplated the scars again, chewing the inside of her cheek as she wondered again what violence had befallen him. Yes, it was likely a war wound, but what had caused it?

And how much did it have to do with the wounded heart Grandmama had so keenly observed?

That would, of course, be the moment that he noticed her. His gaze flickered to hers as he passed, the intensity of the green startling in the brilliant sunlight. She abruptly released her cheek, doing her best to not look as though she had been studying him like some sort of foreign specimen. The last thing she wanted him to think was that she was somehow pining for him.

His step faltered and she could sense his indecision on whether to acknowledge her or not. She was embarrassed at having been caught staring, plus she was still angry enough that she would be perfectly fine if he just kept walking right on past her. But she had no such luck. His lips turned up further in a determined smile—*not natural*—and he dipped his head in greeting. "Good day, Miss Effington. I hope you are well."

"Do you? I wasn't aware that you gave any care as to my state of well-being." Not the way she intended to start a conversation, but her mouth seemed to have a mind of its own. So much for not airing her grievances in the street.

His face tightened, as did his shoulders, and suddenly she was looking at the same Lord Cadgwith she had known for almost three weeks. His joy, whatever the cause, would never be for her. "My apologies. If I could have sent you a note, I would have, but it did not seem prudent to do so."

Such a nice, calm answer, yet all it did was stir up her ire. How galling to know that something she had looked so forward to was an easily forgotten appointment to him. One tossed aside in favor of something more interesting.

"What, I wonder, was so important that you were unable to attend?" It was quite possibly one of the rudest questions she had ever asked, but she didn't feel particularly bad about it just then. If they had stumbled upon each other after the rehearsal, she might not have been so sharp. The day just seemed to be getting worse by the moment.

He tilted his head, eyeing her as one might a slightly unstable bedlamite. "You do realize we never had an actual agreement. It was implied at best."

Is that how things were going to be? Her arms crossed protectively over her chest, but she didn't look away.

"Implied by you, I may point out. You know full well that there was an expectation between us. To say otherwise demeans us both."

Her heart fluttered away in her chest like a scrap of paper caught in the wind. She absolutely hated confrontation; the fact that she would engage in it now spoke volumes about her state of mind.

He sighed, giving a shallow nod. "Fair enough. I wonder, Miss Effington. Did it occur to you how such a meeting—assignation, if you will—would be interpreted should anyone discover it? In the harsh light of day, such a thing seemed terribly ill-advised." His eyes softened, and he leaned forward a bit. "I like you, Charity. I do not wish for harm to come to your reputation. To either of our reputations, really."

Her breath caught in her throat at the sound of her name on his lips. She gaped at him, her ears suddenly ringing like a perfectly struck tuning fork. Had he really just called her Charity? She couldn't believe it. They were on the pavement in the center of town, for goodness' sake! Warmth stole up her cheeks as she stared up at him.

Was that how he thought of her?

For a moment, he seemed confused by her reaction, but a second later pressed his eyes closed and blew out a harsh breath. Leveling his gaze on her once more he said. "My apologies, Miss Effington. A slip of the tongue."

A slip of the tongue, indeed. She was so shocked, she could do little more than bob her head in acceptance of his apology. When he thought of her, was it as Charity, as a woman, and not just the neighbor Miss Effington? Over and over he had pushed her away, only to draw her closer the next time they met. Every time, she became a little more invested. A little more interested.

A little more breathless when he was near.

He shook his head, giving a humorless little laugh. "I don't know why I continually misstep around you. All the more reason to pay special attention to propriety from now on. I do hope you can forgive my clumsy handling of last night."

The door to the hall swung open, and Sophie popped her head out. "Come on, Charity, they're calling us. Oh!" she exclaimed as her eyes darted to where Hugh stood. "Lord Cadgwith, I didn't see you. I hope all is well," she said, her gaze going back and forth between them as though picking up on the charge in the air between them.

"I'll be there in one second, Sophie. Thank you."

"But—"

"I *promise*," Charity said, widening her eyes for emphasis.

Understanding dawned and Sophie straightened. "Oh yes, of course. No problem at all. I'll just be, er, inside. Waiting." With an awkward little wave, she ducked back inside, leaving them alone.

Charity turned her attention back to the baron, who stood ramrod straight only a few short steps away. He looked wary and conflicted and so handsome in the sunshine, her heart couldn't seem to remember its normal rhythm. "Lord Cadgwith," she said, looking directly into his eyes, "I wish you could see that I do, in fact, make a very good friend. And with the minor exception of a broken betrothal, I have lived my life remarkably scandal-free. Do me a favor and have a little faith in me."

She didn't wait to see his reaction. Honestly, she didn't think her nerves could take it after such a bold speech. Turning sharply on her heel, she drew a bracing breath and stepped for the door.

His hand snaked out and caught her wrist before she could go any farther. Gasping, she turned with widened eyes, the skin beneath her gloves nearly vibrating with awareness at his touch.

"I do have faith in you, Miss Effington. It's me I have trouble with."

Releasing his hold, he bowed, his eyes never leaving hers. Her heart broke for the return of the pain she could see lurking there. "Good day," he murmured, his voice slightly raspy. He left then, his long-legged stride carrying him away from her with telling speed.

What had he meant? Did he really not trust himself? He had seemed so brusque, conceited even, in the beginning. Now she wondered what was truly going on deep inside. When he turned the corner and disappeared from view, she drew in a fortifying breath and faced the Assembly Rooms door. She didn't have a spare moment to give the subject the time it deserved. Her trio was waiting.

When she walked in, Sophie was pacing just inside the door. "Oh, thank God. Come along. We've got to go. I want to hear everything, but it will have to wait!"

As Sophie grabbed her hand and dashed back toward the Great Octagon, where the rehearsal was to be held, Charity tried to get her poor skittering heart under control. It was no use. She was a proper mess by the time they collected May and headed for the inner door. There was simply too much going on in her rioting thoughts to have any hope for calm.

"Ready?" May asked, her smile bright and completely unconcerned.

"Do I have a choice?"

She shook her head decisively, making her curls bob. "No."

Charity drew a deep breath, exhaled, then nodded. "All right, then. Lead the way."

"You're distracted."

"Exceedingly." Hugh agreed readily, lifting his chin for Jacobson to have better access to his cravat.

"Is something amiss? I don't mind keeping your schedule, my lord, but you do have to participate in the making of it."

"Yes, right, the schedule. What was the question again?"

Jacobson chuckled, amusement crinkling the corner of his eye. "Does his lordship wish to attend the theater on Saturday evening?" He spoke slowly, enunciating each word. At Hugh's rolled eyes, he grinned and said, "Just making sure you're listening. As for the invitation, remember that Lord Derington has offered the use of his box at the Theatre Royal."

Hugh considered it for a moment. "Yes, actually. Why not?" He was feeling good, after all. It was the best stretch he'd had since the injury—more than a week now with no headache. The theater, with its dimmed lamps and quiet audience, was the perfect way to branch out.

Years ago, he may have scoffed at the thought of attending some boring play. But at that moment, the unmistakable buoyancy of hope lifted his heart at the prospect of spending the evening out in the world. Optimism was a dangerous thing, as was hopefulness, but he wanted to give in to it. To allow himself to feel anticipation again, and excitement.

Almost at once, Charity's lovely face popped into his head. Their encounter today had been unexpected in every way. He'd been shocked to see her, of course, but he certainly couldn't have foreseen the progression of the conversation. From fury one minute to quiet assurances the next, the pendulum had fully swung by the time they parted.

She wanted him to have faith in her. To allow them to be friends. It was foolish and reckless . . . but tempting as hell. Even when they bickered, she still had a certain lightness to her soul that he couldn't help but be drawn to. Nothing had beaten her down in life yet. She'd never known the meaning of the word *devastation*, and he was incredibly glad for it.

Although . . . apparently there had been at least some scandal in her short life. A broken betrothal? Curiosity flooded him all over again as he wondered what exactly had happened. She was young and pretty, certainly from a good family, and of decent means. When not reacting to him, she seemed to have a rather nice disposition. He couldn't imagine her breaking a betrothal, but neither could he imagine a man walking away from her.

With the cravat in place, Jacobson helped him into his forest green waistcoat, followed by the deep gray jacket. Once Hugh was jacketed, buttoned, and properly groomed, Jacobson stood back and inspected him with a critical eye.

"Will I pass muster?" Hugh asked, spreading his arms.

He waited for the customary flippant remark, but instead was surprised to see the batman's thoughtful expression. "Your clothes are perfectly acceptable, my lord, but it is your eyes that make me happy. It is rare to see you in such fine form, sir."

"It is good to feel in fine form." Hugh cleared his throat, shrugging off the somberness. "Now, then, go do whatever the hell it is you do all day while I'm forced to entertain distant relatives."

"Lady Cadgwith's brother is hardly distant, and I believe the card game is meant to entertain *you*," he pointed out, his eyebrow raised. "However, if you are through with my services, I shall avail myself of the *Times* that arrived this afternoon."

"Sure, sure—one of us should be up on current events."

Jacobson excused himself, and Hugh, ready earlier than necessary, wandered over to the balcony door and idly glanced out over the long, narrow garden. The sun had set some half hour earlier, and only the pale gravel path was clearly visible in the twilight. He had yet to make use of the gardens, including as a view. He tended to look up, not out, when enjoying the small balcony.

His eyes roamed to the adjoining garden, separated from his by a six-foot-high stone wall. As his gaze skimmed along, a puddle of white among the dark greens caught his attention. He squinted, trying to discern details in the failing light. A woman sat on a narrow bench, her head bowed and her hands crossed tightly. Charity— it must be. No other finely dressed young woman would be in her garden. He breathed in, a frisson of awareness skirting straight through him.

He watched her for a moment, not daring to move lest he somehow alert her to his presence. Something was wrong. His brow furrowed as he strained to better make out her form. She seemed crumpled, dejected. *Rejected.* What would have upset her so much from the way she had been only hours earlier? When they had met on the street, she had been initially angry, but very much mollified by the end of the conversation.

Straightening, he glanced to his watch fob—still a quarter hour before he needed to leave. He looked back out on her, debating what to do.

It wasn't his place to intrude, but he was absolutely certain something wasn't right. It was in her posture, her position, even the tilt of her head. Her distress called out to something in him. He couldn't say exactly why, but he just knew that she was hurting. The urge to soothe her was almost overwhelming. This was his sweet, infuriating, kind, and spirited neighbor. He didn't want to see her spirits brought low.

He knew all too well the posture of a person in a bad place. He waffled for a moment longer, then made up his mind. Opening the door, he stepped out onto the balcony.

Chapter Fifteen

"If you're lost, I may be able to guide you home from this vantage point."

Hugh waited, negligent grin in place, as her head jerked up at his words. Even from twenty feet away, he could tell he'd been right. Charity was definitely upset. Her body was as tense as a drawn bow, and even with the waning light, there was no missing the unguarded dismay that turned her normally expressive face to a stony mask.

"I'm not in the mood, my lord," she responded, her voice uncharacteristically wooden. She swiped at her cheeks with her ungloved fingers and gave a quiet sniff.

His gut twisted. Had she been crying? Damn it all — what happened to upset her so? He leaned against the railing, offering a subdued smile. "I can see that. However, if I am to be a proper friend, I feel I must offer my services."

She blew out an unladylike breath and leveled unhappy eyes up at him. "And what services would those be?"

There was absolutely no humor or levity in her gaze — or her entire countenance, for that matter. But still, he pressed on. "I'm quite handy with a pistol. Decent with a sword and downright deadly with my fists."

He had her attention now. She blinked up at him, tilting her head to the side. "My lord?"

Keeping his voice deliberately light, he said, "I'm merely pointing out all the handy ways with which I can kill a man, should you chose to make use of my services. Whoever caused those tears clearly doesn't deserve to live."

She gave a quiet, horrified little half laugh, half snort. "Don't tempt me."

He smiled. Good, she was at least not dismissing his company out of hand. "It is my duty as a former officer in His Majesty's Army to protect all of Britain's citizens, particularly lovely young women who've had their hearts broken."

And he would murder the idiot who had caused this—especially if it was a suitor Hugh didn't know about. And, no, he had no intention of examining why he felt so strongly about such a thing.

"Unless you are prepared to take out an entire committee, there is nothing that you can do for me." She sniffled, pulled a square of linen from her lap, and blew her nose. He almost smiled—clearly she felt no need to impress him.

"I'm quite prepared. Now, why don't you come up here where we can plan their demise without tipping off the neighbors?"

She bit her lip, looking up at him with uncertainty. "Such a thing is to be avoided at all costs, remember? God forbid someone sees us conversing." She rolled her eyes at the last word—even if he hadn't seen it, he could hear it in her voice. Throwing his stupid words back at him again, it would seem. He drew the inside of his cheek between his teeth, reevaluating the situation. God, he sure as hell hoped he wasn't somehow the cause of her upset.

With a soft, self-mocking grin, he said, "I think I can withstand the risk, just this once. Now, do come up, or I shall be forced to scale the wall to join you down there, which I really don't want to do. New jacket, you know," he said, pulling at the lapels.

He didn't know where this teasing demeanor was coming from. All he knew was that the faster he could help make her feel better, the faster the knot in his stomach would go away.

With a loud, exasperated sigh, she came to her feet and brushed off her gown. "Very well," she said, retrieving her shawl from the bench. "However, let it be noted that it was at your insistence. I won't have you accusing me of harming your precious reputation."

At least some of her spirit was intact. Biting back a grin, he solemnly nodded. "Duly noted."

What was she doing?

Even as Charity trudged up the stairs toward the music room, she couldn't quite figure out why she was doing so. Hugh had made no bones of his wish to stay clear of her company in the future, and yet here she was, responding to his summons.

She sniffled yet again and rubbed at the remaining moisture on her cheeks. Not that she cared what he thought of her appearance. Yes, she undoubtedly had puffy eyes, a red nose, and pale cheeks. This was how one was supposed to look when one was dealt a crushing disappointment. And, really, he was one reason she was in this mess in the first place. She couldn't prove it, of course, but their encounter surely hadn't helped anything.

She padded past the pianoforte, twisted the lock on the balcony door, and stepped outside. Darkness was rapidly falling, but she could clearly see the baron in the gray light. He leaned negligently back against the black railing, his arms crossed over his chest. He looked immaculate, perfectly ordered, and oh, so handsome with his crisp white cravat and well-tailored jacket. The consummate gentleman, while she no doubt looked like a paper doll left out in a rainstorm. Despite her resolve not to care, she smoothed a hand down the rumpled fabric of her skirts.

"Well?" he prompted, raising his eyebrows in invitation.

"Well, what?" Yes, she was being contrary, but damn it, she was *feeling* contrary. This day had been a total disaster, and being polite wasn't high on her list of priorities at the moment.

"What has stolen the joy from those pretty gray eyes of yours?"

Her stolen joy. If that didn't sum up the way she was feeling, she didn't know what would. Even his unexpected little compliment wasn't enough to raise her spirits. With her disappointment washing over her anew, she fished out the crumpled letter from her bodice and thrust it at him. "Here."

The look on his face was almost enough to make her laugh. One would think she had just, well, pulled a letter from her bodice. She bit her lip. Her mother would have fainted dead away if she could have seen her. But Mama would never know, and she wasn't terribly concerned with the baron's tender sensibilities. "Go on," she said, waving the paper at him.

Visibly working to straighten his expression—and, yes, she did see the humor flaring his eyes—he plucked the letter from her fingers, unfolded it, and scanned the three-sentence note. She could have told him exactly what it said:

*Dear Miss Effington, Miss Wembley, and
Miss Bradford,*

*The committee is honored to have been able to ex-
perience your performance. Unfortunately, we have
discovered that the event has been filled beyond capacity, and we simply cannot find the room for all
registered performances. As the last to register, we regret to inform you that your trio cannot be included
in this year's recitals.*

*With our sincerest apologies,
The Summer in Somerset Musical
Selection and Assignment Committee*

Hugh looked up, his eyes clouded. "What a terrible
disappointment. No wonder you are upset." He held the
letter out to her, shaking his head. "One would think
they would have worked out those sorts of logistics before the process was this far along."

"Oh, I don't for one second believe it is because they
can't seem to find a time slot. How hard is it to tack an
extra five-minute performance to the end of an evening?
No, this was directed to us personally."

Hugh lifted an unconvinced eyebrow. "Personally? I
rather doubt that. Have you managed to offend the committee somehow?"

"No, not directly. But Lord Wexley's daughter is no
friend of mine, and our music was exceedingly unusual,
and Mr. Green already despised us...." She trailed off
when she saw the look on his face. "You think I'm mad,
don't you?" Blast it all, she didn't know why she was telling him any of this in the first place.

"No. Slightly delusional, but not in a bad way."

She scrunched her nose up in dismay. "Delusional!

You didn't see their expressions when we finished our piece. Lord Wexley looked as though someone had switched his snuff with ashes." Actually, at least one of them had seemed intrigued, and two others moderately impressed. But Wexley's look had spoken volumes about how he felt about the performance. Whether Marianne had poisoned him against her or not, the result was still the same: They couldn't perform.

"Then to hell with them."

Her wandering gaze snapped back to his. "What?" she squeaked.

"If they don't want you, you don't want them. Do you really need this? It's just a silly showcase to give bored aristocrats a reason to show off."

Indignation flooded her veins. "I beg your pardon, but I'll have you know this happens to be very important to us. It is not some silly amusement for people with nothing better to do."

He sighed, letting his arms drop to his sides. "Yes, of course. And I know how hard you and the others have been practicing for this. I'm sorry for your disappointment."

Did he ever hear the words coming out of his mouth? The insensitive lout. Not that she should have expected anything different from him. For heaven's sake, he couldn't even be bothered to stay in the room for one song at Dering's dinner. What a fool she was, thinking he might actually be a comfort when she'd decided to come upstairs.

Straightening her spine, she snatched the missive from his fingers and balled it in her hands. "Oh yes. I'm sure you are absolutely devastated to hear that we no longer have a reason to practice."

His brows lowered over reproving eyes. "That's not

fair, Miss Effington. Just because your music isn't for me doesn't mean I don't know how much it means to you."

Annoyance burned in her belly, making her more reckless than usual. She took a step closer to him. "Actually, that's exactly what it means. If you had any idea what it meant to me, you would have never demanded that I stop playing."

The beginning of annoyance tightened his jaw. "Again, that is unfair of you. That was before I had ever laid eyes on you. How could I have known then what I know now?"

He knew full well his dislike for her music went far deeper than that. "Before you knew me, huh? Well, that doesn't explain your fairly running from the room at Dering's party. Or throwing coins at my window in order to beg my silence."

That at least elicited a cringe from him. "I'll admit, that wasn't very well-done of me. You have every right to enjoy your hobby."

Hobby? He had no idea how much music truly meant to her. He simply dismissed it as an annoying way for her to pass time. Her brow furrowed as she glared at him. "What you scorn, I love. What you see as noise, I see as my very heartbeat. What you call a *hobby*, I call my purpose in life. I exist in this world, but I come alive when my fingers hit the keys. You have no concept of the passion I feel for music."

Any lingering humor in his eyes was completely gone now. "Come, now. I may not be passionate about the same things you are, but I understand passion, for God's sake."

Cadgwith? Passionate? He had no idea of the meaning of the word, as far as she could tell. "Do you? Because I have yet to see any evidence of that. All I see is a haunted shell of a man who shuts himself up in his home at every opportunity, and flees the moment things progress beyond his comfort level."

His nostrils flared as he snapped his body upright. *Dear Lord.* The bitter words echoed through her brain, seeming to amplify instead of diminish. She slapped a hand over her mouth, horror widening her eyes. Before she could speak—apologize, grovel, recant, *anything*— he took an ominous step forward.

"Is that what you see when you look at me?" His voice was deadly calm, his green eyes piercing in their intensity. His scars seemed to whiten as his face grew taut.

She shook her head, swallowing convulsively. "No, of course not. I was angry, and—"

"And decided to speak the truth? Ire, like jealousy, loosens the tongue more effectively than any alcohol." He took another step closer, forcing her to tilt her head back in order to meet his gaze. Her heart pounded at the fire she saw burning in his eyes. "You think I know nothing of you, but I *promise* you that you know nothing of me."

"You're right," she said, her voice little more than a strained whisper. "I don't know you. You won't let me. Every time I try to, you push me away."

He was so close, she could smell the spicy scent of his shaving soap, see the pounding of the pulse at his neck, feel the force of his barely leashed emotion. "Did it ever occur to you," he said, his voice quiet, "that I may have good reason to do so? That you wouldn't *want* to know me?"

There—that flash of pain was back. His wounded heart had shown itself again, drawing her to him like a flame beckoned a moth. Sucking in a deep, bracing breath, she boldly took a step forward. "No. Not once."

Only the warm metal of the railing separated them, leaving mere inches between her breasts and his chest. Her skin tingled with the knowledge that if either of them leaned just the slightest bit forward, their bodies would touch.

He gazed down into her eyes, studying her as if trying to divine her innermost thoughts. "Charity," he said at last, his voice full of regret.

"No," she said, cutting off the words she knew he would say, but that she was determined not to hear. "You don't get to back away. Not this time."

He shook his head, and she could almost see him mentally stepping away from her. Not again. She wouldn't let him run away this time.

Without stopping to think, without considering a single consequence, she rose on her toes and pressed her lips to his. He sucked in a shocked breath of air through his nose, the sound sharp in the evening hush. Her nerves rioted at the sensation, making her ears buzz and her stomach drop to the ground at her feet.

Only he didn't move. He didn't respond to her kiss at all. Instead he held himself rigidly still. Her bravery began to waver, especially since she had no idea what to do next. It was as though he were made of granite. Dear heavens, what if he didn't want her? What if he was disgusted by her kiss? Mortification began to take over, and she broke away, dropping back down off her toes. Even though she didn't want to, she couldn't seem to stop herself from looking up into his eyes.

He gazed back at her, his expression utterly unreadable. He hadn't moved, not even an inch. The moment stretched for one second and then two, punctuated only by their breathing. Just when she couldn't take it anymore, when she was sure she had utterly lost her gamble, he came alive, a statue breaking free of his bonds.

In one smooth motion, he swooped down to capture her lips as his arms wrapped fully around her waist and tugged her against him, heedless of the railing between them. She gasped against his mouth, against the roar of nerves that exploded with sensation throughout her entire body. Hugh was kissing her!

More than kissing her. He was consuming her. She rose back onto her toes, her arms snaking around his neck to pull him even closer. His mouth was warm, coaxing but gentle. She breathed in his masculine scent, drowning in the pleasure consuming her every sense. It was the passion she had never experienced, but knew in her heart that it existed.

This was why she had broken her engagement to Lord Raleigh. *This* was the reason she had risked her future for the hope of something she might never find. Hugh's tongue touched the seam of her lips, and she immediately yielded to him. She didn't know what to do, so she simply followed his lead. He tasted amazing, yet for the life of her she couldn't have described it. It was like the smell of the air after a summer rainstorm, sweet and hot. She moaned as their tongues twined and danced, freely losing herself in his perfect kiss.

Not her first kiss, but the first one that mattered.

The first one to send molten heat licking through her veins and butterflies swirling in her belly. It was the kind of kiss that changed everything.

Before she was ready, he pulled away, his chest heaving as he drew in a lungful of air. Darkness had fallen fully around them, cocooning them in their own little world. He looked deep into her eyes, unflinching despite the closeness. "I feel great passion," he rasped, his emotion filling his words. "Much more than I should. So much more than I deserve."

He pulled back farther, allowing his hands to slide along her waist. "I wish I could share your passion, but I can't. It's just not possible."

She was reeling. Clearly he possessed more passion than she could ever have imagined. So why was he denying it? Why was he setting up barriers between them? "Why not?" she asked, confusion coloring her words. It didn't make sense. What was he not telling her? She trailed her hands down his chest and along his arms. Even as she covered his hands with her own and pressed them against her sides, she could feel him withdrawing from her.

"The same reason I should never have kissed you tonight. I'm not . . ." He trailed off, clearly struggling for the right word. His fingers tightened on her waist, and she closed her eyes against the fresh wave of desire that washed through her. Didn't he feel it? The warmth of his skin beneath her palms was thrilling yet comforting at the same time.

Opening her eyes, she peered up at him, but his gaze was diverted toward the indigo sky. "You're not what? You can tell me, Hugh." Her voice was a near whisper in the darkness, barely louder than the pounding of her heart.

He shifted his gazed down to her. Uncertainty wavered in his deep green eyes. She curled her fingers around his hands, pressing her fingernails lightly against his palms. "I know something weighs heavy on your heart. Release it."

He blew out a quiet breath. "This was a mistake. I never should have—"

"Kissed me?" she demanded, her frustration knotting in her stomach. How could he say what they had just shared was a mistake?

His eyes softened and he shook his head. "I can't regret that. It—*you* are perfection. But I never should have let things get this far."

He tried to pull his hands from her grasp, but she held tightly, boldly refusing to let him walk away. "Why not? Tell me what it is about me that makes you continually try to push me away."

"It's not you, Charity. It's me," he insisted, tugging his hands once more. This time she let him go, frustrated beyond words that he couldn't just speak plainly to her.

"If that doesn't sound like a load of horse apples, I don't know what does. If I am so impossible to be with, just tell me and I swear to you, I won't bother you ever again." The words were bitter on her tongue, a stark contrast to the sweetness of his kiss only moments ago. Damn it all, she didn't *want* to leave him alone, but if he was so blasted determined to push her away, then she wouldn't force her company on him.

"It's the truth, damn it. You are sweetness and light and sarcasm and wit. I, on the other hand." He pressed his lips together for a moment before continuing. "I would never be able to offer anything worth having."

God, did he really think that? She rubbed her hands over her arms, chilled by the hopelessness that dulled his eyes and roughened his voice. "That's ridiculous. You have plenty to—"

"I don't," he insisted with such finality, her heart dropped.

She shook her head, at a loss of what to do. Why was he so determined to degrade his own worth? "Why would you say such a thing about yourself?"

He shoved both hands through his hair, dragging it back from his forehead. He stood there for a moment, waging some sort of inner battle as he stared at her in the darkness. She held her silence, openly accepting his scrutiny. Willing him to purge the darkness that tortured him from within.

Willing him to trust her.

At last he dropped his arms to the side and gave his head a little shake. "I'm broken, Charity. And I might never be whole again."

Chapter Sixteen

Christ, he couldn't believe he had actually said it.

While it was unspoken, it was possible to ignore it at times, to pretend that he could be normal and things would someday be all right. But now, to see the truth reflected in Charity's eyes . . . it was worse than he had imagined. Now she would know how pathetic he truly was. He held his breath, waiting for the judgment, the laughter, or, worse, the pity. He was broken, and he would likely remain that way for the rest of his life.

Speaking the words made it that much more real. Yes, he'd recognized the extent of his injury, but admitting it to the woman he desired brought the hopelessness of his situation into sharp focus.

She blinked, confusion marking the normally smooth skin of her forehead with a deep *v*. "I don't understand."

He rubbed a hand to the back of his neck, wishing he'd kept his damn mouth shut. Hell, he wished he were still kissing her. Even now his whole body hummed with the pleasure of it. He wanted nothing more than to forget all that limited him and lose himself in her perfect kiss all over again. But it was not to be. Not now, not ever. "I'm not well. I haven't been since Waterloo."

"But you look—"

"Fine? Yes, I know. My horse was shot from beneath me, and I hit the ground headfirst. There were the visible injuries: Lacerated face." He drew a finger across the scars marking his temple. "Narrow miss of the artery in my neck." He pulled the edge of the cravat down to expose the jagged line at his throat.

"Then there were the more insidious ones. Compressed spinal cord of the cervical spine. Concussion. Internal bleeding. Broken clavicle." He ticked off the injuries for her as his doctors once had for him. "I was lucky. If the battlefield hadn't been such a muddy mess, the fall would have killed me."

"But ..." She shook her head, as though trying to shake loose the words she wanted to say. "Are they not healed? Your injuries, I mean. You seem perfectly fine."

Exactly what everyone always thought. He looked fine, therefore he must be fine. He needed to just snap out of it, to move on and stop being so dramatic. Isn't that what Ian had thought toward the end? Felicity had been more understanding, but Hugh's brother had become more and more impatient with Hugh's lingering illness. He'd never said as much, but every time they were together, Hugh had felt the weight of his brother's silent judgment to pull himself together.

Not that Hugh blamed his brother. He himself was sick and tired of the way he was living—if one could call it living. He only wished he had heeded Felicity's advice when Ian was alive.

"Do I?" He gave a humorless little laugh. "Good to know. It's not something I wish for the world to see. My shoulder healed, as did the scars. But my injuries had consequences. The compressed spine and concussion created a breed of headache I had not known existed."

That first year was still something of a blur in his memory. Thank God; he had no desire to remember or relive those days.

"You suffer from megrims?"

There was the reaction he had been expecting. He could tell she was trying to hide her dubiousness, but he still caught it. Few could comprehend the devastation of one of his attacks. The utter, consuming pain of the sort that racked his whole being, making even the pain of the fractured clavicle seem trivial.

He swallowed and rubbed his neck again, trying to find the words to convey what he meant by broken. "These headaches are to megrims what a cannonball is to a bullet. The pain is indescribable. They last for hours or even days. Sometimes I lose my vision; sometimes I lose movement on my left side. The pounding is so fierce it is as though a blacksmith is using my brain for an anvil. The tiniest bit of light is like an explosion in my head; the smallest sound sheer torture."

And that was where understanding dawned. He could see it in the sudden widening of her eyes, the sucking in of a sharp breath. "Music," she breathed, a wealth of comprehension bundled in the single word.

He gave a single shallow nod. "Music."

She closed her eyes and dropped her chin to her chest for a moment before raising her troubled gaze to his. "My God, Hugh. I didn't know. I had no idea."

"Of course you didn't. No one does, save for my family. It's not something to advertise."

"If only I'd known. I feel a proper shrew now for playing despite your wish for me not to. It's just unfathomable to me what it must be like for you. A life without music, I mean. Does it always bring you pain?"

Just talking about his headaches exhausted him. He

leaned back against the exterior wall, soaking in the residual heat from the limestone. "Not always. But it is one of my triggers, so I tend to avoid it."

"Triggers?"

"I never know when an attack will come, but some things are more likely to cause them than others. Music, particularly higher octaves, is one of the worst. Anything jarring, like riding or long carriage rides, can easily cause them. Sometimes it seems to happen just because I am alive."

He'd never been so open about his constant struggle before. Instead of the shame he might have expected, it was surprisingly freeing. Validating.

"Does anything help?" She seemed genuinely interested, but not in a gawking way. He could see compassion in her eyes. Sorrow for his pain. That was different from pity. Nothing about her empathetic eyes or quiet questions made him feel less of a man.

"So far?" He shrugged, offering a small smile. "The Baths, actually. I've never known such relief. I don't know if it is the magic properties some people seem to believe in or if it's just the relief being weightless affords. The heat seems to help, too."

She smiled back, easy and genuine. "I'm glad for it. Now, if only that pesky neighbor of yours would go away."

If only she knew how much he had wanted that in the beginning. Now? He reached across the railing and slipped his fingers beneath her hand. Lifting it to his lips, he pressed a soft kiss to the hollow between her knuckles. "If only *your* arse of a neighbor would leave you be."

She licked her lips, her eyes riveted on his. "I don't want him to. He just doesn't seem to believe me."

Oh, what those words did to his heart. He laced his

fingers with hers, even as he knew he should leave. "We couldn't be a worse match, darling. I know your music means the world to you. Your heart was broken when the idiot committee prevented you from playing one night. You don't need someone like me around, making things difficult for you."

Her delectable lips curved down. He didn't want to hurt her feelings, but he definitely didn't want her setting her heart on something that could never be. He pressed on, wanting to make his point while she was truly hearing him. "Whoever is meant to share your life is also meant to share your music. God gave you an amazing talent, one that clearly brings you incredible joy in life. *That* is why it was a mistake to let things get this far. It is selfish for me to kiss you when there can be no place for you in my life, and vice versa."

The words were meant to convince her, but they were just as much for him. He needed to remind himself why he couldn't do this. Why he had no business engaging her when he would inevitably have to leave. Why he had to ignore the desire to kiss the frown from her lips, and soothe the turmoil he saw in her gaze.

He gave her fingers a little squeeze before releasing them. Pushing away from the wall he said, "In the meantime, you may count on me being out of the house from two until four each afternoon so you may practice. Will that work?"

She bit her lip and nodded. "Yes, but I hate to put you out of your own home."

"It will do me good. It is past time for me to rejoin society. That's half the reason for me being here—as the new baron, I can no longer hide beneath a rock."

He smiled, pushing away the emptiness that opened up within him whenever he thought of his new title.

"Which reminds me, I shall be out for the rest of the evening, so feel free to play away. Good night, sweet Charity. I'm sorry for your terrible disappointment today. Perhaps something better will come along."

Just as some*one* better would come along. He bowed and walked back inside, feeling strangely better and a hundred times worse all at once. He should never have returned her kiss—he knew that without a shadow of a doubt. No matter how much he'd reveled in their stolen moment, it just wasn't fair to her.

But perhaps there was something he could do for her. Finger-combing his hair back into place, he headed for the door. He may not be able to enjoy Charity's music, but he knew someone who did.

The familiar keys waited for her touch, their neatly ordered black-and-white pattern offering up comfort in Charity's sudden disordered world. But for some reason, she couldn't make herself put her fingers to them and play. It seemed oddly disrespectful.

She simply could not stop thinking of the starkness of Hugh's features as he relayed the true extent of his troubles to her. Staring down at the long, narrow keys, for perhaps the first time in her life, she didn't hear the music in her head.

Silence.

The concept of a life of silence was like the prospect of living without color. Impossible to imagine, dreadful to even conceive of.

But the worst part? Somehow, somewhere along the way, she had started to like the baron. She hadn't realized how much, exactly, until the prospect of any exploration of a future with him was snatched away before it was even fully formed. Before it might have been an intriguing possibility to consider. Now? It was like being told not to think of a pink elephant. Suddenly, all she could think about was where that one precious kiss, that moment of tenderness between them, might have eventually led.

"The artless, crook-pated, milk-livered barnacles."

Charity smiled wanly at May's colorful insult, while Sophie's tinkling laughter was the sole bit of joy in Lady Stanwix's drab olive-painted music room. The colorless day beyond the window was no better, either.

Sophie put her hands to her flushed cheeks. "Oh, my word, you do have a talent for insults. Did your father teach you that? Although if he is even a little bit like your aunt, I can't imagine that being the case."

"Oh, he is nothing like her, thank heavens. But no. One simply picks those sorts of things up in the company of sailors. I shan't burn your ears with the more colorful ones." She gave a wink that made Sophie giggle again.

"Well, it describes the committee to perfection, if you ask me. Charity, you're not letting those awful men get to you, are you?"

Charity's mind snapped to attention. She hadn't even realized it had been wandering. "No. Well, yes, actually, but I'm just generally out of sorts."

She had been completely distracted since her conversation with Hugh yesterday. So much so, even the huge disappointment of the recital hadn't bothered her as much as it should have. She had sat at the pianoforte for nearly two hours, unable to play a single note. All she could think of was the suffering he had been through, and how much of it she had been responsible for. There was no joy in that, and joy was where she found her music.

Last night, all she could feel was sorrow for all the pain that had burdened him for so long.

"Well, if it makes you feel any better, my aunt was quite relieved that they had turned us away. She's been increasingly worried that my guzheng playing would somehow reflect badly on her. So there—we made one person's day." She rolled her eyes, not nearly as offended as Charity might have been if it had been her family member.

"Oddly enough," Charity said, coming to her feet and marching to the pianoforte. "It only makes me want to practice. I don't care if we aren't going to be playing for the recital. I'd rather play alone in this room with the two of you than in front of a whole audience by myself."

Sophie grinned broadly, and made a show of opening her case. "I concur wholeheartedly. After years of playing with my sister, I can honestly say I've never had more fun."

"Excellent," May said, giving a decisive nod. "I couldn't agree more. Oh!" she exclaimed, snapping her fingers. "That reminds me. My aunt was in a particularly good mood, thanks to the committee, and has actually agreed to let me attend the theater this Saturday. Are you going?"

"I am!" Sophie said, looking up from adjusting her reed. "Mama is most eager for me to attend as many functions as possible. 'Rule number one: One must be present if one wishes to make an impression.'"

Charity cocked her head at that particular idiom, and just happened to catch May's lifted eyebrows. Biting back laughter, she said, "Um, yes. That one actually does sound reasonable."

Waving a hand, Sophie said, "Oh, do feel free to laugh. Being obvious is my mother's best-developed attribute. Now, will you be there, Charity?"

"I hadn't planned to, but I'm certain we can work something out. Dering reminded my grandmother that he has a box, and we were to feel free to make use of it. I'll have her send a note this afternoon."

"Then it's settled," May said, plucking a few strings of her zither. "The two of you shall help to make certain that I don't make a fool of myself in my second foray into society. And by that, I mean 'Please come rescue me from my aunt so that she won't drive me to do something I will regret.'"

They all laughed, knowing she was only partly teasing. Not that Charity blamed her—she'd go mad if she had to live with someone like Lady Stanwix. Never had she felt more grateful for her grandmother's sweet support. It really did mean the world to her that Grandmama not only appreciated Charity's playing, she seemed to truly understand how important it was to her.

As she turned back to the keys to begin their practice, she suddenly realized how right Hugh had been last night. To be with a person who couldn't bear her music would be unbearable in itself. Even when she thought she could live without love, she knew she couldn't be with a man who wouldn't support her desire to play.

But somewhere along the way, the baron had started to matter. He had filled her thoughts more than she even wanted to admit to herself, and last night she had positively ached for his pain. He meant something to her.

Quite a lot, actually.

And who said they couldn't be friends, even if there could never be more? She bit her bottom lip, thinking of the incredible kiss they had shared last night. Even now, hours later, her belly did a little flip just thinking about it. It had been so heart-poundingly all-consuming, it was almost impossible not to want to experience that again.

Not to imagine his lips descending onto hers, or his hands pulling her closer, or his tongue slipping into her mouth.

She swallowed, trying to rein in her thoughts. If they were to be friends, they certainly couldn't go kissing like that again.

Still, as determined as she was to preserve their friendship, she couldn't help but wonder: Would one kiss ever be enough?

Chapter Seventeen

After half a decade of doing very little for anyone—himself included—Hugh savored the blossoming warmth that suffused his chest as he walked toward Dering's house.

If anyone could help sway the damn-fool selection committee, it was he. As if the man's rank, social reach, and easygoing charm weren't already enough, Hugh knew that he was already an admirer of Charity's music.

Luckily, the viscount was at home, and in short order Hugh once again found himself in the dark and masculine room that served as Dering's study. It was impossible not to think of Charity, for the last time he was here, she had very nearly gotten them both in a heap of trouble.

Although the thought of being discovered in a compromising position seemed quite a bit less offensive than it had at the time. He swallowed against the odd emotions that particular thought shook loose and smiled in greeting to his old friend. "Dering, thanks for seeing me."

"Of course, of course," he said, extending a paw in greeting. "What can I do for you, my friend? Still planning on coming to the theater, I hope?"

"Yes, I plan to be there." At Dering's invitation, he took a seat in the same chair he'd claimed last time.

"Good to hear. I must say, this city seems to be agreeing with you. You look much restored from even a week ago."

"Indeed." The city was agreeing with him. The waters were better than he could have hoped for, and the company was proving to be surprisingly captivating. Charity's expressive gray eyes and cinnamon hair flashed to his mind. How could someone so wrong for him be so appealing? Was it *because* he had no business being with her that he seemed to be unable to free his mind of her?

Looking his friend in the eye, he said, "I was wondering if you might be of assistance to me. If you are willing, of course."

One dark brow raised in mild interest. "A favor? I'm properly intrigued. Let's hear it."

Suddenly unsure of how to even present the issue without sounding as though he had more interest in it than he should, he adjusted his position in the overlarge chair and lifted his ankle to rest on his knee. "As you know, I am renting a townhouse that is adjacent to Lady Effington and her granddaughter."

Interest flared in Dering's brown eyes. He did nothing more than nod, but Hugh found himself hesitating, trying to come up with the right words. "I happened to discover, quite by accident, that the selection committee of the Tuesday-night recitals has turned Miss Effington and her trio members away."

Dering tilted his head to the left. "Turned them away?"

"They claim they have overbooked the event. After

witnessing Miss Effington's distress, I imagine she is deeply upset by the lost opportunity."

"I see," he said, crossing his arms. His dark brown jacket pulled at the seams, despite its generous cut. Hugh fleetingly wondered if the man still only boxed to keep in shape, or if he had taken up some other activity. His biceps were as thick as tree trunks these days.

"I wonder," Dering said, one corner of his wide mouth tilting upward in barely perceptible amusement. "How does one stumble on such information by accident?"

"Unfortunately, I happened upon her when she had just received the letter. Needless to say, there were a few tears involved."

Dering sat up straight. "Charity was crying?" Any amusement was eclipsed by the scowl darkening his face. "That is something. She's fairly even-tempered, that one."

Hugh bit his tongue. In his experience, Charity was anything but even-tempered. He'd seen anger, upset, laughter . . . passion. He pressed his lips together, hit anew by the memory of their embrace.

Rubbing his palms back and forth, Dering seemed to be debating what to do about the new information. "I wonder, why did you come to me?"

Hugh shrugged. "I know you're a friend of the family. Seemed a damned shame that all their practicing should be for naught." The words were impressively neutral, given the wealth of turmoil the music had caused. "I suppose I thought it was unfair, and someone should do something about it."

"So why not you?"

Laughing, Hugh said, "I am. I'm telling you." Coming to his feet, he offered a careless shrug, meant to convey a distance from the situation that he didn't feel. "Do what you will with the information. I'm sure she'll survive either way."

Dering stood, his frame towering over Hugh. "I'll see what I can do. In the meantime, I feel I should warn you."

With careful nonchalance, Hugh raised an eyebrow. "Yes?"

"If you have any interest in the girl, speak now. Otherwise, I can't promise I won't decide to pursue her myself. I'll admit, she is quite a lovely and accomplished young woman." He shrugged, leaning back in his chair. "A man could do far worse."

Hugh's attempt to remain disengaged faltered, and he took a slow, deep breath before saying, "You old dog. I had no idea you were interested."

Dering's smile grew. "Neither did I. Things have certainly changed since she was a freckle-faced, whip-thin, carrot-haired girl."

It took all of Hugh's willpower to force himself to smile back at the man. Dering would be a perfect match for her. He was wealthy, heir to an earldom, well liked, and a longtime friend of her family. If Hugh wanted the best for her, then shouldn't Dering's surprise announcement make him happy?

"I wish you the best, old man," he answered, giving him a sound whack on the shoulder for good measure. And if he suddenly felt as though he'd taken a punch to the ribs, then he would just have to live with it. He knew a little something about living with pain.

"Well, my dear, don't you look positively divine tonight?" Grandmama smiled as Charity floated into the drawing room, swathed in a cloud of diaphanous pale blue silk.

She wasn't generally one for jewels, but the double strand of pearls dropped with tear-shaped aquamarines that her father had gifted her with on her eighteenth birthday seemed the perfect touch.

"Thank you. As do you. That color lavender was just made for you." With her silver hair coiled into an elegant chignon at the back of her neck, and her exquisite diamond-and-amethyst necklace lying perfectly across her collarbone, she looked as lovely as a painting. Charity cocked her head, realizing that her grandmother actually looked better than she had since before she became sick several years earlier. Her cheeks were tinged a pretty pink, her eyes sparkled merrily in the candlelight, and her shoulders were almost completely straight.

Happiness took root deep down inside her at the thought. Bath was exactly the right place for them just now. Even though Charity had been *un*selected by the selection committee, and the fact she still wasn't sure what to think about the situation with the baron, Charity could say without a smidge of doubt that coming here had been the right choice.

She pressed a light kiss on Grandmama's cheek. There was a time when they weren't sure if she would recover; Charity wanted to be certain to always savor their time together now. Stepping back, she said, "Shall I ring for the carriage?" She started for the bellpull.

"Oh no, dear. I forgot to tell you—we're to ride with Lord Cadgwith."

Charity froze. "Lord Cadgwith?" She couldn't hide her surprise. "The baron is going to the theater?" The sentence came out with the same incredulousness as if she had said *The baron is going to the moon?* After their discussion, she didn't think he would ever participate in any of the larger gatherings.

Grandmama chuckled. "You needn't sound so shocked. It turns out we shall both be Lord Derington's guests to-night, and the baron kindly offered. He is so very courteous. Don't you think?"

"Yes, of course," Charity murmured, utterly dis-tracted. Hugh was going to be joining them tonight? And sitting across from her in a small carriage, with nothing but scant inches and Grandmama's not so watchful eye separating them? Butterflies fluttered to life in her belly, their wings beating a staccato rhythm that matched her heartbeat.

Not the way one was supposed to feel about a friend.

But then, one didn't generally know the taste of a friend's lips.

Glancing to the clock, her grandmother gestured for the door. "Come along. He said he would be ready any-time after nine, and it is already ten after."

The butterflies escaped the bounds of Charity's belly and spread up her chest. What would they say to each other? She put her fingers to her lips, heat seeming to graze them even now. Though she agreed with him that they had no compatibility whatsoever, it didn't stop her heart from pounding all the harder at the thought of be-ing near him.

By the time they reached the front door, Charity was nearly light-headed with the anticipation of seeing him again. Silly, stupid, unwise, but out of her control. She wanted to see him, plain and simple. The butler opened the door for them, and all at once her eyes found him.

Hugh.

He was standing beside the sleek black carriage, wear-ing a well-fitting gray jacket and a handsome pair of bone-colored pantaloons that highlighted his long legs. He came to attention when he saw them, and though he smiled sweetly to Grandmama, there was no mistaking the heat in his gaze as he turned his attention to Charity. The butterflies multiplied, careening around her entire body.

He waited until they reached the carriage before bowing. "Good evening, ladies. It would seem I am to be the luckiest man in Bath, escorted by two such fine women."

"Oh, do go on, my lord," Grandmama said, chuckling gaily. "Such flattery, when you know full well you'll be turning heads, so handsomely turned out as you are." Putting her hand out for his assistance, she carefully ascended into the darkness of the carriage.

When she was properly settled, he turned back to Charity. She worked to calm her breathing. He was as sharply dressed as any of the *ton*'s most sophisticated men, but there was a certain no-nonsense air about him that prevented him from looking foppish. He was all male confidence and quiet composure—a heady combination.

Holding his hand out to her, he said, "Good evening, Miss Effington."

She swallowed. "Good evening, Lord Cadgwith." Her voice was as even and proper as his, despite her rioting nerves. Licking her lips, she lifted her hand to his, allowing her gloved fingers to slide against his with a deliberateness that a casual observer might not think anything of, but that she knew he had to notice. "I'm so glad you decided to come out this evening."

Did she imagine the almost imperceptible tightening of his fingers? She couldn't be sure, not with the way her body was reacting—or, rather, overreacting—to his touch.

"As am I," he murmured, guiding her to the step.

She reluctantly stepped up, unable to delay the inevitable parting of their hands. Was it terrible of her to want to prolong their touch? All too soon he released his hold, allowing their fingers to slip apart. The carriage rocked as he ascended the steps and joined them inside, taking the backward-facing bench.

Their eyes met in the shadowy light of the lanterns hanging just outside the window. As much as she loved her grandmother, she suddenly found herself wishing the woman anyplace but here.

The short half-mile distance to the theater was inordinately long, not only because of the traffic clogging the road, but because of his hyperawareness of Charity's small form only a few feet from him.

Her grandmother kept up a steady stream of conversation, her voice overloud in the small space, but not unpleasant. For the most part, however, her gaze was focused on the busy street beyond the window. That freed Hugh to steal many surreptitious glances at his little redheaded companion. She looked especially lovely tonight. He loved the way her auburn hair just touched the nape of her neck, right at the curve of her shoulder. Her skin was pale and smooth, with light freckles creating a constellation across the exposed expanse of her shoulders and collarbone that his lips longed to map.

When he glanced up, his eyes collided with hers. She unapologetically watched him in the swaying lamplight, boldly meeting his gaze. She didn't smile to negate the intimacy of their shared regard. But then again, neither did he. He couldn't have, not when his heart was pounding with the memory of his lips on hers. Of her body pressed against his chest, and his arms wrapped around her slender waist.

"Isn't that a shame, Lord Cadgwith?"

He snapped his attention back to Lady Effington, at a complete loss as to what she was talking about. "Dreadfully so," he said, assuming she was looking for his agreement.

She nodded approvingly. "I just don't see how they couldn't have found a few minutes somewhere for the girls to play. It's not as though they have a mail coach to catch."

Ah, the recital. Hopefully, Dering would get it worked out, but he wasn't about to say anything to them. If the viscount was able to fix things, then he deserved the credit, and if he wasn't, then Hugh wasn't going to raise their hopes for nothing. "I agree. The organizers have no excuse for such shabby handling of the issue."

"Indeed," she said, nodding once. "And I sincerely doubt that any of the other musicians were better than our Charity."

"Grandmama," Charity admonished kindly, though her voice was raised in deference to the older woman's hearing. "There's no reason to disparage the others' talents. It was merely bad luck that we were the last to register." Disappointment lurked in her eyes, even as she smiled to her grandmother.

God, he hoped Dering was able to work something out. He was counting on the man to come through on this.

Waving a dismissive hand, the dowager said, "Yes, of course. I just feel they shall be missing out on one of the best England has to offer."

Charity chuckled then. "Says the musician's grandmother. Worry not, we three musicians will still play, even if not for the festival."

Lady Effington smiled and patted Charity's skirts. "As

you should." She turned her attention back to the window, humming quietly under her breath. Hugh doubted she even realized they could hear her.

The carriage swayed as they took a corner, and Charity her feet for balance. Her leg brushed against Hugh's, and her eyes darted up to meet his. She didn't, however, move her leg. Neither did he. He tilted his head, holding her gaze. "They are certainly missing out on a very fine talent," he said, his voice a near whisper.

She shook her head. "Is that like the blind complimenting a painter?"

"Pardon?" Lady Effington said, swiveling around to address Charity.

"I asked if Lord Cadgwith had a favorite painter," she replied, her face completely straight.

The dowager turned expectant eyes on him, so he shook his head. "Art is somewhat lost on me, I'm afraid."

She nodded politely and turned back to the moving canvas of the passing scenery. Charity offered a little half grin. "I wonder, my lord, what is it that gives you pleasure? Not art or music or dances or crowds. What are the things that make you smile?"

You. He mouthed the word, not daring to give it voice. She narrowed her eyes, clearly unsure of whether she saw what she thought she saw. He licked his lips and said, "Truly, I find pleasure in quiet things. The distant waves on the shore, holding my infant niece as she sleeps, waking to a day with no"—he paused, almost saying *pain* but thinking better of it—"ill effects of the night before."

"What of friends?"

He almost laughed. What of friends? These days, the only friends he had were the ones who didn't mind a half decade or two between conversations, like Dering and Thomas. He pursed his lips, unsure of how to answer her.

The heat of her leg finally began to seep through the fabric of their clothes. It was oddly comforting. "My brother, Ian, and I were quite close. His widow is a lovely woman whom I would consider a friend. My batman has been with me since the army."

God, it sounded rather pathetic, listed out like that. That was the problem with living at the very tip of England: If one wished to keep to oneself, then no one was going to interfere with that decision. It wasn't as though anyone was just going to drop by, as they did in London and even here in Bath. He'd allowed himself to disappear, to retreat into the darkness and solitude of the old dowager house like some sort of exiled criminal.

"Well," she said quietly, her eyes soft in the muted light. "No matter how things began, nor how they end, I hope that you will consider me a friend."

He wished like hell Lady Effington wasn't in the carriage just then. He wanted to reach across the narrow space separating them and take Charity's hand in his. He wanted to lace her fingers in his and tug her into his lap. He wanted to press his lips to hers and thank her without words for not judging him, even when he judged himself.

Instead, he dug his fingers into his palms and nodded, forcing the corners of his lips into some semblance of a smile. "I will, Miss Effington. And I hope you'll do the same."

Chapter Eighteen

If Charity thought the carriage ride had been sweet torture, the play itself was turning out to be a thousand
times worse. Or was it better?

She squirmed a bit in her seat—again—and attempted
to focus on the actors on the stage. Which was impossible, of course. How could she, when Hugh was directly
behind her, staring at the back of her head, for all she
knew?

To her right, Grandmama sat in the darkness, her chin
resting against her chest after having dozed off around
twenty minutes into the first act. To her left, Dering's
hulking form was a dark silhouette against the even
darker fabric panels draping the walls of their private
box. He had been late, so they hadn't yet had time to
really talk.

She knew Sophie was in the balcony section in the
back, and May was in a box with her aunt almost directly
across the way. All these people that she knew and cared
about surrounded her, and yet all she could think about
was Hugh's presence raising the fine hairs on the back of
her neck.

What would it be like if it were his warm touch on her

neck instead of his gaze? Or, better still, his lips. A chill ran down her spine like a drop of icy water, causing her to shiver. She breathed a sigh of relief when the curtain came down and the lamps were brought back up.

Dering turned to her immediately, rubbing his hands together. "At last we can speak. I hope you will be able to forgive my tardiness. I was attending to a bit of business, as it were."

"Of course," she answered promptly, offering him a broad smile. She needed to start making her way to May's box, since she knew that Lady Stanwix had no intention of letting May mingle any more than necessary. But she could certainly spare a few moments for her host. "Thank you again for allowing us to join you this evening."

"It worked out perfectly. As it happens, the business I was attending to had to do with you."

That got her attention. Her smile fell a bit. "Whatever about?" His smile was self-satisfied and so full of mischief, she rounded her eyes at him. "Dering, you mustn't keep me in suspense."

"Such impatience," he tsked, his baritone voice full of amusement. "If you must know, I had a little conversation with a certain member of a certain committee. I heard a shocking bit of gossip that England's most talented pianoforte player somehow had been overlooked for the Tuesday recitals."

Charity drew in a surprised breath. "How on earth did you hear of that?"

He tipped his head in the general direction behind her, where Grandmama's soft snores were being politely ignored by the baron. The little sneak—had her grandmother slipped the detail into her letter to the viscount when she inquired about his box? "Really, my lord, it was nothing to concern yourself with—"

"Au contraire," he said, raising his voice slightly to be heard over the rising din of the crowd below. "It was a travesty, and it had to be righted. Therefore, it was."

"It was what?" she asked, caution causing her to tamp down her escalating excitement. What had he done, exactly?

"Righted." He looked every bit the cat that had gotten the cream, his lips stretched wide in an expectant smile. "You and your trio are to be part of the inaugural Tuesday-night performances three days hence."

Charity's jaw dropped nearly to her chest as she gaped at him right there in full view of half the theater. "Are you serious? They have agreed to allow us to play?"

Dering gave a one-shouldered shrug, all nonchalance now. "Indeed they have. Not that they had much choice," he said with a wink.

Relief, excitement, gratitude, and a whole host of other emotions swept through her all at once, and she pressed her hands to her chest to keep herself from wrapping her arms around him in a bear hug. "You dear, dear man," she exclaimed, biting her lip and shaking her head. "You couldn't have possibly given me a better gift. I can't even begin to think how I can repay you."

His teasing smugness firmly in place, he patted her arm with one large white-gloved hand. "Fear not. We shall think of something. Undying gratitude is usually a good place to start."

She knew him well enough to know his mischievous ways. With a playful roll of her eyes, she said, "We shall see." Unable to hold in a little laugh, she turned to her grandmother to wake her with the news.

Her eyes landed on Hugh instead, where he sat quietly watching her. Pleasure shone in his green gaze. There was no hint of a smile on his lips, nor any other overt emotion, but she could plainly see his happiness. For her—she knew it even without him saying a word. He alone had seen how greatly upset she had been when she received the committee's rejection. He alone had been there to comfort her when she'd needed it most. Which, somehow, had led to that kiss . . .

She looked away quickly, not wanting to give her thoughts away just then. As she placed a gentle hand to her grandmother's shoulder to wake her, Charity relished the joy spreading from her heart to every nook and cranny of her soul. It would appear she had a hero. Dering always had admired her playing, so it truly shouldn't have been such a surprise.

She just wouldn't have expected him to think of such a thing. He had always been sweet, kind, and considerate, but this was above and beyond. He must have realized just how disappointed she would have been, and had gone out of his way to make things right. But why had he gone to so much trouble? It couldn't have been easy to track down the proper people and persuade them to change their minds.

The unanswered question reverberated in her head as she conveyed the good news to her grandmother. Perhaps there was more to Dering's regard for her than she realized.

Swallowing, her gaze flitted from him to the baron. Two greater foils she couldn't imagine. Dering was as strapping as a Viking, with his dark good looks and charming personality softening what might have otherwise been an intimidating physique. He was sociable, strong, and likable, and, best of all, he honestly loved music. Most especially, he loved *her* music.

He was the kind of match her parents might dream of, especially with their family's longtime friendship. If he had shown even the slightest inclination to marry, Charity's parents would have likely pounced on him by now.

That thought felt jarring as it bounced around inside her, not seeming to find purchase. There was no neat place for it to go, since she couldn't decide whether his attentions would be welcome or not. "Well," she said brightly, suddenly eager to have a moment to herself. "With such glad news, I find I can't bear to delay sharing with my friends. Will you excuse me while I go visit?"

Dering smiled. "Better yet, I can escort you. I've yet to meet Miss Bradford, anyway, so perhaps now is the time, when she will be predisposed to like me." He gave a rakish wink before coming to his feet.

So much for having a moment to herself. "Thank you, my lord. Lord Cadgwith, would you like to join us as well?"

The question rolled off her tongue with hardly a thought. After an entire act of feeling his presence behind her like the static charge of a doorknob in winter, she wanted him by her side. She wanted to feel his arm beneath her hands, and look him in the eye, and know for certain where he stood, both literally and figuratively.

But he, apparently, did not feel the same way. He gave a short shake of his head. "Thank you, but no. I shall stay here and enjoy the company of Lady Effington, I think."

Charity smiled to mask her disappointment. Must he act so distant? "As you wish," she said, her voice overly agreeable to her ears. If he wished to stay here, alone in the half darkness, then that was his prerogative. Patting Dering's arm, she said, "Shall we?"

He was all too eager to comply. "We shall indeed."

It was a special kind of hell, being so close to Charity, and yet being weighed down by the chains of propriety and his own strict rules of conduct he had decided on before ever leaving the house.

She was an acquaintance, nothing more.

And if he told himself that often enough, he may actually begin to believe it.

It would help, of course, if he hadn't spent the past hour focused on her instead of the play. The delicate curve of her ear, the slope of her shoulder, the slender column of her neck—each was a hundred times more captivating than the actors on the stage. He knew exactly how soft her lips were, but the pale skin at the nape of her neck? He regretted now not kissing her there while he had the chance.

His gaze flickered across the open space above the gallery, to the small box directly opposite Dering's. They were all there—Charity and her two friends, the viscount, and Miss Bradford's chaperone. He watched as all but the pinch-faced matron laughed merrily.

He wrapped his hands around the padded arms of his chair and let his fingers dig into the crimson velvet. It was odd, the way he felt just then. Satisfaction for Charity's joy, gratitude mixed with an uncomfortable dose of jealousy for Dering's ability to make it happen, and resentment for his damn body and all the things it had ruined for him over the past four years.

That last one was much keener than he'd experienced before. Perhaps because he'd never wanted the things it had kept him from as badly as he wanted her. He wasn't even sure he had realized just how much she meant to him until he saw her smile at Dering just now. It was an easy, open, carefree smile that spoke of familiarity and comfort. It was the way he wanted her to smile at him.

Bloody hell. He'd leave now if it wasn't for the fact he

had promised the Effingtons to return them home in his carriage.

"What do you think of the play so far?"

Hugh had almost forgotten Lady Effington was still beside him. She sat comfortably in her chair, her slight frame leaning against the chair back. With a polite nod, he said, "Well enough. And you?"

She chuckled, the papery skin around her eyes crinkling. "I'm sure I'd enjoy it if I could stay awake. It would seem these chairs are far too comfortable for my own good."

"Indeed," he said, his hands loosening their grip on the armrests. She was disarming, good company for someone like him. There were no expectations between them. His gaze darted back to the other balcony, where Charity stood with her hand resting on Dering's forearm. *Well, aren't they cozy?*

"Exciting news, is it not?"

He shifted his attention back to the dowager. "I beg your pardon?"

"The news of Charity's trio being included in the recital series after all," she clarified, holding her lorgnette to her eye and peering across the way. "Such a tremendously kind and thoughtful thing for Lord Derington to do." Approval warmed her words as she smiled and lowered the eyepiece. "It does make one wonder."

Hugh gritted his teeth and nodded. It was as it should be. Dering was available, even-tempered, and, most important, completely whole. In a month's time, Hugh would return to Cadgwith, and, God willing, he'd be ready to carry on the mantle of running the estate. "Dering is a good man."

Tilting her head slightly to the side, Lady Effington

turned her full attention to Hugh. "As are you, Lord
Cadgwith."

Hugh blinked in surprise. She always spoke loudly,
but this time there was more forcefulness in her words
than he might have suspected. What was she trying to
say? He wasn't sure he liked the way she was looking at
him, as though she could see straight through his carefully erected walls to the part of him he hid from the
world. "Thank you, my lady," he murmured, shifting in
his seat. With the full force of her gaze on him, he felt
like a wayward schoolboy.

"Do you know, I may not hear everything, but I perceive much." She paused, pursing her lips for a moment.
"Would you forgive me if I overstepped the bounds of
propriety for a moment?"

He quirked an eyebrow, not at all certain he wanted
to hear what she had to say. "By all means."

"At my age, one learns that there are few things more
vexing in life than regret." She leaned forward in her
chair and placed her gloved hand over his. "If there is
something you want in this life, don't be afraid to fight
for it. You don't want to be my age looking back on life,
wishing you had taken a chance."

Softening her earnest features, she smiled and patted
his hand before settling back in her chair again.

Where in the world did that come from? He sat there
dumbly, not even sure whether his mouth was closed or
not. What in the ever-loving hell was he supposed to
say to *that*? Surely she wasn't referring to him and her
own granddaughter. And what did she perceive, exactly, that prompted such a statement? Running his
tongue along the front of his teeth, he finally nodded.
"Duly noted."

He glanced to the opposite balcony, and this time his

eyes collided with Charity's. She smiled easily, not at all embarrassed to be caught looking his way. He offered a fleeting grin in return before averting his eyes to the stage. Damn it all, neither one of the Effington women was doing anything to help his resolve.

And even though he should be unhappy about that, he wasn't in the least. It was almost amusing, really. All these years of running from pain, only to discover that apparently he was a glutton for punishment after all.

Given that this was their final rehearsal before the recital the next day, Charity should have been playing much better than she was. Behind her, May and Sophie were both performing their parts perfectly, but no matter what Charity did, she couldn't seem to keep her mind on the music. As her fingers tripped over the keys of Lady Stanwix's pianoforte, Charity rolled her shoulders, doing her best to stretch the muscles that seemed to be bunching like knotted string at her neck.

The guzheng came to an abrupt stop, followed quickly by the oboe. Sighing, Charity gave up and swung around to face the others. "I'm sorry, ladies. I don't know why I'm playing like such rubbish today."

May stretched her fingers as she eyed Charity. "Well, at least we are in agreement," she said wryly. "Are you nervous?"

"A little. Nothing like the way I was at the selection committee rehearsal, though. There they had the power to stop us from playing. Here we can just enjoy the performance."

Sophie cringed, wrinkling her nose. "I think I always enjoy *after* the performance so much better. At least then I know how well I've done and I can quit worrying. Although if I don't do well, that's when I'll start obsessing about what I should have done differently, so perhaps it's a wash."

"You do know how to give a pep talk, Sophie," May teased, giving an exaggerated roll of her eyes. "Honestly, I prefer to simply close my eyes and forget that anyone else is there. My music is for me. If someone enjoys it, good, but if not, then that is their issue, not mine."

Charity smiled at May's blasé attitude. "That certainly is one way to look at it." She paused, rubbing the tight muscles at her neck and shoulders in an effort to loosen the knots. "Honestly, though, I'm really not that nervous. I'm more distracted than anything."

Sophie's easy grin dimpled her cheeks. "If you mean by the way you keep rolling your shoulders, I can believe it. If we handed you some oars, you'd be halfway to France by now."

"You noticed that, too?" May asked, crossing her arms over the rich sapphire satin ribbon tied about the high waist of her white gown. She leveled Charity with a look that was one part amused, one part exasperated. "I thought you were working on some sort of new seated dance over there. Are you going to make it through tomorrow?"

A blush heated Charity's cheeks. She hadn't realized she'd been so obvious. "Yes, yes, I promise. I don't know why my shoulders are so bothersome today. I feel as though someone draped a suit of armor over me." Usually the discomfort arose when she spent hours bent over her music, paying no mind to posture. But that wasn't it. Could it be that the issues with Dering and Hugh had translated to strain in her shoulders?

The humor faded from May's blue eyes, replaced by concern. "You, my dear, have been working too hard on our behalf. I warned you to take care of yourself last time."

"I know you did," she said with a sigh. "I've tried to, but I think too many things are coming together all at once, and I don't seem to be handling the strain very well."

"What sorts of things?" Sophie asked, pulling the slender double reed from her oboe and popping it in her mouth to keep it moist.

What sorts of things? How to make her friends understand? An incredible kiss from one man; an incredible kindness from another. Her wanting the one she couldn't have and unsure about the one she could. Or, at least, the one who seemed to want her. The blush started to deepen, spreading across her nose and up her neck. "Well, there was quite a bit of change in the past two days. I had originally thought Dering's kindness was just that. But after he called on me both yesterday and this morning, it's becoming clear that he may have greater interest than I realized."

The visit today had been particularly awkward for her, especially since she could no longer pretend he was just dropping by for a friendly visit. There had been something between them that hadn't been there before, and she wasn't sure what to do with it.

May and Sophie exchanged identical, raised-brow glances. May's chair screeched as she pushed back from her instrument and dragged the seat closer to the pianoforte. "And is this interest welcome?"

Ah, there was the true question. She gave a helpless little shrug. "I don't know. He's always been such a good friend of the family. I hadn't stopped to think of him in that way. I don't want to dismiss him out of hand." It was certainly no great love match, but perhaps that was because she hadn't had any time to properly acclimate to the idea.

"And what of Lord Cadgwith? He seemed quite a bit

more interested in you than the performance on Saturday."

May's shrewd question brought forth the rest of Charity's blush; her face probably looked something like a tomato right about then. It was one thing to imagine that he was doing just that; it was quite another to learn the truth of it. Looking to her fingernails, she said. "I don't believe he and I will ever truly suit. I do consider him a friend, however."

A friend. The word sounded wrong on her tongue. Still, she couldn't help but feel that he was distancing himself from her. The ride home from the theater had been spent in utter silence, despite the awareness of his proximity that raised gooseflesh on her arms. He'd made no effort to see her since, and, as far as she knew, hadn't come to the balcony on the chance of meeting outside.

"Mmm," May murmured noncommittally. "I see. Well, I can't do anything about Lord Derington or Lord Cadgwith, but I can help with the suit of armor."

Charity's brow beetled. "You can?"

With a decisive nod, May stood and made her way to the bellpull. She gave it a sharp tug, then turned to face them both, her hands finding her hips. "I can. But only if you keep an open mind. I give you my word you won't regret it."

Not the most confidence-inspiring statement in the world. "All right," Charity said cautiously.

Moments later, the door slid open and a servant stepped in. Smiling broadly, May said, "Please tell Suyin I'd like to see her at once."

Chapter Nineteen

"Mr. Sanburne," Hugh said, standing to greet his unexpected visitor. "What brings you here today?" He walked around the desk and nodded toward one of the chairs sitting in the afternoon sunlight by the window.

The agent held up his hand, smiling genially beneath his white whiskers. "No need to sit down; I won't impose on you for long. I would have sent a message, but I figured the sooner I could get an answer from you, the better."

Interest piqued, Hugh nodded. "I see. Well, by all means, let's hear what news you have brought."

"It would seem, my lord, that one man's misfortune is another man's boon." The agent gave a mischievous little wink, clearly pleased with whatever turn of events had brought him to the house. "The drought in Worcester has hastened Mr. Churmond's need to implement new irrigation canals. He has informed me that he plans to leave town by the end of the week to oversee the process. Which means," he said, leaning forward on his silver-handled cane and raising one white brow, "I have just the place for you to relocate to."

Relocate?

Hugh's lip turned up as everything within him rejected the thought. Why the bloody hell would he want to relocate?

And yet as his brain caught up to his emotions, he knew that this was what he had asked for. Sanburne was beaming at him because the man had managed to come through for him. Hugh's gut tightened as he forced his face to form a gritted smile. "I see. And when will this place be available?"

Sandburne lifted a hand from the silver handle and held up four stubby fingers. His entire countenance reflected his pleasure at the news. He had delivered on Hugh's request, and therefore had every reason to expect approval. Accolades, even. "Four days. He'll be out by Thursday afternoon, and I'll have my staff do a thorough cleaning. You should be able to move in by Friday at noon."

Damnation—so soon? Swallowing against the tightness of his throat, Hugh nodded crisply. "That is good news. Thank you for letting me know."

His tone was even, and despite the lingering feeling of a fist around his windpipe, he stood a little straighter. He was a soldier, damn it. He knew how to lock away that part of him that rebelled against the thought of personal loss and act for the greater good. He'd led his men forward when everything inside of him had screamed to turn back that bloody day on the battlefield, had he not? The casualties were great, but in the end, the battle was won. Simply walking away from Charity should be much easier than that.

Should be.

The tightness traveled down his throat and across his chest, the fist turning to a band of steel. Though he might never admit it, Hugh liked having Charity near, knowing she was only as far as a wall away. Without his permission, an attachment had formed between them. Something inside of him was drawn to her, and he was loath to give that up—even as he gave up the chance to spend time with her, stifling any chance of something developing that he couldn't possibly sustain.

But being this close came at a price. Both to him *and* her. He risked an attack if she played, but when she didn't, she lost something that couldn't be replaced. Each time she refrained from setting her fingers to the keys, she lost a small part of her identity and a further piece of her joy.

He was taking that from her. If he wasn't there, she wouldn't be confined to the two hours a day when he left the house for her benefit. She could play anytime her heart desired, setting free that part of her that needed to be unlocked by her music.

"I thought you might be pleased," Sanburne said, clearly oblivious to Hugh's silent distress. He reached into his jacket and withdrew a slender scroll. "I took the liberty of drawing up the addendum to the current contract. Take your time perusing it, and have it signed and returned to my office by Wednesday, if you please."

Woodenly, Hugh accepted the paper and promptly dropped it on the desk behind him. "I'll see to it. Now, if you'll excuse me, I have some business to attend to." A flat-out lie, but he didn't care. He needed the man to leave.

"Of course. I'm glad to be the bearer of good news." Turning, he took a few steps back toward the hallway before pausing. "Incidentally," he said, tilting his head, "I must say you are looking very well indeed. Our fair city seems to be agreeing with you."

With a mischievous wink, the man made his exit. Hugh

leaned against the desk, listening to the receding foot-steps and the accompanying thump of the cane. Rubbing a hand over the back of his neck, he exhaled a curse.

As much as he had wanted this a few short weeks ago, he hated that it had fallen in his lap. Now he would have no excuse to see her. No possibility of walking outside and running into her or finding himself alone on the balcony with the scent of lavender on the night air.

And Charity would be free to live her life without concern for him again.

That thought steeled his resolve. Skirting back around the desk, he unrolled the contract, dipped the quill in the inkpot, and scrawled his name along the bottom. There— now they could both go back to normal.

Damn it all.

Lord only knew what had possessed Charity to agree to May's proposal. Perhaps it was because right then, Charity would have done just about anything to alleviate the pain in her shoulders. But whatever it was, she was profoundly grateful she had trusted May and allowed her maid to work her magic.

And magic it was. She rolled her shoulders, thrilled to be able to do so without any tightness or strain. After half an hour of Suyin's odd methods of pinching, pulling, pressing, and stretching, Charity's neck and shoulders felt amazing.

As she breezed past Jeffers through the front door, she headed straight upstairs into the music room. A glance at the clock told her she still had an hour left of the time Hugh said he would be out of the house. She was so energized and renewed, she wanted to play freely—and alone—for a while, the way she used to.

She paused to pull open the curtains, letting in the

late-afternoon sunlight, then on a whim opened the door to allow the light breeze to stir the air. The air smelled of roses and sun-warmed earth mixed with subtle hints of the city.

Smiling, Charity sat down at the pianoforte and ran her fingertips across the keys. Their texture was the most familiar thing in the world to her—more so even than her own voice. She closed her eyes and listened, waiting until a melody filtered through her mind. It was lower than her usual pieces—a welcome change from the high notes of the recital piece they had been playing relentlessly.

It was a better fit for the quiet summer evening, with a sultry melody that evoked broad leaves swaying in a warm breeze. Finding the right keys by touch, she began to play. Just as they sounded in her head, the notes were mellow and rich, full of body and resonance, but not at all overpowering. Instead of adhering to proper posture, she allowed her body to sway in time with the music.

As she played, images of her last evening on the balcony with Hugh came to mind. The darkness of the night, the smell of his skin, the heart-pounding kiss that even now made her stomach flip. It was all in the music, the entire story laid bare for anyone who dared to interpret it.

Why was it this song that came to her fingertips? Why not something tied to Dering, or anyone else who was a better match for her? The answer was clear in the un-named composition. He resonated with her, just as an exquisitely tuned instrument could fill an entire hall with pitch-perfect music. They were like two perfectly harmonious notes on entirely different octaves. It was difficult to make them work since the spread was too far for most people's tastes, but when played just right, the beauty of it could give one gooseflesh.

As she hit the final notes of the piece, she held the

keys down until the last bit of sound had been wrung from the notes, then let the dampers fall at last. It was lovely. Smiling, she opened her eyes and lifted her hands from the keyboard.

"That's different."

She gasped, her hands flying to her chest as her eyes darted to the balcony door. Leaning forward with his elbows on the black wrought-iron divider, Hugh smiled as though it was the most natural thing for him to be standing there listening to her play.

For some inexplicable reason, a wave of shyness washed over her, and she looked to her hands before garnering the courage to face him again. "I like different. It keeps things from becoming stagnant." Questions burned within her: What had he thought of her song? How long had he been listening?

But she asked neither of these. Instead, she rose and walked to the balcony, offering him a small smile. "I hope I didn't bother you."

His dark blond hair lifted in the breeze and fell across his forehead as he shook his head. "I only just caught the end of it as I returned home. Was it one of your own?"

"Yes. Unpolished," she added, since she suddenly felt self-conscious about the unscripted piece. "I was rather making it up as I went."

His eyes were as warm as the setting sun, and his half smile did something to her pattering heart. "It was beautiful. Truly. You're blessed to have such a talent."

Pleasure at the comment warmed her cheeks and she lifted her lips in a small grin. She never thought he would use the word *beautiful* to describe her music. The simple praise meant more to her than any of the accolades lavished on her over the years. "Thank you. Occasionally I'm inspired to try something different."

She could only imagine what he would think if he knew the kiss they had shared had inspired it.

"Are you excited for the recital tomorrow? Or nervous?" He ran a hand through his hair, pushing it back from his forehead. She stifled the desire to stop him. She liked him when he was slightly disheveled and relaxed. It was just more *him*.

"A little of both, I suppose. I didn't play my best this morning, but by the time I left May's home, things had improved." She leaned against the doorframe, thinking better of standing on the balcony with him in the early-evening light. From where she stood, she could feel the heat radiating from the limestone after an entire day of soaking it up, and incongruously it made her shiver.

"A little? Looks as though you are shaking in your slippers to me." His low voice was only half teasing. Even though he smiled and made light with her, she could sense a reserve in him. It wasn't that he was serious or unhappy, just somehow weighty.

She rolled her eyes, attempting to keep things light. "Very funny. Honestly, I'm so happy to have the opportunity to play. As I'm sure you know, I couldn't have received a finer gift. Let's hope the audience agrees."

"They'll be delighted, I'm sure." His voice held conviction, as though there was never any doubt. As though he truly believed it, despite his condition. "Dering did them all a great service by having your trio reinstated."

"I owe him a debt of gratitude," she murmured. And she did. But Dering was *not* the person she wished to talk about just then. He didn't have a place out there on the balcony. Not when Hugh stood before her, all quietly handsome, supportive, and sweet. It was their place—Hugh's and hers.

She tipped her head to the side, taking in his gorgeous

green eyes and pale complexion, trying to read his mood. "How are you feeling? No attacks, I hope? I haven't seen you in days."

It was none of her business, but the question was out now. She worried about the solemnity that kept his eyes from sparkling as she knew they could.

"No attacks," he said with a single shake of his head. "Though if I have one tonight, I shall place the blame squarely at your feet." Teasing Hugh was back, and she couldn't help but smile.

"Well, if I'm to be blamed, you should have come earlier so you could at least have made it worthwhile."

"I wish I had. The tune was haunting, in a good way. Not like a ghost, but like a memory that slips in and out of one's subconscious."

The description caught her off guard. It was perfect; not something she would have expected from him. She wondered again if he realized what had inspired the piece. She bit her lip, debating the wisdom of saying something, then decided to throw caution aside. "Perhaps it *is* a memory. What does it remind you of?"

Did he notice that she couldn't seem to hit the casual tone she had reached for? How could she, when she was standing mere feet away, her heart pounding as she imagined closing the distance between them, rising on her toes, and pressing her lips to his? Would he push her away? Or kiss her back like he had last time? That thought sent a tiny shiver through her body.

He didn't say anything right away. Instead, he watched her, his eyes nearly unreadable as they swept over her face. Her lips parted as she drew in a quiet breath. She didn't mind being the object of his scrutiny—not when she could do the same. She liked looking at him, taking in the subtle nuances of his features. Each aspect of his face was attractive to her, from the bisected eyebrow to his straight nose to his perfectly formed lips. Even his scars were beautiful, a physical reminder of his strength and bravery.

After a long moment, he said, "A very good memory. One I doubt I'll ever forget."

The soft rasp in his voice called to her. She swallowed, wanting to step out on the balcony, closer to him, where she could reach out a bare hand and trace the sharp line of his jaw. It was a desire so strong, she curled her fingers into fists at her side. "If it is a good memory, then I'm happy to have sparked its recollection."

Chuckling softly, he said, "You spark much more than that."

Her eyes widened. Not a statement she would have expected from him. She tried to think of something clever to say, but of course nothing came to her.

As if realizing how intimate things were fast becoming, Hugh straightened to his full height, allowing his hands to rest on the divider. "I shouldn't keep you. I did want you to know that I thought that piece was beautiful. You should be very proud."

She swallowed, forcing herself to follow his lead and allow the moment to pass. "You flatter me. Your high opinion means more than I can say, particularly given the circumstances. I shall think on that as I try not to let my nerves get the best of me tomorrow."

His smile was relaxed and natural. "You'll do marvelously. I only wish I could be there to support you."

"So do I." Though she felt the heat of a blush stealing up her neck, she didn't regret her words. They were the absolute truth.

He sighed, his smile still in place, and held out his hand to her. She didn't hesitate, despite the daylight. She stepped onto the balcony and lifted her hand to his. Neither of them wore gloves, and the slide of her skin against his sent a thrill all the way down her spine. His fingers were warm and gentle as they closed around her hand.

Their eyes met as he lifted her fingers to his lips and pressed a feather-soft kiss to the sensitive skin of the back of her hand. "Good luck, sweet Charity. I look forward to hearing how everything goes."

She nodded, her heart skittering as he squeezed her fingers before releasing her hand. Licking her lips, she said, "Tomorrow night, perhaps?"

He hesitated and she held her breath, wanting him to say yes. Finally, he gave her a short bob of his head. "I'll see you then."

The contract was signed. The move was mere days away. Soon they would both continue on with their wholly separate lives. But as Hugh stepped into his bedchamber and closed the balcony door, one thing stood out in his mind among all the rest. *There are few things in life more vexing than regret.*

Lady Effington's words of wisdom meant something. He was walking away, so there was no worry of anything more developing between them. Tomorrow night would be the perfect way to say their good-byes, especially since Charity would undoubtedly be in a good mood following the recital.

He hadn't been exaggerating about her music just now. It truly was incredible. She had a talent that he knew was rare, even if he couldn't enjoy it the way others might. He loved seeing the pleasure in her eyes when he complimented her—as if his opinion actually meant something to her.

It had been a long time since anyone had valued his

good opinion. Being shut away in the dowager house did not exactly open one up to admiration from anyone. He scrubbed a hand over his face, rubbing at his eyes.

It had been two weeks since his last attack—practically a lifetime. It was so damn tempting to feel as though a normal life was within his grasp. What if, just once, he released the fear of unbearable pain, and allowed himself to truly enjoy an evening?

What would he do if he could do anything? If he could step outside the constant threat of his injury and live without regret? He thought of Charity's sweet presence, the way she somehow managed to steal the breath from his lungs with a single innocent look, and knew exactly what he would do.

"Jacobson," he called, knowing the batman wouldn't be far.

A few moments later, the man appeared in the door. "My lord?"

"I think it's time for a little something different."

Chapter Twenty

"I must say, it is awfully nice to see you looking so well," Grandmama said, pulling Charity's attention away from the passing storefronts. The older woman had that wise, all-too-knowing look about her that immediately raised Charity's brows.

"Thank you," she said, unable to keep the slight question from her voice.

Chuckling, her grandmother replied, "Yes, that was a compliment. And you are most welcome. I just wondered, perhaps, if there was anything in particular making those lovely cheeks of yours so rosy."

"It must be the new gown," she said, smoothing a hand over the exquisite peach silk gown that had been completed only this morning. The clean lines and simple design allowed the beauty of the fabric to shine on its own merit.

"Which is glorious, but doesn't account for the sparkle in your eyes."

"I'm excited, Grandmama. I have a big recital in less than an hour. I think my eyes are supposed to sparkle."

She folded her hands primly in her lap. "I'm certain

that must be it. Or perhaps it has something to do with a certain gentleman."

The blush she had been fighting came full force to Charity's cheeks. "I have no particular gentleman, as I am certain you know full well."

"Mmm. It's interesting, actually." She plucked at her rich amaranth skirts, idly arranging them. "I had thought you had interest in a certain neighbor, but now that Lord Derington went so very out of his way for your benefit, I wonder if perhaps you don't have a particular gentleman. Perhaps you have *two* who have captured your interest."

Well, this was a rather mortifying conversation. "For heaven's sake, Grandmama, I do *not* have two gentlemen! Lord Cadgwith is a friend; nothing more, I assure you." She wasn't about to mention how much she wished he *were* more. "And I don't even know what to make of Dering right now. He has always been a kind and generous man. I imagine when you told him of my disappointment with the selection committee, he thought it a challenge to change their minds."

Grandmama's silver brows came together in confusion. "Whatever are you talking about? I never told Lord Derington about the committee's decision."

Charity blinked, as confused as her grandmother appeared to be. "But when I asked him how he knew, he nodded to you."

The crimson feather affixed to Grandmama's turban swayed as she shook her head. "Not I. I have more discretion than that, thank you," she said primly, lifting her chin.

At a loss, Charity just stared at her. She was sure of what Dering had said. He had given that devilish little grin, then nodded over Charity's shoulder where her grandmother sat. She froze suddenly, the air whooshing from her lungs.

Hugh.

He'd been off to the side, but he had been the only other person in the box. More important, he had been the only other person she had told about the committee.

She exhaled, falling back against the squabs as her heart pounded in her chest. Hugh had gone to Dering. But why? Had he been gossiping about her? Sharing the intimate moment when she had unburdened her heart to him?

Was gossip to follow her everywhere she went? With the exception of her run-in with Marianne, things had been so wonderful this summer. The people here were kind and interesting and no one seemed interested in spreading tales about her as they had in London.

Her brow furrowed. She would have never imagined Hugh would be the type to wag his tongue. And to what end? He couldn't have known that Dering would take it upon himself to help her. Had he been regaling his old friends with tales of his silly neighbor?

No, she couldn't believe that of him. Or, rather, she wouldn't. He'd been so kind since that night, sharing his own secrets with her. Surely she was missing something. Not that it made her feel any better—he'd still shared her heartbreak without permission.

"Figure it out, did you, dear?" Grandmama's question was quieter than usual.

Swallowing against the lump forming in her throat, she offered a small smile. "Not exactly. Hopefully I can speak with Dering about it tonight after the recital."

And afterward, she'd see what Hugh had to say for himself. She didn't wish to jump to any conclusions, but he certainly had some explaining to do.

At last, they pulled up to the Assembly Rooms, their carriage one of a dozen queuing along the curb. Grandmama alighted first; then Charity followed her out into the drizzle. The tiger held a wide black umbrella above them and walked them the few feet to the entrance. It seemed as though half of Bath was already in attendance, with men and women perfectly coiffed and in their finest clothes clogging the corridor and milling among the chairs already set up in the Ballroom.

The performers were to meet in the Card Room, which would serve as a holding room of sorts before the recital. They were a bit late, so Sophie and May were probably already there. Leaning close to her grandmother's ear, she raised her voice above the crowd and said, "Where would you like to sit?"

She lifted her lorgnette to one eye and perused the vast space. "Ah," she said, dropping the eyepiece. "I believe I see Lady Stanwix near the front of the room. Perhaps I could cheer her up a bit." She winked, and Charity had to bite back a laugh.

"A Herculean task, but if you're up to it."

They wove their way through the crowd to greet the lady in question. Charity's courage wavered a bit as she realized just how many people would be watching them. *She* loved the piece they were to perform, but who was to say what the audience would think?

"Good evening, Lady Stanwix," Charity said as they approached her chair. "Is this seat taken?"

She looked over to them, her frown firmly in place beneath the voluminous fillet of twisted satin and pearls wound about her head. "Good evening, Lady Effington, Miss Effington. I am an island unto myself tonight. You may sit wherever you choose."

"Oh, Victoria, how you flatter me." Grandmama's

perfectly correct tone betrayed none of the sarcasm her gray eyes imparted.

Charity bit down hard on her lip, stifling her laughter. Grandmama would be good for the stodgy old woman. After making sure her grandmother was properly settled, Charity headed off toward the Card Room, nerves rippling deep in her belly.

She had never performed in front of this kind of crowd. It was always private musicales or impromptu recitals like the one at Dering's dinner party. Even if it was just her and her pianoforte, she'd still be nervous.

As she approached the Card Room, a woman in a blush pink gown emerged from the ladies' retiring room and Charity's heart fell. *Marianne.*

She slowed as she saw Charity, her lips lifting in a cold smile. "Miss Effington. How interesting to see you here. And in peach again, I see." She shook her head sadly, as though terribly disappointed in her.

"Miss Harmon," Charity said with a shallow nod. "I'm not sure why it should be interesting—we are to perform, after all."

"Yes, so I heard." She patted a hand to her golden curls as if Charity's presence would somehow have sent them askew. "I do hope you and your little trio know what you are doing. My father is so very concerned your tender sensibilities will be injured when the audience reacts poorly." She sighed, offering a terrible impersonation of commiseration. "He did try to protect you from such an eventuality, but it's out of his hands now."

Even as Charity ground her teeth against the desire to shove Marianne from her way for saying such deliberately mean things, a small part of her worried that what she said was true. The fluttering in her belly turned to trembling as her fingers grew cold.

"Luckily for him, I don't need a keeper."

"He's no keeper, Miss Effington. Much like an excellent modiste," she said, looking pointedly at Charity's new gown, "he's a man with taste and good opinion who wished to save you from yourself."

Clutching her fists at her sides, Charity absolutely refused to be cowed. Or, at least, not to let Marianne believe she had been. Standing up straighter in an effort to appear confident, she smiled falsely. "Thank goodness someone with higher rank and better taste had something to say about it."

It was the boldest, rudest thing she had ever said to another person. As Marianne's features contorted with affront, Charity nodded and swept past her, her chin lifted as high as a queen's.

Oh, Lord, she was a terrible human being. How could she have said that out loud? Yes, the woman deserved it, but still. She pushed her way into the Card Room, heedless of polite greetings or decorum.

She spotted May easily, thanks to her height and proliferation of light blond hair. Sophie was beside her, and waved when she noticed Charity.

Hurrying to their sides, Charity grabbed them each by the arm and yanked them close. Catching her breath, she said in a desperate whisper, "I may or may not have just said something mortally offensive to Marianne Harmon."

"Blast—you beat me to it," May said, completely unfazed.

Sophie's eyes widened. "What did you say, and what did she do? I mean before, to earn it, not after, in reaction. Though I want to know that, too, come to think of it. If I know Miss Harmon, I'm quite certain it was warranted."

Charity's fingers were icy within her gloves. Warranted or not, she already felt terrible. "She wasn't pleased, that's for certain. She basically said it was a shame her father failed at his attempt to save us from ourselves."

"Calm down," May said, patting her hand. "I can feel your fingers trembling. Whatever you said couldn't have been half as bad as she deserved. Save us from ourselves, indeed."

Charity gave a humorless laugh. "You don't understand—I *hate* conflict. I'm a peacemaker at heart."

Lifting her blond brows conspiratorially, May said, "Well, then, I'd say it's about time you came out of your shell."

"Misses Bradford, Effington, and Wembley?"

They turned as one as Mr. Green looked over his spectacles at them. "You are our first performance this evening. Follow me, please." He turned and headed for the door, not even pausing to make sure they complied.

Charity's heart thundered so powerfully, she placed her hand over her chest to keep it from leaping out. She wasn't ready, not yet! Not after that encounter, with the taste of her vulgarity still fresh on her tongue. But Sophie and May both grinned hugely. "Shall we?" May asked, sweeping a hand after Mr. Green's retreating back.

And just like that, they were walking from the room, through the darkened doorway leading to the Ballroom, and onto the small raised platform that the orchestra had performed on during the opening ball.

Panic bubbled up in Charity's chest as they curtsied before the audience, accepting their polite applause. Against her better judgment, her gaze roamed the assembly, taking in the hundreds of eyes leveled on them. She felt light-headed as all the doubt and worry about the performance seemed to assail her all at once.

She quickly made her way to the pianoforte, grateful she played an instrument that required her to be seated. Unfortunately, it was turned so that she could still see the audience if she looked up. She closed her eyes, drawing a fortifying breath for the work to come.

When she opened them, her gaze fell to the back of the room, where a single man stood by the wall. His posture was ramrod straight, his legs planted firmly, and his hands clasped behind his back.

Everyone else in the room fell away in that moment as she realized he wasn't some apparition conjured by her stressed mind. Hugh was here, looking her right in the eye, his lips curled slightly in an encouraging smile.

Her heart felt as though it had expanded, pressing against her ribs. He was here! He had come here, to his most hated of venues, and she knew without a shred of doubt he was there for her.

Only for her.

Her nerves, rioting just moments earlier, calmed to a slight hum. Even from half the room away, she could feel his confidence in her, feel his absolute assurance that they would do well. She smiled then, just for him.

Without looking away, she settled her fingers over the proper keys, opened her mind and heart to the music, and began to play.

The traffic had been congested as hell, the night damp with rain, and the hall filled to overflowing, but none of that mattered worth a damn the moment he laid eyes on Charity as she stepped out on the stage.

Her gown was made of a rich peach fabric, making her skin even more beautiful in the golden light of the three grand chandeliers illuminating the space. He had already been enchanted just by seeing her, but when her eyes found his, it was as though lightning had stretched across the room to strike them both.

He held his breath, waiting as she positioned her fingers over the keys. He could feel the expectation in the room, sense the curiosity of the audience as the place grew quiet. Then, all at once, music began to fill the room.

It was the same music that had tortured him mere weeks ago, with its tinkling high notes and odd oriental influence, but tonight it was pure magic. No one made a sound as the song, so familiar yet so foreign, poured forth with palpable emotion.

He closed his eyes and listened, remembering the years when he had danced with abandon at many a ball. He retreated to that time in his mind, before the pain and worse—the anticipation of pain—had tainted his every breath. In that moment, he wasn't thinking of the possible repercussions, wasn't tense with the expectation of agony. He was light and free and beyond pleased to be there, listening to Charity in her element.

He followed every note, admired every run, and gave himself over to the experience. She was brilliant. Light and sweet one moment, forceful and demanding the next. The others played beautifully as well, but to him, it was all just support for Charity. When the last note rang out, he opened his eyes and found her gaze almost at once. She was smiling broadly—wholly different from the bundle of nerves she had been walking out on the stage. He smiled, wide and unabashedly, and began to clap.

The rest of the audience quickly followed suit, their admiration clear in the muffled sound of a thousand gloved hands clapping. Miss Bradford stood first, followed quickly by Miss Wembley. With a blush turning her cheeks a becoming shade of pink, Charity stood last, and the women curtsied.

When she straightened, Charity's eyes immediately found his once more. Her smile radiated, triumphant and joyful, and he grinned broadly in return. The master of ceremonies emerged onto the stage, breaking the moment.

Hugh slipped away then, ducking into the entry hall and heading for the door. His head was lifted, his shoulders square as pride unfurled within him. She had been brilliant. Beautiful to watch and incredible to listen to.

He already knew it was a very bad idea to come, had known it from the beginning, in fact, but, damn it all, it was worth it. To support her in the one thing he had been able to help make happen for her. There was a bit of selfish pride in that, too. Without their talk, without the kiss that had moved him in ways he'd no longer thought possible, he never would have been able to do this for her.

It was fitting that he would be leaving her on that note. In a few hours, they would meet again, most likely for the last time. Anticipation for that moment drove his measured steps faster as his boots tapped smartly on the marble floor.

When he was only a handful of feet from the door, it swung inward and a man rushed inside, pausing to shake the moisture from his jacket. Apparently the rain had picked up. Damn, he didn't want anything to get in the way of his agreed-upon meeting with Charity.

The newcomer pulled off his hat and raked a hand through his brown hair, which was pulled back at the nape of his neck. Hugh squinted his eyes. The man looked familiar. He handed his outerwear to the waiting footman and glanced to where Hugh stood.

"Sorry. Am I in— Wait a second," he said, his light blue eyes lighting with recognition. "Danby, is that you?"

The voice more than the man's appearance was what jogged Hugh's memory. Deep and clear—and prone to singing, if Hugh remembered correctly. "Lord Evansleigh, I'll be damned."

"It's been a long time since Harrow, but not so long that you can't call me Evan. Heard you went off to the war a while back. Still in the army?"

Hugh gave a twitch of his head in the negative. "Sold my commission a few years back. Unfortunately, I'm no longer Danby, either. My brother, the rat bastard, decided to pass the baroncy to me sooner rather than later."

Evan's jovial expression fell a bit, and he shook his head. "Damn sorry to hear that. I've done a dreadful job of keeping up with current events this past year." He waved a dismissive hand. "Family matters. Still, no excuse for missing the news of Ian's passing. My sympathies."

The lump that always appeared at talk of his brother rose in his throat. "Thank you. It's been more than six months now, but I'm still not quite used to it."

The genuine sadness on Evan's face was a nice change. So many gave that momentary sympathetic look, then breezed right over the topic. Evan looked as though he actually understood the pain of losing someone so close. "Don't know if one ever gets used to such a thing, I'm sorry to say. But we do move on and find ourselves at such places as music festivals in an until recently passé, landlocked city in the middle of a particularly hot summer."

The wry humor Hugh remembered from their school days was still there. He smiled and clapped the other man on the shoulder. "Perhaps the grief has impaired my judgment, but I have recently come to my senses and am heading home."

"And I shall head straight into the fray with open arms," Evan responded without a moment's hesitation. "It was excellent seeing you again."

"And you, sir. Hopefully we can find a minute to catch up over a drink or two." Fishing in his pocket for the calling cards Felicity had had made for him, he handed it over. "Do feel free to call on me at your leisure."

As Hugh headed into the rain, he thought of his brother and the life that had ended too soon. There were no guarantees for the time they had on this earth. As a soldier he had known that, but, then, he and his men had volunteered for that position. They'd done so for the greater good of their country, which at least made the deaths seem less senseless.

There was no such consolation with Ian. A simple meal of seafood—one of hundreds over his lifetime—and minutes later he was dead. An acute allergy, the doctor had said. One that had developed out of nowhere, and, just like that, all their lives had been turned upside down.

Hugh turned his head up to the rain, letting the cool water wash over his face. Lady Effington had said it earlier, and now his brother's experience was cementing it in Hugh's mind.

No regrets. While he would never ruin Charity for the happy future she deserved, he intended to make the most of this night. For this one moment in time, she could be his. He'd be damned if he was going to waste what little time they had together.

Chapter Twenty-one

Happiness, joy, pride, exhilaration, relief, vindication—there simply weren't enough words to describe the emotions pinging around inside of her. Charity squeezed the other girls tightly in an exuberant three-way hug as their laughter rose to the high ceiling of the otherwise empty ladies' retiring room.

"Have I told you ladies that I love you? Because I most certainly do," Sophie said, both cheeks dimpled with her enormous smile. "And you should be happy—I've said those words only to my sisters, up until this moment." Her eyes darkened momentarily before she broadened her grin and squeezed each of their hands. "We shall be unstoppable now."

May nodded, her blue eyes as bright as sapphires despite the dim light. "Indeed. For the first time in months, I actually am glad for my father abandoning me in this country."

"Me, too," Charity agreed, her cheeks aching from the grin that hadn't left since the moment they finished the recital. "Remind me to thank him for having such forethought."

May's laugh was rueful. "I'll be sure to do that. I must

admit," she said, dropping Sophie's hand and linking arms with Charity, "you had me a bit worried."

"Only a bit?" Sophie interjected, raising her eyebrows. "I thought she might have a fit of vapors right there on the stage. But you fooled us both. One moment you were a quivering mess, and the next you were the consummate professional, cool and collected as a cucumber. Well, cool as a cucumber; I don't think they are all that collected."

Warmth bloomed in Charity's chest as she bit her lip and shrugged. "Let's just say I realized there were those in the audience who wished nothing but the best for me. For us."

She still couldn't believe he had actually come. Knowing how much he had risked to be there, she couldn't help but adore him for it. The way he had looked at her tonight . . . She swallowed, savoring the sparkling sensation shimmering through her belly.

That look had been special. Not quite the expression that had prompted her to call off her betrothal last year, but it had potential. Lots of it.

May disengaged their arms and leaned back, squinting her eyes as she inspected Charity's face. "Mmhmm. There was one particular audience member who looked *especially* supportive."

There was no stopping the blush, and Charity didn't even try. "You saw him?"

"Of course! He was sitting front and center beside your grandmother—how could I have missed him?"

Sitting beside her grandmother? Who was May talking about?

Before she could think of something to say, Sophie giggled. "Impossible to miss him, if you ask me. He was like a mountain among men, though an exceedingly well-dressed mountain. You could just see how proud he was of us. Or you, rather. I'm sure he barely noticed May and me." She winked as she nudged May playfully.

Dering? Charity hadn't thought of him one bit since the drive here. Guilt dulled the fizziness a bit. He had done so much for her, and she had somehow completely missed his not inconsiderable presence directly in front of her. "I'm certain he was enjoying the performance, per his hard work to ensure it happened."

"Oh yes, clearly," May said, giving a lighthearted roll of her eyes. "Are you trying to say you've not yet decided what to do about the viscount's attentions?"

Charity grabbed the statement like a lifeline. "Yes, exactly. Now, come. We must get back to the recital before people think we are poor sports for not listening to the other performers."

With one last group hug, they exited the retiring room and headed down the corridor leading to the Ballroom. String music filtered in from the hall, and Charity's ears picked out the distinct tones of two violins and a cello, all played with perfectly adequate skill. As they rounded the corner, Charity noticed a large figure leaning against the wall, facing in their direction. Dering's handsome face lit with an easy smile as their gazes met.

Of course. She seemed destined to be unprepared for everything this evening. Offering a polite smile, she slowed as she approached. "Good evening," she said in a low murmur, not wanting to disturb any of the audience members seated close to the doorway.

"It is, isn't it?" he said, holding his hand out to her. She obliged, and he pressed a perfectly proper kiss to the back of her gloved hands. He gave her fingers a little squeeze before releasing them and turning to the other girls. "Miss Bradford, Miss Wembley, a pleasure to see you again."

"And you," May replied, while Sophie smiled her acknowledgment. "Charity, would you excuse us for a moment? I believe I left something in the retiring room."

Without waiting for Charity's reply—one that would have attempted to keep them by her side—the pair of them spun on their heels and padded back in the direction from which they had just come.

Blast. With nothing else to do, she turned her attention back to the viscount. He truly was handsome, despite his well-over-six-foot frame. Or, as many seemed to think, because of it. He was a presence to be reckoned with. On another man, such broad shoulders may have seemed intimidating. For her, there was a certain protectiveness about him. He was a good man, even if it was taking her a while to adjust to his sudden interest.

She offered him a small smile. "I hope you enjoyed our performance. After your kindness, we especially wanted to do well."

Not a lock of his black hair dared to move as he nodded. "Without exaggeration, it was one of the finest performances I have ever had the pleasure to sit through. Very unique. Unexpected, but still quite elegant." He lowered his face closer to hers and said, "Just like you."

His warm breath stirred the fine hairs at the nape of her neck, and despite herself, she shivered. It was an exceedingly fine compliment. No one had ever called her elegant or unique, and certainly not both. This was a man who truly appreciated her, and, judging by the unconcealed admiration in his eyes, in more ways than one.

She relaxed a little, giving a small shrug. "You are entirely too generous. And I mean that. Without you, we would have been relegated to the audience tonight." The conversation in the carriage earlier came back then, and she bit her lip, not sure how to ask the question on her mind.

"Yes?" he prompted, raising his eyebrows.

Well, he certainly was perceptive. Clasping her hands in front of her, she said, "I was just curious. How, exactly, did you find out about the committee, after all?"

He shrugged, unperturbed. "Don't recall the exact details. A conversation with your neighbor led to a discussion of the committee's decision."

Something inside her shifted, upsetting the balance she strove for. Hugh had indeed been the one to talk about her. How much had he revealed? An unsettling sense of betrayal unfolded deep inside her. "It's a wonder my ears weren't ringing. You two must have had quite the discussion. I wonder, though—how did you come to the conclusion to help?"

At this, his muscles relaxed, and he smiled a sweet, reassuring grin. "For you, my dear Charity, I would happily move mountains, let alone the hearts of wayward committee members."

"So it was your idea? To act on my behalf, I mean?" She tried to hide her earnestness, but his answer to this question in particular was important to her.

He tilted his head to the side. "But of course," he said, his confusion clearly marking his surprise that she would think otherwise. "I couldn't let you suffer on the whim of one stodgy old committee member."

So there it was. Hugh had gossiped, and Dering had reacted with kindness and honor. As thankful as she was to him, she was equally, if not more, hurt by Hugh's indiscretion. After the way the *ton* had treated her, she had learned to treasure privacy. She never would have shared such a private part of herself with him if he hadn't opened up to her. She thought she could trust him, but clearly she was wrong.

Her laugh was slightly bitter. "Lord Cadgwith must have been properly horrified about encountering my less than sophisticated state that day."

Dering chuckled, clearly thinking he was laughing with her. "Oh yes—I heard all about the tears. Some men are intimidated by such a thing. I see it as an opportunity to play the hero." He winked, obviously poking a little fun at himself.

The betrayal of her confidence was beyond upsetting. It was absolutely unacceptable. Why had he come here tonight, anyway? Why did he have to make her feel as though she was the most important woman in the world one minute, and a silly fool the next?

She was tempted to leave him waiting tonight, just as he had once done to her. To simply not show up and let that speak as to how important he was to her. But as much as she would love such a statement, she knew she wouldn't follow through. Not when so much of her wanted to see him, ached for it, in fact.

Drawing a breath, she looked up to meet Dering's dark gaze. He was the real hero in this. She reached out and placed her hand atop the deep gray velvet of his jacket. "You do play it so well, my lord. Thank you for the kindness. I certainly hope I can return it someday."

He covered her hand with his, the heat radiating from his palm through both their gloves. "As do I."

Her heart gave an unexpected flutter at the earnestness she saw in his eyes. Tomorrow—she could think on this tomorrow. Tonight she would deal with her neighbor.

*   *   *

It seemed to take hours for them to make it home that evening. Between the performances that ran long, the traffic, and the rain, it felt as though everything was conspiring against her and her plans. When at last they pulled to a stop in front of their rental home, Charity fairly bounded from the carriage and into the house.

It was well past one in the morning, and the house was dark and quiet. She'd donned her simplest gown, and thankfully had actually been able to get it buttoned up, despite her lack of stays. She tiptoed her way to the music room, relieved that they had such a small staff. Rain tapped at the windows, dampening her spirits along with the soggy night.

She set her candle on the pianoforte and hurried to the windows, her slippered feet silent on the wood floor. Holding her breath, she pulled aside the curtain and peered into the night. There must have been a full moon behind the thick layer of clouds, because pale shimmery light offered at least some illumination. She scanned his part of the balcony.

Nothing.

Blast. Had the rain driven him away? Had he given up waiting as she bided her time for the house to settle down? Or had he simply never bothered to show up, like last time? She bit down on her cheek, her brow beetling. No, he didn't get to stand her up this time. They had an agreed-on time and place, and, by Jove, she had the right to give him a piece of her mind after what she discovered from Dering.

Indignation rose inside her, and she glanced about the room, looking for something small, hard, and movable. Her eyes landed on the handful of coins she had collected the day Hugh had used them to get her attention. Well, turnabout was fair play, was it not?

Snatching them from the window ledge where she'd laid them out, she marched to the door, yanked it open, and stepped out into the rain. She squinted as fat drops landed on her cheeks and forehead, and quickly selected a coin. The windows of his bedchambers were as black as ink, with no sign of him being awake. Rubbing water from her eyes, she lobbed the guinea at the nearest pane.

It clattered off the damp glass with enough noise to make her cringe before falling harmlessly to the ground. She held her breath and waited, listening for any sound besides the shushing of the falling rain, and looking for any signs of movement from within.

Nothing.

She threw another coin and then another, over and over until she'd exhausted her supply. By then, the front of her gown was soaked and cool droplets were flowing freely down her scalp. Blast him. Why was he doing this to her again? Why had he shown up tonight, looking so handsome she could hardly breathe, and watched her as though she was the only person in the entire room? Why did he want to toy with her like that?

Just as he had toyed with her when he'd divulged her private conversation to Dering.

She clenched her jaw, trying to force back the hurt. Had she just imagined their connection the past few times they had encountered each other? Heaven knew she hadn't imagined their kiss, but had she been alone in thinking the walls between them had started to come down? That was the worst of it: believing they shared something meaningful, only to discover he held no such conviction.

Her hands went to her hips as she glared at his unmoving curtains. They had a meeting, damn it all, and she intended to keep it. She was already drenched, angry, and considerably poorer than she was before she'd stepped outside. What was one more sin against propriety?

Taking a deep breath, she tied her skirts into a knot at the bottom, grasped the divider with both hands, and scaled it in one less than graceful move. She may be mad—absolutely, completely mad—but she was committed now. Reaching out, she grasped the doorknob, gave it a twist, and pushed open the door.

Chapter Twenty-two

Pain. Pure, hellacious, constant.

Truly magnificent in its ability to consume him. There was no light, and still he squeezed his eyes shut tightly. He hadn't eaten, and yet his stomach roiled dangerously, threatening yet another bout of vomiting.

He couldn't take it. If he cast up his accounts one more time, his head would surely explode with the unfathomable pressure that screamed for escape like steam from a violently boiling teapot. He burrowed deeper beneath the covers, desperate to escape the pounding pain. No anvil had ever suffered greater blows than his brain now endured. Over and over, as regular as his heartbeat. He had enough time to recover for all of half a second before the next blow came, stealing his breath and turning his stomach with its intensity.

Sweat dampened his pillow as he pressed his face into it. Every hair follicle seemed like a raw nerve ending, chafing each time he moved.

This was the real him.

This pathetic, crumpled, helpless being racked with the sort of pain he had never imagined possible back when he was whole. This had been him for half a decade, and it would be him for the rest of his life.

How long had it been? And hour, maybe two? His breath came out in a tortured hiss. He knew from experience he had hours to go yet.

A lifetime.

He swallowed against the nausea, but his mouth kept salivating. *God, not again. Please, not again.* He gritted his teeth, even as the tightened muscles intensified the stabbing at the base of his skull. To his immense relief, the nausea abated and he slowly relaxed his jaw.

The Baths had offered hollow, teasing hope. A promise that things might get better, but he'd known it had been a hopeless pursuit. He'd allowed Felicity and the damn quack doctors here to lull him into a false promise, and this was what he got for it.

Pound, pound, pound, pound. Squeak.

He froze, listening to the distinctive sound of a door swinging on its hinges. What the bloody hell was wrong with Jacobson? He knew better than to come in during an attack. His job was to stay the hell away. Hugh willed the man to leave, much too wretched to actually speak.

"Hugh?"

He squeezed his eyes closed that much more tightly. Was he hallucinating now? That was Charity's voice, whispering in the back of his mind. It was barely audible above the intense throbbing in his brain, but he knew it was her. Had his brain redoubled its torture with a two-pronged attack? Physical agony combined with emotional anguish? *Here's all the things you'll never have, and here's why, you sorry bastard.*

He kicked at the covers, suddenly hotter than Hades. The cool air gave scant relief as it washed over his sweat-dampened skin. He pressed the heels of his hands against his temples and pushed as hard as he could.

Was that a gasp? Impossible to tell. Could have been his own, for all he knew. He writhed to the side, desperate to find a position that would quiet the pounding.

Water splashed—he knew he heard that. With every bit of strength he possessed, he cracked his eyes open, squinting into the gray light cast through the wall of windows. A movement beside his bed drew his attention to a human-shaped outline. Water splashed again; then a cool, wet cloth was draped across his forehead.

"Shhh, don't fret," the soft voice crooned. *Charity.*

Christ, what was she doing here? The throbbing intensified—he wouldn't have believed it was possible—as he instinctively shook his head. "Charity," he rasped, his voice dark and ragged. "Go away."

Cool hands pressed against his cheeks. "I won't. What can I do to help?" Her voice was barely a whisper, but he could hear the pity.

Self-loathing threaded into the blanket of pain and agony already suffocating him. Now she knew how pathetic he truly was. "Nothing," he said, wincing at the sound of his own voice.

She didn't move. Was she staring at him? Looking on as one might observe a burning building—part horror, part fascination? He couldn't escape her, even as he didn't want to face her. Drawing his cheek between his teeth, he bit hard as he struggled to turn away from her. He braced for the crashing, rhythmic blows that assailed him as he moved. Even so, it was worth it. At least she could no longer see his face.

He breathed out a harsh breath, grateful to be turned away from her. He didn't give a damn that she was presented with the bare expanse of his back. If she didn't want her sensibilities offended, she shouldn't have let herself into his bedchamber.

"Oh, Hugh," she murmured, her voice heavy with regret. "I'm so sorry."

The scent of her lavender fragrance reached his nose, and he braced for the nausea. Smells of any kind were generally disastrous when he was in this state. But it didn't come. Even as the pounding continued its relentless beat, the scent was almost soothing. Comforting.

Almost as much as it was unwelcome. "Leave me, please." In his weakened state, there was no stopping the pleading tone in his voice. How could he? He was bloody desperate.

She retrieved the cloth that had fallen away when he moved and dipped it in the basin beside his bed once more. The sound of the excess water hitting the surface as she wrung the thing out made him recoil. He'd long given up cursing the rain, but this he freely cursed in his mind.

She laid the linen across the back of his neck, pressing it gently against his spine. The slacking of the pain was minimal. He fought against the urge to relax against her touch. It was wrong. Damn it all, she shouldn't be here.

She didn't say anything, hardly even made noise at all as she settled on the bed beside him, her movements slow and gentle so as not to jostle him. And that was where she stayed for the next hour. Silent, unmoving except to rewet the cloth and lay it across him every so often, she stayed beside him as the waves of pain crashed, as the nausea came and went, and as he steadfastly ignored her.

Somehow, fatigued by the fight and lulled by the constant rain and the quiet presence beside him, he drifted off into a fitful sleep. When he awoke, the first hints of dawn filtered into the room. The pain was a dull, manageable throb, and he exhaled with relief, exhausted beyond measure. For a moment, he wondered if her presence had been some sort of convoluted dream, but one long breath proved the theory wrong.

The lingering scent of lavender remained, as light as a memory but real nonetheless. He closed his eyes and shook his head. *Bloody hell.* So much for having a night of no regrets.

"For a woman who is supposed to be celebrating, you are awfully quiet today, Charity." May's eyes reflected concern as she offered up a plate of biscuits.

Charity waved off the plate and mustered up a tired smile. "Please forgive me. I slept dreadfully last night." Celebrating was the last thing on her mind just then. She was tired, yes, but that had nothing to do with the emotions weighing her down this morning.

"Dreadfully?" Sophie repeated around a mouthful of ginger biscuit. She hastily swallowed and tried again. "Why ever would you sleep so poorly? I was so relieved everything went so well, I slept like the dead. Well, I suppose the dead don't sleep, so perhaps I should say *like a baby.* Although I remember my sisters' wails in the middle of the night when they were infants, so let's just say I slept well. Regardless, the recital was a smashing success, and if that doesn't earn a sound night's sleep, I don't know what does."

Sophie's tangent managed to raise a small grin on Charity's lips. "Yes, I know. I can't really say what had me up half the night." A very literal statement.

Taking a sip of tea, May gave a slight shrug. "Perhaps it was the weather. I don't know how you English deal with the constantly changing weather. Rain or sunshine: Pick one and stick with it." She winked, smiling teasingly.

Charity cupped her tea in both hands, savoring the exotic blend of spices that May had dug out to celebrate the occasion. She wished it were as simple as the weather. Her heart still ached for the suffering she had witnessed last night. She'd never seen anything like it. Like everyone else, she had endured the odd megrim, but this was in an entirely different realm. A candle compared to fireworks. A pebble to a boulder. How he had endured such attacks for so long was beyond her ability to comprehend.

And it was incredibly hard to accept the fact that his pain had been her fault. He had come to the recital just for her; she knew that without any doubt. Despite the fact he had told her before that her music was a trigger for him, he had still come. And she had played her heart out, putting everything she had into that song. It was all for him, whether she admitted it at the time or not. She had wanted him to see her at her best.

And because of it, he had been punished severely.

It was ironic, really, that the very best part of her should ultimately bring about the worst in him. Guilt weighed down her shoulders and wrapped around her heart. Had her music caused an attack before, too? Had he suffered more than once for her blithe attitude in the face of his objection to her playing?

She hoped not, but suspected that he had.

But, of course, she couldn't share any of this with the others. It wasn't hers to share, really. She wouldn't betray his darkest moment, no matter how much she loved and trusted her friends. She sighed and nodded. "Yes, I suppose it could have been the weather. Hopefully I will sleep better tonight."

May tilted her head, as if not quite believing that. Did she see through Charity's attempt to be lighthearted this morning? "Should I call for Suyin? I'm certain she would be happy to help you relax."

"No. Oh, wait," she exclaimed, sitting up straighter as May's words about how the servant's techniques had helped her mother sprang to mind. "Yes, please do. If you don't think she'll mind, that is."

May had specifically said the therapy she called *tui na* was designed to help with both body aches and headaches. What if there was something she could teach Charity that would help Hugh? She was willing to do anything to help prevent such terrible pain befalling him again. Perhaps helping him now could somehow make up for the suffering he had endured because of her.

"Of course not! She's passionate about her art. Don't tell my aunt," May said, lowering her voice with a wicked grin and leaning in, "but she's been giving the maids treatment. They've never been so sprightly."

Charity could only imagine how Lady Stanwix would react if she learned her staff was indulging in the Eastern therapy. She smiled back at May and said, "Thank you, then. I know it will help." At least she hoped with all her heart it would.

When he agreed to move to the newly available townhouse, Hugh never imagined he'd be willing the day to come more quickly. That, however, was exactly what he was doing as he listened to the sounds of the household making preparations below.

He'd spent the late morning at the Baths, despite feeling rather ridiculous about being there. He didn't know why he was even trying, not when its so-called magic remedy had failed him so completely the night before. But as he had settled back into the steamy water of the private bathing room he had rented and breathed in the sulfurtinged air, he realized that he had not only grown accustomed to it, but he actually found it quite pleasant.

The truth remained that he had gone well over two weeks in relatively good health, and that wasn't something he was willing to toss aside.

Relaxing his tired shoulders, he had let the heat and buoyancy of the water soothe and cradle him. Why hadn't he thought to float in the ocean more, like he had during his childhood? It was a hell of a lot colder than springwater, but at least it would have relieved some of the pressure. It was something to try when he returned home.

Home.

The word echoed in his head now as he sprawled on the chair in his bedchamber, still a little weak after having walked home and changed again. Soon he would have to return to Cadgwith, whether he was well or not. He would have to fully take up the mantle of his responsibilities, and try to be even a tenth of the baron his father and brother had been. Right now, that small goal seemed beyond his reach.

Charity's soft touch came to mind, and he closed his eyes and exhaled deeply. She had somehow managed to make things a little more bearable last night. It didn't sound like much, but it was more than anyone else had ever managed to do. But that assistance had come at a cost. Dear God, what she must think of him. How on earth could he ever look her in the eye again, knowing she had seen the part of him he was so deeply ashamed of?

He glanced to the clock as it occurred to him that this was the time that he had promised to leave to her so she could play. Why wasn't she doing so? Had her day been so thoroughly thrown off after last night? He rubbed a weary hand over the back of his neck. Perhaps she was with her other trio members.

Sighing, he came to his feet and pulled open the door

to the balcony. Something metallic glinted in the bright white light of the overcast day. A coin. He bent to pick it up, only to find a half dozen more littering the stone floor below the window. He shook his head, gathering them all in his hand and curling his fingers into a fist.

She'd stolen his trick. What on earth had possessed her to climb the rail when he hadn't come to her bidding? Why did she care so much? Of course, she must have been disappointed when he hadn't been waiting for her, but to go to such lengths? He shook his head. God knew he wasn't worth that sort of effort.

The door to her side of the balcony rattled and opened, and her sweet, freckled face appeared as though conjured by his musings. Her gown was a simple white muslin, with a dark green ribbon tied at her slender waist and a matching ribbon woven through her auburn hair. She looked fresh and lovely—exactly the opposite of how he felt.

Her eyes betrayed her uncertainty, even as she smiled softly. "Good afternoon."

He bowed his head in formal greeting. "And to you, my lady."

She opened the door fully and slipped outside, squinting in the bright light. "How are you feeling today?"

Of course—what else could they speak of other than his infirmity? It would have been hanging over their heads otherwise, but, still, he bloody hated that it was there at all. "Right as rain. You?" Flippant was better than pitiable, right?

The corners of her lips turned down. "I'm well," she said, slight hesitation evident in her response. She must have sensed his reticence in discussing what had happened last night. An awkward silence settled between them, as uneasy as a poorly balanced house of cards.

He cleared his throat, wishing he weren't such a damn

ass. Wishing there were a much more pleasurable reason for her to be in his bedchambers last night, for God's sake. "Why aren't you playing?" The question came out more as a demand than a genuine interest. He gentled his tone and tried again. "It's supposed to be your free-play time of the day, after all."

She looked down and shrugged. "I should think that'd be obvious," she replied, her words quiet.

He blew out a frustrated breath. Bloody hell—she wasn't playing because of *him*. "No, it's not obvious. What would be obvious would be for you to be doing what you love. You shouldn't have—" He stopped, raking a hand through his hair. "You shouldn't have to make allowances for your invalid neighbor. Please don't stop on my account."

Shaking her head, she said, "How can I not? I can't bear to think I would bring you such pain."

His chest felt as though a spring coiled tightly within him. He would not allow her to take any responsibility for his problems. Without thinking, he fell back into his old officer pose, his legs planted shoulder distance apart, his spine ramrod straight, and his hands clasped smartly behind his back. "You didn't bring me anything. If either one of us needs someone to blame, we've only to look as far as Saint Helena to the little emperor himself, or even the French soldier who shot my horse out from under me."

His words were blunt, meant to cut through the building regret he saw in her troubled gray eyes. "I was an idiot yesterday. I acted as though I hadn't a trouble in the world. I pushed too hard, did all the things that I haven't done in a long time, and inevitably I paid the price for it. My only regret," he said, the word sticking in his throat, "is that you had to witness my episode at all."

*   *   *

Despite his curt tone and rigid stance, she knew he was still suffering inside. He couldn't completely block the emotion he felt from his beautiful green eyes. Despite his clear intentions to push her away, she intended to help him, whether he wanted her to or not. Charity licked her lips, trying to think of the best way to explain it. Best just to be candid. "I think I can help."

For his part, Hugh raised an eyebrow imperiously. Doubtfully. "What will help is for me to know that you are not sacrificing on my behalf." He sounded more like the man she had known in the days shortly after their first meeting.

Well, she knew better than to believe the defensive attitude. Ignoring him completely, she said, "Have you ever heard of *tui na*?"

He blinked, suspicion creeping into his expression. "Doesn't sound familiar. A musical term, perhaps?"

"Not at all." Stepping closer to him, she forced him to meet her eyes before going on. "It's a form of Eastern medicine. A sort of physical therapy that concentrates on the body's energy flow. There are special places on the body that are connected to this river of energy, and *tui na* taps into those places to bring energy to the deficient place, which brings about healing." The words came out in such a rush, she knew she sounded like she was babbling. But she wanted to say it all before he had a chance to judge, which she knew he would do.

He gaped at her for a moment, his face blank. "You're joking."

She shook her head. "No, I'm not. May's lady's maid practices it, just as her family has for eight generations."

"Ah," he said, nodding as though it all made sense now. "Not joking. Just mad. If you believe that, I have some snake oil that should work wonders for whatever ails you."

She scrunched her nose at him, putting her hands to her waist. "I am not mad, thank you. It's a genuine method; in fact, she used it on me for my sore shoulders. It was odd, but worked beautifully."

"Oh, good. I am glad to know it can help minor twinges in the shoulders. I'm sure it will work wonders for my skull-pounding attacks." There was no missing the sarcasm in his voice.

Frustration seized her. Why was he being so belligerent? "It's not just my shoulders. It helped May's mother tremendously before she died."

"I see. Good to know I could feel better before *dying*." He released his hands from behind his back and crossed his arms instead.

He was dismissing her out of hand, as though she were some sort of fool. "If you'd just tr—"

"Try it?" he said, his harsh words cutting her off. "I have tried just about every quack doctor and miracle cure out there. From bloodletting to willow-tree bark to neck stretching and tinctures, tonics, and salves. I think I'll sit this one out, thank you."

She wanted to growl with the frustration rising within her. "You're not being fair, Hugh. Give me a chance to show you, at the very least." Suyin had emphatically explained that it took years of study and practice to be properly qualified, but she had at least relented enough to show Charity a handful of basic maneuvers. She was hoping it would be enough to convince him to seek out a practitioner.

But she was getting nowhere. In fact, she could practically see him putting up a wall between them.

"My issues are my own, Charity. I don't need you concerning yourself with them. The only thing that you can do to make me feel better is to march that meddling self of yours back into your music room and play your blasted music."

Her shoulders fell as disappointment dimmed her excitement. "I don't want to play. The music isn't in me right now." It was the God's honest truth. She felt hollowed out by the knowledge that she'd been a part of his pain. Blast it all, all she wanted now was to be a part of his healing. Why wouldn't he give her a chance?

A bit of the irritation slipped from his eyes, and she caught a glimpse of the despair that she knew was lurking deep inside him. "Now is as good a time as any to tell you that I am moving to a different townhome on Friday. And, so help me, if I think you are martyring yourself in order not to disturb me, I will banish myself from here for the next two nights, even if it means sleeping in the carriage. So," he said, bracing his hands on the divider and leaning forward, "I suggest you go have a seat at that pianoforte of yours and do what you do best."

He was leaving? So soon? The rest of his speech went right past her as she stared at him in shock. Why hadn't he told her about this? She had only just begun to really know him. She wanted to dig deeper, to uncover the real Hugh, the man beyond the facade he shows the world. She wasn't ready for him to leave yet. "Why are you moving?"

His eyes softened then, and his shoulders fell as he blew out a breath. "An opportunity arose, and I took it. It's best for both of us, I think. You can play all the day through, and I can be as antisocial as I want." He offered a small lopsided grin.

She pressed her eyes closed, helpless to identify the emotions swirling in her belly like autumn leaves in the wind. Shaking her head, she looked up to him once more. "I truly do not know what to think of you. One minute you are gruff and standoffish; the next sweet and sensitive. You kiss me one day; push me away the next. Let me into your confidence, then betray mine."

His brows snapped together at the last one as though she'd reached out and slapped him. "What the devil are you talking about, betrayed your confidence?"

His surprise seemed so genuine as to give her pause. Was it really so inconsequential to him that he didn't remember? All the disappointment and upset she had felt last night came roaring back to her again. She crossed her arms tightly over her chest. "I know that you were the one to tell Dering about the selection committee. And not just their decision. Apparently, Dering felt compelled to help me after hearing about my *tearful* reaction."

Hugh's eyes shuttered then, and she knew in that moment that it was all true. He had gossiped about her like some sort of busybody old maid. "My apologies. Your heart was broken."

Her heart was broken? *That* was his excuse? "So you decided to spread tales of my heartbreak during a lull in the conversation? Jolly good entertainment, was it? Did you describe how silly I looked, crying about some meaningless recital?"

She looked away and scoffed, outrage heating her blood. "I suppose I should be grateful. Without your lack of discretion, Dering never would have taken it upon himself to try to help me." Even as she strove for sarcasm, she fell closer to something resembling bitterness. The hurt was impossible to disguise.

"Charity," he breathed, the single word holding an abundance of feeling. He reached out to stroke a finger down the back of her arm, and she couldn't help but lift her gaze back to his. For the first time, she detected the genuine compassion in him that pulled her to him again and again. "I swear to you, I wasn't flippant with your confidences, and I certainly wasn't gossiping about you."

His touch was addling her brain, and she found herself leaning forward. Resolutely, she straightened, stiffening her spine and lifting her chin. "The facts would appear to say otherwise."

His hand settled on her upper arm, his touch featherlight and exceedingly gentle. If she wanted to pull away, she could have at any moment.

But she didn't.

His eyes were too mesmerizing, his touch too perfect. As if sensing her hesitation, his other hand slid up her opposite arm. She swallowed, her heart skipping a beat at the warmth of his skin against hers. Despite her efforts to remain firm, her resistance was crumbling like a day-old scone.

Holding her gaze, he said, "I knew of one person who could help you, one who already respected and admired you and your talent. I felt he could do what I couldn't: find a way to overturn the committee's asinine decision." He dipped his head and said with quiet conviction, "You *deserved* to play."

He shouldn't be telling her this. He should allow her to think the worst of him and let the ties be cleanly cut. But seeing the hurt darkening her eyes and wrinkling her brow was more than he could bear. Damn it, he didn't want her thinking her private moments were being bandied about the gentlemen's clubs, for God's sake. That she wasn't important enough to deserve his discretion, or that she was something to be used for entertainment.

"You— You told him so he could help me?" Her words were cautious, unsure. She looked at him through narrowed eyes, as though trying to gauge the truth of his statement.

His fingers slid across the soft skin beneath the delicate cap sleeves of her dress. "Yes. On my honor as a soldier, it was my only purpose."

She worried her bottom lip for a moment, then asked, "Why?"

Why, indeed? He gave a little, mirthless laugh, then pulled her lightly toward him. She came freely, even as the insecurities flashed in her eyes. "You are a truly amazing person, Miss Charity Effington. Never, ever doubt that. I want more than anything for you to be happy."

Shaking her head, she said again, "But why?"

A hint of lavender flavored the air as he leaned down, against every sane thought in his head, and pressed his forehead against hers. "Don't make me answer that," he whispered, tortured by the closeness of her lips. Teased by the scent of her breath. Tormented by the rioting effect she had on his every nerve.

Her chest rose and fell with a speed that proved that she felt the pull between them as strongly as he did, and he knew without a shadow of a doubt that her heart pounded every bit as violently as his. He'd never been so tempted in his entire life, so powerfully drawn, so utterly desperate to press his lips to hers and claim the kiss his entire body was screaming for.

Her lips parted as she breathed short puffs of air. Each exhale fanned across his lips, teasing him with the taste of her, the damp heat of her. He thought he knew the meaning of the word *torture*, but this was over and above anything he had ever experienced. The burning need within him was exquisitely sharp, delectably raw.

He fought against the desire, holding his muscles rigidly in check as he willed himself to release her. To step away now before it became impossible to do so.

"Hugh, please," she breathed when he wouldn't move, her sweet voice a whispered plea. "Kiss me."

Chapter Twenty-three

He'd always considered himself to be a strong man. When that was taken from him, Hugh knew he was still an honorable man, one who would always choose right over wrong. But he'd never anticipated a woman who was a mere fraction of his size would be his downfall.

Almost of their own volition, his hands stole up her slender shoulders. He traced the smooth line of her neck, lingering over the pulse that fluttered as rapidly as a hummingbird's wings. With exquisite slowness, he cupped either side of her face and tilted her head up until barely a half an inch separated their lips. Unable to stop himself, he pressed his mouth to hers in a kiss so longed for, he groaned aloud.

She opened to him at once, her tongue eager to dance with his. In that moment, his senses were alive in a way they hadn't been in ages. He explored the velvety warmth of her mouth, reveled in the taste of her, and memorized the feel of her lips. His desire was so heady, he could hardly think, could hardly do anything but experience her.

But he had to think. He couldn't let them get carried

away. He couldn't give in to the pleasure; Charity deserved more than that.

With that thought, he drew a deep, steadying breath, drawing on every bit of strength he possessed in the world, and pulled away from her. She gave a breathy little sound of dismay, opening her eyes to look at him in slightly dazed confusion. "Don't stop," she breathed, nearly toppling his resolve.

Offering a small smile, he shook his head. "First I want you to play for me, sweet Charity, and then I shall kiss you again."

He pressed a firm, lingering kiss to each corner of her mouth before releasing her. His heart still pounded like a runaway horse, and he grasped the warm iron railing between them to keep from wrapping her up in his arms.

She blinked at him, her pupils huge and rimmed with a thin circle of gray. She breathed two long, full breaths, each one bringing the tops of her breasts above her bodice. Christ, she would be the death of him.

Her tongue darted out and swept her lips before she raised her gaze fully to his. "Promise?"

Pressing a hand to his heart, he nodded once. "On my honor."

Exhaling a whoosh of air, she nodded. "Very well. Tonight, after I return from our dinner party, I shall play." She reached out, slipped her fingers over the top of his waistcoat, and tugged him an inch or two closer. "But I warn you, if you are not there this time, I may very well have to kill you."

He pressed his lips together to stifle his unexpected grin. "I'll strive to avoid such a fate."

Until that evening, Charity had never understood the true meaning of the word *anticipation*. All night it was like a hot, brilliant light filling her chest, invisible to others yet impossible for her to go even a moment without acknowledging it. It shimmered and sparkled the entire evening, distracting her from conversation and robbing her of her appetite.

Now as she crept down to the music room, wearing the same easily donned gown she had the night before, she couldn't recall a single conversation she had shared. Even the other guests were a blur in her memory. Her heart pounded as she approached the darkened room, her candelabra providing a flickering golden path.

Hugh may have thought to bribe her into playing again, but what he didn't know was that she had her own bribe in mind. She'd play for him, but in return she planned to make him take her ideas seriously. The only way to do such a thing, in her mind, was to get her hands on him first.

A fresh wave of nerves swooped through her chest at the thought of trying the *tui na* techniques on him. Laying her hands across his shoulders, burying her fingers in his hair, tracing the length of his spine. She shivered as she turned the small brass knob and let herself into the room. If nothing else, this night would definitely be memorable.

The pianoforte sat dark and dignified before the windows, moonlight gleaming on its polished surface. A whisper of music had come to her in the carriage, something completely different from anything she had ever played. It was like nothing she had composed before, not even the song that had come to her when Hugh had listened to her play earlier in the week.

She set the candelabra on the casing and padded barefoot to the door. Unlatching the lock, she pulled it open . . . and there he was. Leaning against the railing, he wore only a pair of buckskin breeches, a white linen shirt open at the neck and with the sleeves rolled to his elbows, and a pin-striped waistcoat.

Though not quite smiling, his lips were relaxed with a slight upward tilt at the corners. The front of his hair fell casually across his forehead, obscuring the scarred brow that she had come to love. "Good evening," he said simply, his eyes reflecting the dancing candlelight. He was so beautiful in the moonlight, she had to work not to stare.

"You came," she said back, shyness springing up out of nowhere.

He straightened, and she was struck anew by his long, lean build. Without the bulk of his jacket, his narrow waist and slender hips were on full display, and his broad shoulders were accentuated by the cut of his waistcoat.

"I'd hate for you to have to resort to murder, so I decided to actually show up this time." He did smile then, setting her at ease.

She stepped back and invited him in with the sweep of one arm. These past two nights, she had been more reckless than in all the rest of her days combined, but still she didn't hesitate. Grandmama slept like the dead and was an entire floor away, and if any of the servants happened to hear the music, they knew better than to interrupt her.

"Wise choice," she said, keeping her voice low. There was reckless, and then there was *reckless*. There was no need to tempt fate.

He chuckled softly. "I thought so." Glancing around the room, he motioned toward the settee. "Should I sit?"

"If you like." Her nerves were catching up with her. It was one thing to be alone in a man's bedchamber when he was suffering and needed comfort, and quite another when he was hale and hearty and looking directly at her with an intensity that made her stomach give a little flip. Swallowing, she made her way to the pianoforte and sat down. "Are you certain you are ready for this? It's not too late to forfeit this part of the evening."

"Should I leave, then?" he asked, one eyebrow lifted as he offered an innocent smile.

Oh, he knew exactly how much she wanted his kiss. It was all she could think about since they parted, as she was sure he well knew. And though she *would* give it up if she thought it would bring him pain again, she was more and more convinced that the low, dark, soothing music that had been forming in her mind would actually be calming to him. What little higher octave notes it contained were so pianissimo, they'd be more of a whisper than anything. What she played tonight would be completely different from her normal style.

Yes, she was nervous—about the song and the kiss— but excitement flitted through her as well.

Instead of answering him, she closed her eyes and let her fingers rest on the cool, smooth keys. For a moment, all she could hear was her own thundering heartbeat. She breathed deeply several times, in and out, in and out. Finally, her heart began to calm, and the echoes of the song from earlier became clearer and clearer. Her fingers slid down the keyboard, coming to rest at the lower end of the scale. She scooted down the bench to compensate for the unusual position.

When she was ready, she took one last fortifying breath, depressed the keys, and began to play.

Her touch was light, a sweet caress designed to make the notes whisper forth. There were none of the forte notes she generally tended toward. Instead, she embraced the dolce style, so delicate as to be ethereal. The soft, round tones married together as she played, combining to create a sort of lullaby. As she gave herself over to the music, her mind filled with dark, slowly evolving images.

Shadows in the night, cast by silvery moonlight through softly swaying leaves.

Gently drifting clouds sliding along an indigo sky.

Undulating wisps of wood smoke curling from a chimney in the predawn hush.

The shapes elongated and narrowed, rounded out and stretched thin. Her hands moved over the keys with a grace she'd never before possessed as she gave life to the music within her. She allowed each note to stand, to rise from the steel strings from which it was born, and roll out like ribbons from a maypole, caught in a night wind.

She forgot all about the nervousness that had plagued her earlier. About the anxiety and anticipation. There was nothing but the two of them in a room of flickering shadows, surrounded by the gently wrought notes of the instrument that was as good as tied to her soul.

The music was dark and sensual in a way she had never heard—not from her fingers nor from anyone else's. There was a sweetness as well, gentle notes teased from her right hand, carefully dulled by the tenderness with which she played.

She could feel him in the music. Could recognize his true spirit in the restrained passion of the melody. She was there as well. Lifting him up, offering harmony, quietly entreating him to trust her.

The air stirred at the back of her neck, and she felt his weight settle onto the bench beside her. He didn't touch her, didn't say a single word or try to interrupt her. She played on, even as she breathed in his now-familiar scent. This song wasn't just for him, as she originally thought. It was for both of them. It comforted her in a way she hadn't expected. Somehow she knew, with absolute assurance, that this music wouldn't hurt him. She could feel it in the calmness of his presence, and in the beauty of the notes themselves. It offered peace.

She offered peace.

When the last note faded to silence, she opened her eyes and straightened. Hugh had settled onto the bench, his back to the pianoforte and his body slightly twisted in her direction. He watched her in the wavering light, his expression one of reverence.

For a moment, neither of them spoke or even moved. From this angle, with them half-turned toward each other, she couldn't see the scars that branded him. Even so, she knew the greatest suffering lay just below the smooth, unblemished skin of his right temple. She was in awe of his strength, amazed how he soldiered on in life. Could she do the same if she was stricken by the episode she had witnessed?

Probably not.

Her eyes fell to the side of his neck, where Suyin had shown her how to massage. Charity had to find a way to make him trust her enough to try.

Finally he moved, sliding his right arm across her front in a way that sent waves of sensation through her middle. His hand settled at her waist, as naturally as if they had always sat this way. "I've never heard anything so beautiful," he murmured, his voice barely more than a whisper. "I hope you never, ever stifle that part of yourself. Not for a neighbor, not for committees, and, most especially, not for me."

The heat of his hand seeped through the fabric of her gown and chemise, warming her skin. No stays armored her against his touch, and she was suddenly enormously glad for that. She nodded, since words were quite beyond her grasp.

"Now that you have followed through on your promise, it is only fair that I fulfill mine." Even as he said the words, his gaze dropped to her lips.

The kiss. She drew in a ragged breath, hoping he couldn't hear the hammering of her heart. His hand left her waist and traveled up her body until it came to rest across the sensitive skin of the side of her neck. Gently, slowly, he tugged her to him, drawing her inexorably toward him. The heat of his skin against hers was like a drug, as intoxicating as it was addictive.

Just as their lips were about to meet, when his eyes had darkened to midnight and desire hung between them like a palpable force, she paused and whispered, "Wait."

At the single word he froze, blinking. "What is it?" His voice was raspy, filled with barely leashed passion and a hint of concern.

She put another inch between them, trying to recapture her wits. If she was to help him, she had to be smart about it—a reality her rioting insides wanted nothing to do with. "Just give me two minutes. Two minutes to touch you any way I want. After that," she said, swallowing audibly, "then we'll have both earned that kiss."

Confusion flickered in his eyes, but he didn't resist. She pulled his hand from her waist, bringing it to her lips for a soft kiss before coming to her feet. She didn't break their contact as she stood and slipped behind him, trailing her fingers up his arm and across his shoulders. She was pressed in the narrow space between the bench and the pianoforte, but it was enough. When she settled both hands on his shoulders, he tensed at once, almost as if waiting for a blow. She leaned down until her lips were close to his ear and whispered, "Trust me, Hugh. Please."

*   *   *

Trust her?

It wasn't Charity he was worried about. His body was wound tight as a spring, wanting more than anything to lose himself in her. A kiss, he could handle. He'd already decided they would share one kiss, and he would leave. It was all he had promised her, and it was all he felt he could give and still be able to walk away.

But clearly she wanted something different from him. Something more. She was asking him to trust her, and even as he felt his iron control slipping, he nodded. He simply couldn't deny her whatever it was she wanted from him.

With much effort, he relaxed the taut muscles of his shoulders, releasing a pent-up breath as he did. Almost at once, her hands began to move. She pinched the ridge of his shoulders between her thumbs and palm and gently but firmly pulled up. She slid her hands back and forth, plucking at his muscles as she moved. It felt surprisingly good. He further relaxed, leaning forward slightly to offer better access.

She continued for a while, her motions rhythmic and repetitive, before sliding her hands to his neck. There, she pulled back the collar of his shirt, exposing his skin to the room's tepid air. Starting with her thumbs against the base of his neck, she pressed upward, following the rise of his spine. Her cool fingers slipped into the hair at the nape of his neck again and again, sending showers of sensation cascading down his back each time.

The motions she employed over and over were odd, but not unpleasant. *Definitely* not unpleasant. Yes, the small, constant motions felt quite nice, but her hands against his body were the best part. He relaxed against the pleasure of her touch, nearly groaning when she returned to his shoulders, putting fabric between them once more.

How long had it been? A minute? Five? He couldn't say. All he knew was that he loved the feel of her hands on him. It teased even as it satisfied, awakening something deep inside him that had been missing a long time.

When he couldn't take it anymore, he raised his hands and captured her wrists just as her fingers slipped into his hair again. He tugged, dragging her arms down the front of his chest until her cheek was nearly flush with his. "Enough," he said, his voice as raw as sandpaper. "My turn."

Chapter Twenty-four

A thrill ran straight down Charity's spine, then clear to her toes and back. There was something incredibly sensual about touching him the way she had, even though the purpose had been entirely innocent in nature.

Anticipation poured through her body as he released one hand and guided her around the bench with the other. Without any warning at all, he tugged sharply, pulling her straight into his lap. One arm cradled her across her back as his other hand went to her waist. This time there was no hesitation. His lips crashed down on hers in a kiss so passionate, she moaned aloud. He pulled her closer still, holding her securely against him as his hand squeezed her waist possessively.

She felt safe in his arms, adored and protected and so desired, her skin felt scorched wherever they touched. His tongue delved into her mouth, and her heart raced all over again. To be surrounded by his heat, his touch, his smell, his taste — it was pure heaven. As their tongues twined and danced, she wrapped her arms around his neck, wanting to be even closer to him.

She savored every second, not wanting to think about him moving away or them returning to their respective homes. She wanted to live in this moment forever, with her heart racing and her skin tingling, with his lips warm against hers and his arms wrapped around her as if he never wanted to let go.

Dimly, she was aware of the clock chiming twice, tolling the hour. Hugh must have heard it as well. He ended the kiss then, resting his forehead against hers as they both panted for breath. Already she missed the delectable heat of his lips against hers.

"God, Charity," he rasped, hugging her to him before pulling away. His eyes roamed over her face before meeting her gaze. He shook his head. "What you do to me."

Good. She liked knowing he was every bit as affected by her as she was by him. "If it's anything like what you do to me, I think we may be in trouble," she said, then boldly indulged herself by pressing another kiss to his mouth. And then another.

He groaned against her lips, the sound half torture, half satisfaction. "I was right when I said you'd be the death of me." In one smooth movement, he lifted her to her feet, then came to stand beside her. "Which is why I must go while the possibility still exists."

Having him leave was the very last thing she wanted. In fact, she couldn't recall ever wanting to be with someone more than she did him in that moment. "A few more minutes?" She looked into his eyes, silently pleading for him to stay.

"For God's sake, don't look at me like that." He lifted her hands and kissed the backs of each one. "I am clinging to the very last thread of my gentlemanliness."

That thought sent a renewed thrill down her spine, making her shiver. "Is that a bad thing?"

He gave a gruff laugh, releasing her hands and raking his fingers through his hair. His hand settled at the back of his neck as it so frequently did. She tilted her head, considering his pose. Was his injury flaring up again? Concern beetled her brow. "How is your head? Are you feeling ill effects from the music?"

The wry amusement fled and he gave a quick shake of his head. "No, I'm fine."

But his words were brusque. Defensive even. Would he tell her if he was hurting? Why hadn't she thought of that when she'd allowed him to lift her to her feet? "Are you certain? You're rubbing your neck as though—"

"I'm tired," he said curtly, dropping his hands to his sides. "I'm not going to break after having shared a kiss."

"But perhaps the music—"

"The music was fine. I told you that already." His nostrils flared slightly as he drew in a breath. "Your music was lovely, and I am perfectly fine," he said, his voice calm and even. And detached. "But it is quite late, and I should go."

Charity's shoulders sagged. He was pushing her away again, blast it all. It was as though he had thrown up a screen between them. She briefly considered asking him to stay, but she could already see what his answer would be. Lifting her chin, she nodded. "Very well."

Within moments he was gone, leaving behind nothing but the lingering scent of his shaving soap and the soft notes of his song still echoing in the back of Charity's mind.

Hugh closed the door to his balcony with a curse. Unbuttoning his waistcoat, he yanked the thing off and tossed it on the chair by the window. He stalked to the liquor cabinet, selected a bottle at random, and splashed two fingers' worth in the nearest glass.

Nothing like sharing a kiss hot enough to melt his boots, only moments later to be reminded of his infirmity. For God's sake, he had done nothing more than touch the back of his neck—a *habit*, by the way—and the first thing that had sprung to her mind was that he was about to have an attack.

If he had kissed her properly, the embrace should have wiped away thoughts of anything other than of the two of them tangled in each other's arms. But no. Clearly his illness wasn't far from her mind if it had popped forth so quickly. He knocked back the glass, swallowing half the contents in one gulp.

He was right.

She'd never see him as anything more than a man to be pitied. That's why she'd played that song, wasn't it? Wholly altered from her normal music in deference to him? And the ministrations to his neck and shoulders, too. While he had been half-crazed with desire, she had been thinking of helping him. Treating him as though he were a patient, not a man.

His decision to move had been the right one.

Sounds from next door filtered through the wall, and despite himself, he held his breath, listening. The low, deep tones were faint, but he instantly recognized them.

Charity was playing for him.

"Really, dear, you need not stay with me if you'd like to join your friends." Grandmama patted Charity's hand kindly before settling back in her usual spot on the sofa in the drawing room. "I'm perfectly happy to write my own correspondence."

Charity smiled as best she could, stifling the urge to yawn. "I think I'd rather stay in this afternoon. Though the tea and biscuits at the Pump Room does sound lovely, I think a quiet day at home sounds entirely too good to pass up."

Then maybe she could recover from yet another dreadful night of sleep. Her head hadn't hit her pillow until nearly four o'clock in the morning. She had been too restless to even begin to think about sleep. Instead she had played. For more than an hour, she had let the music pour from her.

She suspected that Hugh would be able to hear her, but it was his song, composed for the sole purpose of soothing him, and she did not believe it would hurt him. She played because the music wanted to come out and because it was the best way she knew to deal with her emotions. It had helped, somewhat.

"Well, if you are quite certain, then my eyes would be most grateful for your offer."

Charity rose and took a few steps toward the escritoire, when a commotion from below stopped her in her tracks. A man's voice, a scuffle of footsteps, the slam of the front door. Her eyes widened as she turned to the door.

"My heavens," Grandmama exclaimed, "what is all that racket?

Charity couldn't drag her eyes from the door to answer her grandmother. Only one thought would form in the humming chaos of her mind: *Could it be Hugh?* Was he for some reason demanding to see her? Her heart leaped nearly out of her chest, and she braced a hand on the back of the nearest chair so as not to lose her balance from the sudden light-headedness. She sternly tried to grab hold of her imagination. Why would he be here, after the way they had parted?

But as footsteps hammered up the stairs and the commotion below continued, she couldn't stop the surge of anticipation at seeing him again. The door opened, and a tall man appeared outlined in the corridor. He took one step inside, and disappointment washed over her, followed immediately by confusion. It wasn't Hugh at all.

She shook her head, her brows pinching together. "Papa?"

Chapter Twenty-five

Charity couldn't remember a time when her father had ever been spontaneous. If he had planned to come visit, he would have dutifully sent a note days in advance. He was methodical like that.

For a moment, fear tightened Charity's throat. Dear heavens, what if he had somehow learned of her illicit meetings with Hugh? Biting the inside of her cheek, she forced the thought away. It wasn't possible, surely. Grandmama looked every bit as surprised as Charity felt. No, this had to be something else. For some reason, the thought did not put her at ease.

He walked toward them, pulling off his leather riding gloves as he approached. His dark hair was slightly mussed—unheard-of for him—and several dried drops of mud spotted his cheeks. "Charity, Mother," he said in greeting, his voice strained. "My apologies for showing up unannounced. I felt the news I bear should be delivered in person."

Dread instantly sluiced through Charity's veins, and she quickly reclaimed her seat. "What has happened?" she asked breathily, knowing full well she wouldn't like his answer.

Grandmama sat up straight, worry clouding her eyes. Her hand fluttered to her chest as she said, "My word, Marcus, what is it?"

He dropped his gloves on the sofa table and sank into the cheery blue-and-yellow-striped chair across from Charity's. "I received word in the middle of the night via express post that after several days of fruitless labor, Cousin Burton's wife, as well as their infant, have both perished in the rigors of childbirth."

Supper was a very quiet affair that evening. The dull scrape of utensils on the primrose porcelain and the clinking of crystal goblets on the wood dining table took the place of any real conversation as the three of them kept to themselves.

Papa had decreed that they should leave as soon as possible for Bromsgrove, but, thankfully, Grandmama had insisted that they required at least a full day for proper preparations, so plans were made to depart Saturday morning at first light. The household had been thrown into turmoil, with every one of the servants dashing up and down the stairs and from room to room as they worked furiously to prepare for the departure.

As Charity took her first bite of the dessert course — cheesecake topped with summer berries and a dollop of raspberry sauce — Papa cleared his throat purposefully, and she glanced up to find him eyeing her.

"There is a matter of some delicacy that must be discussed before we depart, I'm afraid."

A wave of caution rippled along her insides, and she carefully set down her fork and dabbed her mouth with her napkin. "Oh?" His choice of words wasn't what gave her pause, but rather the way in which he spoke them. He sat stiffly in his chair, his chin slightly raised as his dark eyes locked with hers. He had adopted the tone reserved for declarations and orders—the kind meant to brook no arguments.

"The recent turn of events is, without doubt, terribly tragic. However, while I would wish it on no one, the fact is it has occurred, and I believe that there is good to be found in the situation."

Charity gaped at him, unable to contain her disbelief. Her gaze flickered to Grandmama, who had frozen in the process of setting down her goblet. Blinking, the older woman lowered the vessel with the utmost care and lifted her chin in the exact way her son had. "'Good,' Marcus? Surely there is no good to be had in the death of a young woman and her child."

He cleared his throat again, betraying a hint of his discomfort. "Not in the deaths, no. But in the resulting circumstances, yes. The truth is, Burton is my heir, and it is in both our interests to see to securing the line. To my everlasting shame, I failed to secure the title by way of my own offspring. But it is my belief that, given the change in circumstances, that travesty may now be righted."

So many thoughts and rogue feelings whirled through Charity at his words, she couldn't even speak. She knew she was a part of his "everlasting shame." He bitterly regretted her sex, and that after the trauma of her birth, Mama had never again been able to carry another child. To his credit, he had still managed to love her, in his own way, but she always knew his disappointment was there.

It was then that the true point of his statement hit home. *No, it can't be.* Even he, her impossibly pragmatic and thoroughly duty-conscious father, couldn't be *that* unfeeling.

She swallowed against the tightness in her throat and said, "What exactly are you saying, Papa?"

Grandmama's eyes darted back and forth between them, alarm clear in the deepening lines of her forehead. Papa didn't flinch beneath their scrutiny. "I'm saying that Burton will need someone with great compassion and kindness in the coming days. Whatever your faults, Charity, I believe you to be equal to the task of comforting him during this difficult time."

She didn't believe for a moment he was concerned only with Mr. Burton's mental well-being. "To what end?"

Papa's eyes narrowed slightly, not quite ominously, but certainly in warning. "Don't be naïve, daughter. You are moderately intelligent. You must have figured out that this leaves us with a very unique opportunity to reclaim the title for my descendants. Being available to Burton in his time of need will undoubtedly leave you well positioned. If you perform well, by this time next year, you could be married."

Perform well? Charity recoiled against the notion.

"Marcus, show some respect, please," Grandmama said, her voice booming in the quiet of the room. "The woman and her child are not yet even buried."

"Mother, I don't need you making a bigger fuss over this than is warranted." He sent her a stern look, clearly warning her not to challenge his authority. "We hardly knew the woman, and there is nothing wrong with making the best of a sad situation."

Yes, she could tell just how sad he thought it was. Charity's mind raced, desperate to think of a way to change her father's mind. For God's sake, the thought of preying on a grieving widower was beyond distasteful. And that was saying nothing about the fact he was easily twice her age. She didn't dislike him or wish him ill, but the thought of marrying him? She cringed. *Impossible.*

Especially now. Not after she had truly glimpsed passion. Hugh may have his faults, but no one had ever made her feel as he had. She craved his company like a starving man craved sustenance. When they weren't together, still her mind was on him. When they were, everything in her longed to touch him, to kiss him—even just to talk to him.

She shook her head, meeting her father's stubborn gaze. "Please, Papa, such a thing wouldn't be seemly. I think we must respect Mr. Burton's mourning period, at the very least." If she had a few more months, she'd surely be able to dissuade him from this track. Especially if she could garner her mother's support.

"Are you forgetting that Mr. Burton is not only a wealthy man, but an heir to a prestigious title? If you think eligible females from miles around won't be setting their caps for him, you are sorely mistaken." His chair screeched as he pushed back from the table and came to his feet, tossing his napkin on his plate.

"This is not a debate, Charity. You had your chance to find a suitable match. First there was that ill-handled business with Lord Raleigh, then an entire second Season wasted without a single offer. You have as much responsibility to this family as I, and I will not sit by and allow this opportunity—this *once-in-a-lifetime* opportunity—to pass us by."

Panic closed its fist around Charity's heart, and she threw a desperate glance to her grandmother. This couldn't be happening. Not now, not when she had only just found the man who made her heart sing.

Grandmama eyes were filled with empathy. She pressed her thin lips together for a moment, then jerked her gaze back to her son. "But what of her suitor, Marcus? He's made his intentions clear."

Charity sucked in a breath, shocked at her grandmother's pronouncement. Good heavens, did she know? Did she sense the growing bond between Charity and Hugh? Almost against her will, her eyes flickered to her father to gauge his reaction. He looked every bit as stunned as she felt, with his eyes widened and his lips parted.

He shifted his gaze to Charity, blinking several times before saying, "I've heard nothing of any such suitor. Explain yourself."

Charity floundered, unable to find the words to explain her feelings for Hugh. Grandmama broke the silence, tone conciliatory. "It has only just recently come to light. Lord Derington is quite committed, however. I believe he would make an offer, given time."

Lord Derington? By some miracle, Papa had turned his attention to his mother, so he didn't witness Charity's gobsmacked expression. Dully, her wits came back to her, and she closed her mouth and did her best to clear her expression. Of course Grandmama would think that. Dering had been calling several times, wearing his intentions on his sleeve.

"Derington is interested in our Charity?" The question bordered on incredulous, and he turned back to Charity with renewed interest. "Is this true?"

Mutely, she nodded. Technically it was true, but she didn't love Dering. She couldn't imagine ever kissing him the way she had Hugh. Or being wrapped in his arms, or playing for him alone by the softly wavering light of a handful of candles.

"I see." Papa slowly reclaimed his seat, his brows lowered in concentration. She knew exactly what he must have been thinking. She could marry Mr. Burton and keep the title in the family—something Papa had pined for her whole life—or she could marry the wealthy and well-connected viscount, who was heir to one of the oldest earldoms in the kingdom.

Choices, choices, she thought resentfully. She was grateful to her grandmother for trying to offer her a way out of her father's manipulations, but neither option held any appeal at that moment. There was only one option she could imagine, but after Grandmama's declaration, Charity couldn't contradict her now. Not yet, anyway.

Papa stroked his chin thoughtfully, despite having shaved his longtime beard last year. "Well, this is something to think about. Allow me to consider the situation, and we'll talk again tomorrow."

"Very good," Grandmama said, setting her napkin on the table. "Charity, let us leave your father to his port. I think we all have much to think about tonight."

Her words were such an incredible understatement, Charity had to stifle a bubble of hysterical laughter. Yes, let them all retire to their rooms and decide her fate. She followed her grandmother dutifully, but even as she did, resolve straightened her spine.

Let them think it over; *she* was going to do something about it.

"Pardon me, my lord."

Caught in the act of woolgathering, Hugh blinked, coming back to the present. His batman stood patiently in the door of the study, a mischievous smile curling his lips.

"What is it, Jacobson?"

He'd been thinking about Charity, imagining what she might think of Cadgwith. A completely worthless contemplation, and he was rather annoyed with himself for indulging such a thing. He shuffled the papers he was supposed to be looking at, as though he'd been interrupted thinking about something important.

"I believe you are being summoned."

Hugh cocked his head. What the bloody hell was that supposed to mean? "You *believe* I am being summoned? By what, a ghost?"

Amusement flickered across the man's face, and he lifted a shoulder. "Perhaps. After all, I'm not sure who else would be knocking at your bedchamber wall."

Hugh shot to his feet before he could think to temper his reaction. Jacobson chuckled, earning a glare from Hugh. "Oh, do shut up," he growled, straightening his jacket unnecessarily.

His batman raised his hands. "Apologies. I'll just go make myself scarce."

"Yes, you do that," Hugh said, refusing to feel ridiculous for his reaction. He waited until his batman was out of view before dashing up the stairs to his bedroom. He paused, but didn't hear anything. Perhaps . . . He glanced to the balcony door, though it was impossible to see anything in the posttwilight darkness. Crossing the room, he drew a breath, opened the door, and stepped outside.

She was there, her hands resting on the outside railing, looking over the darkened gardens below. Candlelight from the open door behind her illuminated her back and turned her hair to shining copper. She looked ethereal in her simple white gown, and he stepped toward her, all his promises to himself to keep his distance crumbling to dust.

She turned her head and looked at him, and when he caught sight of her expression, his heart dropped.

Tension radiated from her entire countenance, from her stricken eyes to her pale cheeks. No hint of her sweet smile touched her beautiful lips. "What is it?" he asked, dread pooling in his stomach. God, had someone discovered their rendezvous last night? Had he been seen slipping over the balcony divider? Or, worse, had something happened to her grandmother?

She closed her eyes and breathed out a harsh breath. "Thank God you're still here," she said, her relief palpable. She glanced back at the music room briefly before stepping closer to the divider. "I knew you said you'd be here until Friday, but when you didn't answer, I thought..." She trailed off, shaking her head.

"Charity, please tell me what is the matter." Seeing her in such distress was killing him.

"Oh, Hugh, I don't even know where to begin." She rubbed a hand over her eyes, weariness draped over her shoulders like a cape. "My father came today with some dreadful news. My cousin—second cousin, that is—anyway, his wife has died in childbirth, and we must leave at once to go to Bromsgrove."

"I'm so very sorry for your family's loss," he murmured. A second cousin's wife didn't sound so close, but perhaps they had shared a special bond. Regardless, any such death was a tragedy. "Is there anything I can do for you before you leave?"

Her brows came together and she shook her head. "No, you don't understand. While I am deeply saddened for my cousin's loss, I hardly know him. Although if Papa has his way, that will change very shortly."

She looked on the verge of tears. He tried to puzzle through what she had just said, but it didn't make a bit of sense to him. "And that's a bad thing?"

"Yes," she exclaimed, as though he had just guessed the winning answer in a rousing game of charades. "A very bad thing. Mr. Burton is my father's heir, and now his wife is gone. Therefore, Papa is determined that I should marry the man."

Marry him? Hugh reared back, beyond shocked at the statement. First, the man's wife had just died, and the viscount was already arranging his next marriage. Second, the idea of Charity marrying anyone else was an unexpected slap across the face. The very thought made his chest constrict.

Which was wrong. She wasn't for him, so clearly she must marry someone else. Taking a deep breath in an attempt to loosen the band that seemed to have wrapped around his chest, he said, "That does seem very bad form."

She blinked at him, dumbfounded. "Bad form?" She shook her head, looking at him as though he had said the surface of the sun must be mildly warm. "My father wants to marry me off to a grief-stricken widower — or anyone for that matter — and all you can say is 'that it is bad form'? I thought . . . that is to say, when we kissed . . ." She faltered again, glancing down before meeting his eyes once more. "Have you no care for me at all?"

Christ, if ever there was a loaded question, that was it. Did he care for her? More than anyone he had ever known. She'd come to mean entirely too much to him in the past few weeks, and he didn't know what the hell to do about that. All he knew was that her future could not involve him. His would always involve her, since he doubted he would ever be able to forget her or the astonishing effect she had had on his battered heart, but he would not allow her life to be ruined by yoking herself to a broken man.

"Of course I care for you, Charity. But this is very much a family matter. What did your grandmother say?"

Her fingers fiddled anxiously with a delicate little

handkerchief. "She told my father I had a suitor who was ready to offer for me."

Hugh froze. Had the old woman been referring to him? She had seemed to recognize something in him when they went to the theater. But he'd never, ever intended to offer. "Oh?"

Her eyes narrowed. Clearly he was not reacting the way she had anticipated. "So now my father is debating whether I should be foisted off on my cousin or handed over to the higher-ranking Lord Derington."

Bloody, bloody hell. The most selfish part of him rebelled violently against both options. He bit hard on the inside of his cheek in an attempt to rein that part of him in. He had no say over who her future husband should be. None at all. "And what is your preference?"

"My preference?" Astonishment dripped from the words. "I should think you of all people should know my preference. Or do you think I regularly invite gentlemen into my music room in the dead of night?"

This conversation was never going to lead to something good. He knew better—he bloody well knew better than to allow things to progress between them as they did. He had known he was making a mistake when he'd met her last night, far before their lips had even met. He'd done things wrong again and again, and now he was reaping what he'd sown. "Of course not. But we've already discussed this, Charity. You have your music, your family, and your whole life ahead of you. The two of us are wholly incompatible, and that will never change."

"Do you not feel the pull between us? Do you not feel the passion when we are together?" Her eyes flashed in the dim light as her hands curled tightly over the railing. "I left a perfectly *compatible* betrothal because I knew that he would never look at me as though I was the only woman on the planet. The way *you* looked at me yesterday. For that, I would happily live with *incompatible*."

"You say that, but you don't know—"

"I know that I love you," she exclaimed, shocking him into silence.

She *loved* him? But ... that wasn't possible. He was far too damaged to ever be worth that. He shook his head, unable to accept her words. "There's a difference between love and lust."

She gasped, rearing back as though she'd been struck. He'd never felt more like a bastard in his whole life, but he couldn't back down. She deserved better, and *anyone* was better than him.

Instead of the fury he expected, compassion crept into her eyes. She leaned forward, straightening her shoulders. "I know what love is, Hugh Danby. I didn't until I met you, but I do now. I love you. Your physical limitations don't matter to me. They have nothing to do with who you are. I dare you—look me in the eye and tell me you don't love me. Tell me that you don't want to marry me and spend the rest of your life with me."

His heart hammered painfully in his chest, robbing him of the ability to catch a proper breath. She was wrong. She thought it didn't matter, but witnessing one episode was nothing compared to living with it an entire lifetime. Even now, he could feel the telltale tightening of his neck muscles. The pressure was starting to build, and in less than an hour he'd be prostrate with pain. More helpless than a damned infant.

He would not sentence her to a lifetime being chained to a man like him. She felt desperate now because of the pressure her father was putting on her. A whole wealth of issues could be overlooked when one was of that mind-set. He was certain she'd be able to work out a solution that didn't involve him if she just gave herself a little time.

He knew what he had to do.

With sudden, vivid, perfect clarity, he knew that there was only one way to ensure that she would accept that they weren't meant for each other. For a moment, he just looked at her. He drank in her unique beauty, all those little things that made Charity, Charity. The freckles dusted across her face; her full, welcoming lips; and kind, expressive gray eyes. The curve of her cheekbones; the perfect shell of her ear. And his favorite of all, her beautiful, thick, glossy hair, the color of which he hoped would always linger in his memory.

Purposefully, he gave his head a negligent little shake. "We shared an attraction, my dear. Nothing more, nothing less. You're a lovely girl, but I don't love you and I certainly don't wish to marry you."

The lies burned a wretched path down his throat and straight into his gut. He fought to keep his expression slightly sympathetic but with an edge of condescension. The pressure in his head swelled, promising physical devastation to go along with his mental anguish tonight. Good. He deserved the punishment for allowing things to reach this point, where short-term heartbreak was the kindest thing he could offer her.

Unshed tears shimmered in her eyes as she stared at him, aghast. She shook her head, tiny little insignificant movements that spoke volumes as to her disbelief.

Hugh knew strategy. As a former officer, he knew damned well that sometimes the death knell wasn't a punch, but a subtle idea planted with finesse. Charity would never believe him if he acted as though she suddenly didn't mean anything to him. The trick was to simply make her think that he didn't care *enough*. "If it will help, I'll be happy to speak with Dering on your behalf. I believe your grandmother is right; with a little encouragement, he'll no doubt offer for you."

His words hit their target with deadly accuracy. The tears spilled over then, each one a separate dagger to his heart. His muscles bunched at the back of his neck, ominous warning of what was to come, but still he held his questioning expression, as though waiting for her to actually answer him.

At last she stepped back, holding her head high even as the tears rolled down her cheeks. "You're not the man I thought you were," she said, her voice a tight whisper.

His point exactly.

Chapter Twenty-six

"We're here, we're here," Sophie called, breezing into Charity's bedchamber with May just behind her. "Your note sounded quite dire, so we came prepared. Biscuits, lemon drops, freshly ordered tea and," she said, digging around in the little basket on her arm before pulling free a silver flask with a flourish, "brandy!"

"And I suggested poppet dolls, but Sophie vetoed the idea." May rolled her eyes teasingly.

Charity had never been so glad to see the pair of them. She'd sent the missives only an hour earlier. Desperate not to run into her father, she had spent the morning holed up in her bedchamber, trying to figure out what on earth she should do. Her heart ached terribly, a physical pain that hadn't lessened in the least since Hugh had broken it to pieces with his callous words last night.

Her eyes were dry and scratchy, her nose was runny, and she knew she had to look a proper disaster. She offered the others a wan smile—the best she could muster. "Thank you for coming so quickly. I know it's early, and you both are dears for coming to my rescue."

"Who says all knights have to be men?" May said, coming to sit on the bed beside her.

"Um, I'm pretty sure the king says it," Sophie teased, sitting on Charity's other side. "But we plan to fix things nonetheless. So let's hear the whole story, start to finish."

Sighing deeply, Charity did just that. She didn't hold back this time about anything. Somewhere in the middle of the tale, she had paused long enough for a maid to bring in the tea service, but other than that, she was able to get the whole story out without interruption. Fairly remarkable, considering Sophie's penchant for chatter.

When she was done, she curled her arms around her pillow and hugged it to her chest. "So that's it—the whole dreadful story. Now, tell me what to do."

"Run off to a nunnery?" Sophie said, compassion softening her normally cheery brown eyes.

"The Church of England doesn't have nunneries," Charity said with a tiny smile. "Though if I wanted my father to disown me, joining a Catholic convent may be the way to go."

May shook her head. "No music allowed—you'd go mad as a loon in a week." Sighing, she shook her head. "I hate this for you, Charity. Why is it men always seem to make a muck of things for us?"

"God-given talent," Sophie replied, her normally light tone surprisingly sharp.

Coming to her feet, May paced back and forth in front of the bed. "I think what we need to know is, what do *you* want, Charity? If you could have any solution, what would it be?"

A more complicated question, Charity couldn't imagine. "I'll have to think about it."

"No," May said, stopping directly in front of her, her blue eyes boring into Charity's. "Don't think. Answer with the first thing that comes to your mind. *Now*."

"I don't—"

"*No thinking.* What do you want?"

"I want *Hugh*," Charity cried, the words torn from the deepest part of her. "I want him the way I thought he was. Not the way he turned out to be." Regret stung her eyes, bringing tears with it, but she refused to let them fall.

May nodded, sitting back down and putting an arm around Charity's stiff shoulders. "If the Hugh you thought you knew is off the table, then we must move on to the second-best solution." She somehow managed to be gentle and firm at the same time. It was helpful, having someone so pragmatic by her side.

Sophie let her slippers drop to the floor and tucked her feet up under her skirts. "You did seem to quite like Lord Derington. And he at least likes you back. Plus you've known him for ages, and he does love your music."

Charity nodded. All of these were true. To another, it might actually be a dream match. But if she'd wanted that sort of match, she could have just married Richard. And why hadn't she? Because she knew, deep down, that they would both be miserable in the long run.

Giving her head a little shake, she said, "No. I don't want to marry Dering. If I cannot marry for love," she paused, swallowing against the fresh wave of heartache, "then I might as well marry for duty."

Silence reigned as the three of them let that statement sink in. Duty. She'd always done what her parents ultimately wished of her. With the notable exception of ending her betrothal—which, thankfully, had never been announced—she was a biddable daughter. She wouldn't have even come to the festival if they hadn't liked the idea.

"It's my father's greatest wish that the title remain

with his direct descendants. After twenty years of disappointment, I have the ability—or at least the possibility—to grant his wish."

The words brought hollow comfort. Finally, a chance to make right her ultimate mistake: being born a female. And if she couldn't marry for love, that was at least something.

"Are you certain? Because you could always stow away in my bedchamber," May said, her tone teasing but her eyes quite serious. "My aunt would never notice you were there."

Charity released a tiny laugh and shook her head. She wanted children someday, so remaining a spinster certainly was not an option she wished to consider. "No, but thank you. At least I'll have several months to change my mind while Mr. Burton is in mourning." Though she very much doubted that would be the case.

Sophie tilted her head, eyeing Charity quietly. "So does that mean you have reached a decision?"

Closing her eyes against the sadness and keen sense of loss that echoed in her empty heart, Charity nodded. "It appears I have."

"It has come to my attention, good sir, that you are in need of having your last rites read."

Hugh cracked open a single eye to see the blurry image of Felicity's damn brother standing over him. Groaning, he turned on his side, pulling the pillow over his eyes. "Go away, Thomas."

"Three words never yet uttered by a woman, thank God." The sound of screeching wood on wood rent the air as he dragged the chair over to the side of the bed.

Hugh gritted his teeth. He was going to kill the pup. "Get out," he said, enunciating each word with as much malice as he could muster after a night of hell—his second in a row, in fact. The dull throb in the back of his head was practically a caress compared to the past thirty-six hours.

Thomas chuckled. "Unfortunately for you, I tend to act contrary to orders. It's why I chose to go into the church; would've never made it in the military."

Damn the irreverent arse. Flopping onto his back, Hugh shoved the pillow aside and glared at the intruder. "What the hell do you want? Can't you see I'm sleeping?"

"I *can* see that you're sleeping. Which is interesting, because you were supposed to be out of this place by noon, and it was my understanding you were moving out yesterday. There's a new tenant who's quite anxious to claim it."

Blowing out a harsh breath, Hugh sat up and squinted at the clock across the room. One thirty-two. In the afternoon, judging by the sunlight bullying its way past the curtains. He cursed under his breath, then reached for the nearly empty glass of whiskey sitting on the bedside table. It was stale and warm, but it would do.

"Cursing and drinking spirits in front of a man of God?" Thomas tsked, shaking his head slowly from side to side. "At the very least, offer to share, you ill-mannered miscreant."

Hugh offered the good vicar a rude gesture before rubbing his hands over his eyes. He felt like absolute hell, and only half of it had to do with the hellacious attack. Knowing he'd hurt Charity, no matter how honorable the reason, gutted him in a way he hadn't imagined. "Why are you here, anyway? What's it to you that I'm late vacating the place?"

Extending one finger he said, "First, we're practically family, so we must look out for one another. Second," he said, holding up two digits, "I was worried when Jacobson said he was concerned about you. And three"—he paused long enough to pull his flask from his inner pocket and take a swig—"you're in my house now, my friend."

That got Hugh's attention. "You're moving in? How did you manage that?"

"The good earl thought he might like to attend the festival after all. Therefore I'm putting down stakes until he gets here. A good son does what he must," he said with a waggle of his eyebrows.

With a sigh, Hugh spun his finger. "A little privacy, if you please."

Thomas obliged, coming to his feet and walking to the balcony door. Hugh threw aside the covers and pulled on the clothes he'd tossed to the floor the night before.

"What a handy balcony," the vicar mused, pulling aside the curtain for a better look. "Especially given the lovely young ladies I saw leaving the adjoining townhouse last time I was here."

Before either of them knew what had happened, Thomas's face was smashed against the window, with Hugh's full weight thrown across him. With his forearm pressed forcefully against the younger man's back, Hugh hissed, "If you so much as look at the woman next door, so help me, I will throw you from this balcony on your sorry arse."

Coming to his senses entirely too late, he pushed away, staggering back several steps. Thomas whipped around, fury darkening his perpetually jovial eyes. "What the *hell* was that about?" He jerked his shoulders, angrily righting his jacket.

"Christ, I'm sorry," Hugh breathed, raking both hands through his hair. What was *wrong* with him? Charity wasn't even there anymore. According to what she'd told

him, they would be hours down the road toward Bromsgrove by now.

"Sorry?" Thomas gaped at him in disbelief as he
checked his nose for blood. "I'm going to need a better
answer than that. I'm only just managing not to draw
your cork as it is, you bastard."

He exhaled harshly, dropping down on the chair in
front of the windows. "I am a bastard. I've made a bloody
mess out of things with the girl next door, and I overre-
acted."

"For Pete's sake, man, if you have a claim on the girl,
you've only to say so." Shaking his head, he went straight
to the liquor cabinet and poured a generous glass of
scotch.

Hugh gave a dry, mirthless laugh, laying his head
against the leather padding. "No claim. You of all people
should know I'll never have a claim on any woman."

Thomas's glass halted halfway to his lips. "Why's
that?" He sounded genuinely curious.

"Did you happen to see me when you came in? The
worthless, prostrate man buried in his bedclothes, sleeping the afternoon away?"

Shrugging, the vicar took a swallow of his drink before answering. "Not so unusual. At least you have a
good excuse. Most men are just recovering from a night
cavorting when they look like that." He shot Hugh a
devilish grin. "And when I say *most men*, I mean *me*."

Damn it, he didn't need anyone trying to make him
feel better. "I don't need you turning me up sweet, Tom.
I know what kind of man I am."

Thomas gave him a sideways glance, assessing. "And
what kind is that?" The question was mildly spoken, but
his eyes held true interest.

"Let's be blunt, shall we? I'm practically an invalid.

Half a man, if that. You know what my attacks are like. No woman deserves to be married to someone so wanting."

Thomas's eyebrows shot up. "There are so many things wrong with that sentence, I'm not even sure where to start." He held up a finger while he downed the rest of his drink, then set the empty glass on the bureau with a firm snap. Grabbing the chair he had dragged to the bed earlier, he lifted it in both hands, carried it to where Hugh sat, and set it directly across from him. "Right, so here's my best go: You suffer from a chronic ailment caused by massive injury sustained whilst in the service of our great country, defending those of us too lily-arsed to do so ourselves. That makes you a hero, whether you like it or not. Your condition does not make you less of a man; it proves that you are *more* of a man. More of one than I'll ever be—that's for damn sure."

"I'm not a—"

"No," Thomas said, holding up a staying hand. "Hear me out or, so help me, I will claim that punch I still owe you."

Hugh pressed his lips together, none too happy. He *hated* being called a hero. It was as ill fitting as a child's tunic. But if Thomas felt he had something to say that would make the man feel better about this little tête-à-tête, then by all means, Hugh would keep his mouth shut.

"Here's the thing, Hugh. We all still love you, whether you feel worthy or not. Based on what you've said, I wonder if this woman doesn't feel the same way."

Charity's declaration echoed in Hugh's mind. *I know what love is, Hugh Danby. I didn't until I met you, but I do now. I love you.* His gut clenched, knowing what happened next. Recalling the words now brought him nothing but pain. "She deserves more, Tom." She deserved to play her music as loud as she wanted, and dance the night away at every ball she wished to attend. She deserved a strong, able-bodied man to keep her and protect her.

"Does she think so?"

The muscles of Hugh's cheek flexed as he leveled flat eyes on his friend. "It doesn't matter. I wouldn't saddle an enemy with me, let alone Miss Effington." And, really, thanks to their last conversation, she wouldn't have him now, anyway.

Thomas tilted his head to the side and put a contemplative hand to his chin. "Does she know about your attacks? I mean, *really* know about them."

Hugh nodded curtly. "Much to my dismay, yes. She witnessed one several days earlier. Much like you, I couldn't make her leave, either."

"What? She didn't run screaming for the hills? Interesting."

Rolling his eyes, Hugh dropped his chin to his fist and pointedly ignored the meddling vicar. He wasn't about to share anything about that particular encounter. Almost a week later, and he still felt the sting of humiliation that she'd seen him at his worst.

When Hugh didn't say anything, Thomas leaned forward. "Would you feel the same way if she were the one with the ailment?"

"Of course not," he said defensively, before he could stop to think.

Smirking, Thomas nodded. "Then you have your answer."

"Stop trying to analyze me with your faulty logic. It's not the same. I'm a man. I'm supposed to be the strong one." Why was he even having this conversation? His decision was made, Charity was gone, and life would go on.

"You know," Thomas said, relaxing back against the chair as though he hadn't a care in the world. Which he didn't, as far as Hugh could see. "I may not be the best vicar in the world, and I may not know all the muddled parts squished into the middle of the Bible. But I certainly remember the beginning. *Then the Lord God said, 'It is not good that the man should be alone; I will make him a helper fit for him.'* Genesis, two eighteen."

Hugh blinked, astonished at the authoritative way with which the man spoke. His heart pattered unexpectedly as the vicar's point seemed to hit home in a way that nothing else before ever had. She *had* helped him. She had sat by him in his worst hour, even when he didn't want her to, and made things better. She had insisted again and again that she wanted to be with him.

Thomas went on, his voice quiet but firm. "You didn't die on that battlefield for a reason, Hugh. Don't live your life as though you should have. It sounds to me like God had a helper in mind just for you. Don't be an arse and turn your back on the both of them."

Thomas's words had an uncomfortable ring of truth. Over the years, Hugh had wished more than once that he had died a proper death on the battlefield instead of lingering in this state. But since coming here, since meeting Charity, he had lived more in the past four weeks than he had in the previous four years. She had brought him life again.

He swallowed against the emotion that clogged his throat, attempting to get ahold of himself. "That is by far the most sermony thing I have ever heard you say."

"I have my moments. Always better to be underestimated and pleasantly surprise people than to get their hopes up and disappoint," he said with a wink. "Now, am I to assume I have gotten through that thick skull of yours?"

"Amazingly, I think you might have." His mind whirled. What should his next move be? All he knew was that she had gone to Bromsgrove to Mr. Burton's home. Should he write a letter? Wait for her return, if indeed she was even coming back? No, neither of those was good enough.

He had to go to her.

Whatever it took, he would find her. He knew now that he couldn't bear the thought of her going even a minute longer than she had to thinking she wasn't loved. He hoped only that he hadn't ruined things so thoroughly that she'd refuse to see him. And that didn't even touch on the problem of timing. With the recent death, he couldn't very well barge into a grieving stranger's home and demand to see her.

Pushing to his feet, Thomas offered a brief nod. "Well, then, if you'll excuse me, I think I'll go find a decent whiskey at the club to wash out the taste of that swill you stock."

Hugh stood, momentarily setting aside the dozens of questions yet to be answered. "Sure, sure. And, Thomas?"

The vicar paused, lifting an eyebrow in question.

"Thanks." Hugh's throat was oddly tight as he spoke the single word.

Thomas nodded, smiling easily. "Just be sure to invite me to the wedding. I want a good look at the woman who nearly earned me a broken nose. If," he added, his eyes sparkling with mischief, "you can get her to forgive whatever asinine thing you did to push her away in the first place."

Yes, there was definitely that. As Hugh offered a salute to his friend, his mind turned back to all the things he had to consider. First, he needed to cool his heels for a few days to allow a little time for the family's grieving. In the meantime, he needed to figure out a way to prove to Charity that he was making a good-faith effort to look to her as a helpmate. After the way he had spoken to her, he would need more than words and a small trip up north to convince her of his earnestness. And even if it she didn't require it of him, he required it of himself. Of all the things he thought she deserved in a man, respect should have always been one of them.

He wanted her to know without a shadow of a doubt that not only did he love her, but he respected her, her ideas, and her interests. And that he wasn't always going to be an overbearing arse. Striding for the door, he made his way downstairs to the study, not caring a whit that he wasn't fit to leave his bedchamber in his rumpled state of dress.

If he was going to do this right, he had a few letters he needed to write and not a moment to waste.

Chapter Twenty-seven

"**M**ay I join you?"

Charity looked up at her grandmother's over-loud query. She'd been so lost in her thoughts, she hadn't even heard the woman's approach. Nodding, she patted the empty space on the bench beside where she sat. "Of course."

Laying her shawl down first, Grandmama settled onto the stone and sighed. "My, isn't this quite the view? You can see the entire valley from here."

"Indeed," Charity said, offering a small smile. From their vantage point at the edge of the dowager house–turned–guest cottage's small gardens, they could see the whole of Mr. Burton's sprawling estate. The grounds truly were beautiful, especially today, when the sun had found its way out from under the clouds more often than not. Situated in a verdant valley and surrounded by rolling, forested hills, the land looked as pretty as a painting.

The main house, Bromsgrove Manor, stood proud and tall in the middle of it all. It wasn't overly large, but with its classic styling and elegant stone facade, it was exceedingly pleasing to the eye.

Settling her hands primly in her lap, Grandmama said,

"It is a home that any woman would be pleased to be the mistress of, I should think. For the meantime, at least. At some point, Mr. Burton will have to move to Durham, of course."

Charity nodded but held her tongue. Her grandmother was right, of course. It was hard to imagine any woman not being delighted to call the home her own. And yet Charity herself could muster no enthusiasm. She was doing exactly what came naturally, offering kindness and whatever assistance she could to the grieving Mr. Burton, but thanks to her father's intentions and her agreement to abide by them, she felt terribly ghoulish. What kind of woman preyed on a man in mourning?

Thank goodness Mama had insisted that they stay in the lovely, generous-sized cottage that had once served as a dowager house. She had been firm that Mr. Burton should be allowed at least some space during this difficult time. Despite his status as her father's heir, the truth was they hardly knew him, and it was disconcerting to try to comfort a near stranger in his time of need.

"It's so nice that you are able to play such peaceful music for Mr. Burton. Quite a change from your normal repertoire," Grandmama observed, turning her gaze from the view in order to look at Charity. "The song you played yesterday, was that new?"

Something between embarrassment and defensiveness rose in Charity, not toward Grandmama, but toward herself. She should have been able to forget the man who had broken her heart by now. A full week had passed, and she worked hard to put him from her mind.

Or so she had thought.

But when she sat down at Mr. Burton's incredibly gorgeous pianoforte yesterday, of its own volition Hugh's song had flowed from her fingertips like honey, sweet and dark and full of such emotion that tears had pricked the back of her eyes as she played.

Her cousin had praised her warmly, admiring her skills and asking about her favorite composers. But as they had spoken, all Charity could think of was the night in her music room when she'd poured her heart into the composition meant for the man she loved.

And how the very next day, he had tossed her aside.

Swallowing, she forced a smile for her grandmother. "Just something I had been mulling over the past two weeks or so. I wanted something . . . different." The piece had been meant to soothe the baron, not that it mattered in the end. Still, the melody played again and again in her mind over the last week, and it was cathartic to play it out loud.

"You certainly succeeded." Sighing, Grandmama let her gaze return to the valley. "Oddly enough, it reminded me of my Raymond."

Charity drew in a surprised breath. "It did?"

"Quite." She was quiet then, appearing for all the world to be enjoying the scenic grounds, but her eyes were unfocused, and Charity knew her mind was somewhere else entirely. After a few moments, she continued. "I told you before how when we met, he carried so much sadness deep inside. What I didn't say is that it took months for me to break down the walls he had built around his heart." She shook her head, clearly lost in the memory of her long-ago, newly wedded self. "There were times when I didn't think it was worth it. When I wished I could accept that he simply wasn't interested in anything but a respectful, distant marriage. But then I would catch a glimpse of that hurting heart of his and knew I couldn't give up."

She smiled at Charity, sadness and fond memory softening her eyes. "I'm so glad I didn't."

Unexpected tears welled up behind Charity's eyes and she glanced to her lap to hide them, blinking rapidly in an effort to make them go away. She had tried with Hugh. Their situation was wholly different from her grandparents'. She and Hugh were not only not married, but Hugh had also quite plainly told her they had no hope of ever being so. And, really, after learning that he'd only just been toying with her from the start, she wouldn't want to marry the man.

Still, the music played deep within her, calling him forth in her mind stronger than ever.

"I've learned a lot in my lifetime," Grandmama continued, her voice surprisingly quiet. "The best things in life are worth fighting for. And for more reasons than one. Living with regrets is no way to live—even if that means disappointing those we love in the short-term. Some decisions are simply too important to leave to others."

Charity could scarcely believe her grandmother's words. What was she saying? Was she encouraging her to ignore her parents' wishes for a match with Mr. Burton? Even as her heart grasped onto the idea, her mind rejected it. She had thought she had loved someone, but look how well that had turned out. Her heart still ached from the disappointment and sorrow of that night. It was safer to simply follow the path laid out for her.

As for regrets, her only one was not recognizing the baron's true feelings—or lack thereof—until it was too late.

"Oh, my," her grandmother said, pulling Charity from her thoughts. "I would so love to see the view more clearly. Could you be a dear, please, and fetch my lorgnette from my bedchambers? My maid will know where it is."

"Of course," Charity said, coming to her feet. She could use a little time to gather herself after the unexpected conversation.

She followed the winding gravel path back toward the house, paying little mind to the roses and shrubbery filling the garden to capacity. Ducking beneath the proliferation of white-bloomed climbing roses draping the arbor, she followed the bend around to the side of the house and came to an abrupt halt.

Dear heavens!

Her breath caught in her throat as her hand flew to her mouth. *Hugh!* He stood directly on the path in front of her, his shoulders smartly squared and his head held high. He didn't say anything at all; he just stood there, waiting for her. Letting her decide what to do next.

Her heart felt as though it had sprouted wings and was attempting to take flight. The sight of him was a double-edged sword—exquisitely sweet and unbearably painful. His last words to her reverberated in her brain, stealing the joy that had sprung to life at the sight of him. Why would he be here? What more pain could he possibly cause her?

It occurred to her then that her grandmother had been a part of this.

Cautiously, she stepped forward, unable to look away from the sight of him. He had never looked so strong and tall, so thoroughly self-assured. When she was half a dozen feet away, she stopped. "What are you doing here?"

His cravat was impeccably tied, his jacket finely brushed. She fleetingly wondered how he'd managed to make it there without having ruffled a single hair. He offered a crisp, perfectly executed bow. "I came here with the hope of further investigating your character, Miss Effington."

Indignation wrinkled her brow as she gaped at him. What in the world? "My character," she repeated, certain she had heard him wrong.

He gave a single nod. "Indeed. I've recently come to know mine quite a bit better, you see. According to a sage old vicar, I am a presumptuous fool with enough self-pity to fill a boat and enough shortsightedness to run it aground. After much consideration, I have come to the conclusion that I agree.

"Therefore," he said, taking a casual step forward, "I thought I could benefit from discovering a bit of your character. Specifically, how are you at forgiveness?"

Despite her effort to keep her head about her, a spark of hope cruelly flared to life, deep in the darkest part of her heart. Shoring up her defenses against the man who had broken her heart barely a week ago, she crossed her arms over her chest and said, "That depends."

"On?"

"Whether or not it has been earned."

A slight breeze rattled the leaves around them, making the light dance across his handsome face, illuminating in turn his nose, cheeks, and every jagged rise and dip of the scars. His green eyes never wavered from hers, nor did his soft, sweet smile. "Allow me to throw myself upon your mercy first; then we shall see about the rest."

He took another step toward her. "First and foremost, please let me express how fervently sorry I am to have hurt you. Especially since, I am ashamed to say, it was quite purposeful."

Her brows came together at his words. *This* was an apology? Had he come here to make things worse?

His next step brought them close enough that if she extended her hand, she would touch his chest. She curled her fingers into her skirts to keep herself from doing just that, though she didn't know whether she would push him away or pull him closer, given the chance.

"The truth is, sweet Charity, I lied. When you asked me to tell you that I didn't love you, every fiber of my being was crying out for the chance to tell you I did, but my stubbornness couldn't allow me to tell you the truth. And the truth is," he said his voice low and earnest, "that I *do* love you. More than I thought possible, more than I imagined I ever could. It's because of you that I even know how deep love can be."

Charity's heart nearly leaped from her chest. She pressed her eyes closed, savoring the words on his tongue, turning them over again and again in her mind. Could it really be true? Why would he have come all this way if it wasn't? Still . . . She opened her eyes and met his gaze fully. "Then why lie? Why hurt me like that? Why abandon me in my most needful time?"

Watching him as closely as she was, she recognized the regret in his eyes when it came. He shook his head and blew out a long breath. "Because I believed, truly and honestly believed, that you deserved better."

"Better?" she whispered, her heart aching for the pain she heard in his voice. "What could possibly have been better than marrying the man I loved?"

He smiled then, sadness still weighing his tone. "Marrying anyone else. Or so I thought. All I knew was that I wanted you to have a husband who was whole and hearty and able to love and care for you in the manner that you deserve. With my attacks, I was convinced I could never be that man." He gave a shrug. "So I did what I thought was best for you."

Her hands went to her waist then as she glared up at him with indignation. "That is the most ridiculous, selfish, stupid thing I have ever heard, Hugh Danby." Breaking her heart because he somehow thought he was unworthy? As though she were some great paragon, and he a lowly pauper.

He grimaced. "So I've been told. Which is why I have come to beg for your forgiveness. But first," he said, reaching into his pocket and pulling out a handful of coins, "I come bearing bribes."

A smile lifted her lips as she looked down at the coins in his hand. She had no doubt they were the ones he had thrown at her window, and she at his. With delight wending its way through her veins, she held out her palm and accepted the money.

"That, Miss Effington, was bribe number one. And here is bribe number two: Shortly after you left, I went to your friend Miss Bradford. After her initial surprise, she has agreed to indulge my somewhat unorthodox request."

"Which is?" she asked, curiosity getting the better of her. She couldn't *wait* to hear the story from May's point of view.

"Assisting me in hiring a *tui na* practitioner. If you think it will help, than I am willing to try it. I trust your judgment, Charity, and will strive to never again discount your opinion out of hand."

She was more than impressed—she knew very few men who would ever do such a thing. "Thank you. It means a lot that you would listen to me."

"Interesting that you should mention me listening to you," he said, his bisected brow lifting mischievously. "My last bribe is this: I have written my sister-in-law in Cadgwith. At this very moment, she is likely happily in her element, employing a designer to refurbish the dowager house into a proper music space. She's also preparing the guest rooms, as it is my hope that you—and your family, of course—will come to Cadgwith. I'll need your expertise to test the new pianoforte, after all."

He took one more careful step and looked down at her candidly. "I know my limitations, but I never wish for them to limit you as well. In fact, I believe that with you by my side, I can strive to be the kind of baron I wish to be. I already know that you have made me a better man. We may have to make adjustments and allowances, but it is my intention that we shall never be limited in the things that matter.

"If you should decide to overlook my stupidity of the last time we spoke, and bow to the *considerable* bribes I now come bearing in both penance and good faith, it is my greatest wish, Charity Effington," he paused, taking her hand in his, "that you would consent to be my wife."

Charity's mouth fell right open. Could this truly be happening? She looked up into his beautiful, completely earnest green eyes, happiness whooshing through her like a strong wind rushing through fallen leaves. "Where was this person a week ago?" she asked, shaking her head in wonder.

"Busy learning a few hard lessons, I'm afraid."

A thought occurred to her then, pouring cold water over her warm delight. "But my father! I've already committed to his wishes."

Nodding briskly, Hugh said, "Yes, I'm fully aware of the conversation I must have with him. But before I did anything, I had to gain your forgiveness . . . and hopefully your hand, however tentatively. Did I succeed?"

She nodded, sniffling even as she smiled. "Yes."

"Yes?" he repeated, his eyes sparkling brilliantly in the shifting sunlight.

"Yes—on both accounts."

Yanking her into his arms, he swallowed her up in a

tight embrace, laughing as he did so. He kissed her forehead, then her nose, and finally her lips, making her positively melt into him. It was over all too soon, as he pulled away and straightened with purpose. "I suppose it is time for me to speak with your father."

He squeezed her hand before releasing her, and a part of her mourned the loss of his touch. Already anxiety was eclipsing her joy of a moment ago. She knew her father; she couldn't imagine him being receptive in the least. Especially not after she had agreed to his plans. And, perhaps worse than that, she had never even mentioned Hugh to him. She stifled the urge to groan aloud—this was *not* going to go well.

Hugh stepped back, then brightened when he looked over her shoulder. "Oh, and one more thing I hope you will forgive," he said, tipping his chin in the direction of the arbor.

She turned to see Grandmama walking toward them on the path, her gown visible through the climbing rose branches. Charity swiveled back to face him. "Yes, I was wondering how she fit into things."

"I arrived two days ago and have been staying at the Heath and Heather. I couldn't very well just show up unannounced, so I took the liberty of sending Lady Effington a note." He glanced at her again and smiled. "She was always quite sympathetic to me, I think. She helped me determine the best time to talk with you."

Two days! How had her grandmother kept such a secret? She wondered now if she'd been watching Charity, looking for signs that she'd be amenable to his suit. Had the new piano piece played a part in her decision?

They waited until Grandmama reached them, and then Hugh offered them both an arm as they went around to the door. Charity's heart pumped wildly as worry and excitement and all sorts of other emotions built within her.

What happened next truly would determine the rest of her life. Hugh looked down at her then and smiled, confidence coming off him in waves. "Have faith, sweet Charity. If there is one thing I'm good at, it's being stubborn."

For the first time since she'd known him, she fervently hoped that was true.

Chapter Twenty-eight

He should have been worried. He should have been anxious. He probably should have been doubting his own wisdom, judging by the thunderous look on Lord Effington's face.

But Hugh was none of these things.

At that moment, he had the sort of clear-eyed, razor-sharp lucidity that he hadn't experienced since his days as a commanding officer. It was usually right before battle, when everything was at stake and he alone had to make a decision. In those moments, his vision seemed to narrow to only the things that were of the utmost importance, and at that exact moment, the thing he saw most clearly was Charity.

Or, more specifically, the future he desired with her.

Facing his combatant, he offered a respectful nod. "Please accept my sincerest apologies for my regrettable timing, my lord, but following my conversation with your daughter before her departure, I felt that time was of the essence."

Hugh's one advantage was his height, which prevented Charity's father from glaring down at him, as he so obviously wanted to do. Standing with one hand gripping the edge of the library's small mantel, Effington's dark gaze bore into him. "Time was of such essence that you couldn't allow my family to grieve in peace during this difficult time?"

Hugh had to tread lightly here. He couldn't risk alienating the man, but he wanted the viscount to know exactly where he stood. "It was my understanding that if I waited much longer, Miss Effington's affections might be pledged elsewhere."

Silence. The older man pressed his lips together, clearly displeased that Hugh possessed this particular piece of knowledge. "Say your piece so we can be done with this business."

Nodding, Hugh looked him directly in the eye. "I'm in love with your daughter, my lord, and I have come to ask your permission to seek her hand."

Effington's knuckles whitened on the mantel, and Hugh fleetingly wondered if the marble would crumble beneath his grasp. The older man's nostrils flared as he shook his head. "I know absolutely nothing about you, save for your name and your appalling disregard for propriety. That, sir, does not recommend you or your purported love."

It was a valid point. Effington knew nothing about him and had every right to be dubious of him. "Then allow me to expound. I recently inherited the Cadgwith barony. The estate earns more than five thousand a year, boasts three miles of private shoreline, and features a house fit for a king—literally. It was renovated in advance of King George the Second's 1750 visit, to be worthy of His Majesty's presence."

Lord Effington's steely countenance offered no encouragement, but Hugh plowed on. "I served for three years in the service of our king as an officer in the army during the war. I know what it means to fight for what you believe in. I know that there is only one thing in life that truly matters when everything is stripped away: love. Love of country, love of family, and, most powerfully of all, the love of the woman who holds your heart.

"After I was seriously injured at Waterloo, I sold my commission and returned to Cadgwith. But I have never forgotten those lessons learned on the battlefield. I may not be able to make Charity the next Lady Effington, but I can cherish her every day for the rest of my life. I can love her and give her children and spend my every breath in the pursuit of making her happy."

Hugh took a step forward, wanting the viscount to see his earnestness and hear his resolve. "I swear to you, on my honor, that she shall never want for anything as my wife. She shall have the choice to travel as much as she chooses, the freedom to invite anyone she wishes to our home, and the ability to play and create her music to her heart's content. She'll have status, respect, and, most especially, love. I come to you, with all due respect, my lord, to ask for her hand in marriage."

Silence reigned for the space of several seconds, each one ticked off by the jarringly loud clock in the corner. The viscount's features were grim, his mouth pinched in displeasure. "I cannot allow it. This so-called love is entirely new to me, sir. I think you overstate my daughter's affections. She never once mentioned you, not even when discussing possible suitors not one week ago."

The door swung open then and Charity sailed into the room, her cheeks already flushed before she even said a word. "That is a mistake that I wish to rectify immediately."

Charity's blood thundered in her ears as she held her head high, meeting her father's rounded eyes. She had never, ever stood up to her father before. Even after breaking her betrothal, she had confessed her sin with great regret. If she'd had to ask permission, she would probably be married to Richard today. But for Hugh, she could do this.

Her joy at hearing his words, at knowing the way he was standing up for them, had nearly brought her to tears. Even now she didn't dare look at him, for fear she'd be overwhelmed. Today she had finally seen the officer that he had been. The proud, honorable soldier who had sacrificed so much was still alive and well in him, if a bit worse for the wear. This was the man she had sensed in him, even when he'd lost sight of it himself.

She drew a deep breath and approached her father. "I wish to marry him, Papa. He is the man I always dreamed I would find. He is honorable and selfless and willing to admit when he is wrong. I feel whole when I'm around him, as though some long-barren place in my heart is filled when he is with me."

Shoulders stiff and face stern, her father sliced a hand through the air. "Charity, this is not the time or place to be discussing this. This man has put us all in an untenable situation, and I will not allow this to continue."

"*He* is not the one to put me in an untenable situation," she said, hardly able to believe she was saying such a thing to her father. But she couldn't be silent anymore, not when so much was at stake.

Reaching out, she took her father's hand in hers, willing him to see the sincerity in her eyes. "I love you, and I wish to honor you, but I will never be able to fix the fact that I was not born a son. I beg you, release me from my promise to pursue Mr. Burton, and let me marry the man I love instead."

Papa blinked several times, his eyes darting back and

forth between Charity and Hugh. She gently squeezed his hands, forcing herself to remain silent, to give him a chance to process what she had said.

Finally, his dark gaze settled on hers. His nostrils were wide with affront, but his eyes held the first hints of indecision. "You would rather move to the end of England, hundreds of miles from your mother and me, and give up the life and lands you have always known, than wed Mr. Burton and know that your future and that of the viscountcy were settled?"

She didn't hesitate. "Yes, Papa. The title will always be in flux. As you well know, there is no guarantee that I would have a son. What I can guarantee is that I would be miserable if I married Mr. Burton. I will always know that my heart is elsewhere, and would regret it for the rest of my life."

Papa's jaw clenched as he narrowed his eyes, studying her. "And if I forbid a match with Cadgwith?"

Charity's heart squeezed as she drew a desperate breath at the very thought. Her eyes darted to Hugh's, and he held her gaze but didn't interject. Slowly, she turned her attention back to her father. The first man she had ever loved. The first man she had ever disappointed. The man she wanted so much to please, but who may try to stand in the way of her happiness.

She looked down at his hand, still held in her own. Could she ever really choose between her father and the man she loved? Even as she thought the words, she knew what she had to say. Raising her gaze, she entreated him, "I love you, Papa. And I love Lord Cadgwith. I should hope that neither of you would ever stand in the way of my love for the other." Her dulcet tones echoed the low, sweet melody of the song she had composed for Hugh, the one she had titled "Shadows in the Dark."

"Well said, my dear." Grandmama's voice cut straight through the tension in the room. They all turned to the doorway where she stood proud and tall, despite her diminutive form. "Marcus, I have been wrong about many things in my life—including where my granddaughter's affections might lie," she said with a brow raised in Charity's direction, "but of this I know I am absolutely right: There can be no regret when love prevails."

Papa pulled his hands away and stepped back. "Mother, this is none of your concern. Please leave it for—"

Mama appeared behind Grandmama, her hands firmly on her hips. "For whom? For us?" Her apple cheeks nearly matched her red hair. Charity's heart swelled—her mother always avoided conflict.

"Catherine," Papa exclaimed, surprise widening his eyes. Neither his wife nor daughter had ever stood up to him or challenged him in any way.

"I'm sorry to intrude, but it seems as though this is to be a family discussion." She paused, setting her gaze directly on Charity. For her part, Charity didn't look away. Instead, she poured all of her emotions into her expression: hope, determination, and, most of all, love. She wanted to share it all with her mother, for her to know and understand exactly how Charity felt.

Drawing a steadying breath, her mother stepped around Grandmama and went to her husband's side. "Do you remember Charity's relief last year when she parted ways with Lord Raleigh? Yes, I've been eager for her to find a match, but I knew it couldn't be just anyone. I kept hoping she'd find someone who would make those beautiful eyes light up."

She linked an arm with him and resolutely turned them both to face Charity straight on. "Well, look at her now, Marcus. Can you be the one who steals the light from her eyes? Because I confess, I cannot."

Papa looked at her for a long moment, really *looked* at her. So many things flickered in his expression, she didn't know what to think. She held her breath, accepting his inspection, and prayed he would be persuaded instead of angered by their arguments.

Finally, he pressed his eyes closed and exhaled a long breath. When he opened them again, his answer was there in his resigned gaze as he looked around at the gathered crowd. "Very well," he said, his tone flat. "If it is your wish, I will not stand in your way. When we return home, I shall have the contracts drawn up."

Disentangling himself from his wife's loose hold, he strode from the room, leaving them in shocked silence. For a moment, all Charity could do was stare after her father, listening to the pounding of her own heartbeat.

She had won. She had actually won.

Slowly, savoring the burn of anticipation unfurling in her belly, she turned her gaze to Hugh. His eyes were shining, absolutely glowing with the happiness that seemed to radiate from deep within. He was hers at last!

"Well, then," Grandmama said, chuckling softly, "I think perhaps you might like a moment alone with your betrothed."

Her betrothed. Tears of joy pricked her eyes as she smiled. "Mama, Grandmama, I don't know how I can ever thank you enough."

"Just be happy, my dear," Mama said, swallowing her up in a warm hug. "I should have done something sooner. I knew from my time here that you and Mr. Burton wouldn't suit. Forgive me?"

"Of course," Charity replied, giving her an extra squeeze

before pulling away. "I know how much it took for you to come in here like that. It means the world to me."

"Yes. Well, your grandmother is right," she said, wiping tears from her eyes as she smiled. "We'll give you two some time alone."

Within moments, they were gone, and Charity was alone with Hugh at last.

When she turned to him, he opened his arms to her, and she rushed into them.

His lips found hers as they embraced, and they kissed as though they weren't standing in the middle of Mr. Burton's guest library. As though the door wasn't wide-open, and broad daylight didn't illuminate the room's every corner.

She clung to him, nearly weeping with joy as they held each other tight. The kiss was bold and unapologetic, more powerful than any they had yet shared. No more hiding in darkness. No more lurking around like thieves in the night.

He was hers and she was his, and from that moment on, they would face everything the world had to throw at them together. Finally, Hugh pulled away and smiled down at her. "After the way we began things, I should have known I had a warrior on my hands, but still, you impressed me."

She smiled and rose on her toes to kiss him again, breathing in his wonderful scent. "I was thinking the exact same thing."

Epilogue

"That's new."

Charity squeaked in surprise, her fingers abruptly ceasing their play. She swiveled on her bench to find Hugh lounging in the doorway, looking devilishly handsome in the early-afternoon light. She grinned and started to greet him when all at once she realized why he was there.

"Oh no! What time is it?" Her gaze darted to the clock. Of course, she was late again. She was supposed to have gone back to the main house ages ago to change for the festival. It was just that she was *so* close to finishing her niece's lullaby, she had gotten a little carried away.

He smiled knowingly and shook his head. "Time for you to change, my dear. The villagers would have my head if I didn't bring their favorite baroness, as promised."

His polished black Hessians tapped a neat beat on the hardwoods as he made his way across her cheery little music room. The warm ocean breeze slipped through the open windows, ruffling his hair and catching at the folds of his expertly tied cravat. His features were relaxed, an easy smile lifting the corners of his lips. There were two faint purple half-moons beneath his eyes, remnants of his episode two nights ago, but otherwise his skin was golden and his eyes bright.

"I wouldn't miss it for the world," she said, accepting his proffered hand and allowing him to pull her to her feet. He tugged harder than necessary, bringing her flush against his chest. She lifted an eyebrow, "And I can see for myself that you are feeling very well today."

These days, his attacks were less and less frequent and blessedly mild. Between his ocean swims and *tui na* therapy twice a week—not to mention her own efforts at massage, though those always tended to end in tangled sheets and secret grins at the breakfast table—his life was rarely interrupted by pain anymore. When the episodes did happen, they had a routine of sorts that helped to lessen it before it got out of hand.

She liked knowing that she could help him. He had brought so much joy to her life, it felt good to be able to reciprocate.

"I am," he said, sliding his hands over her hips before clasping them just above her derriere. "I'm actually looking forward to socializing, believe it or not. Although," he added, dipping his head to nuzzle her neck, "I could be persuaded to be a bit late."

She shivered, gooseflesh peppering her arms as his hot breath fanned across her skin. Never mind the fact they had been married for months; she still couldn't get enough of him. "Mmm, don't tempt me." Even as she said the words, she tilted her head, granting him greater access.

"Why not?" His lips followed the slope of her exposed shoulder as his hands tugged her firmly against him.

Why not? The reasons slipped away from her grasp as

she closed her eyes in pleasure. It was always like this with him. He could rob her of all sensible thought with little more than a simple touch, and she loved him all the more for it.

"Ahem."

Charity's eyes popped open at the unwelcome intrusion. She started to pull away, but Hugh didn't move an inch, firmly holding her in place. "Go away, Felicity," he called out.

"Oh no," she said, laughter coloring her words, "we must leave within the hour if we are to arrive on time. Lady Effington clearly knew what she was doing when she sent me to fetch the two of you."

Ah, Grandmama. Charity should have guessed. Grandmama claimed she had accepted their invitation to move to Cadgwith because of the medicinal qualities of the fresh ocean air, but Charity suspected she enjoyed keeping an eye on two of them. Which was just as well, since Charity liked keeping an eye on her grandmother whenever Squire Baumgartner came calling. Which, incidentally, was probably why she was anxious to leave for the festival. Charity grinned at the thought.

She looked up at Hugh. "I suppose I should go and dress."

Sighing greatly, Hugh pressed one last kiss against her lips before turning to address Felicity. "Fine, fine. Take her away if you must."

Felicity grinned all too knowingly. "So sorry to have interrupted your fun," she said with a wink. By now Felicity was every bit as close to her as a sister, but it didn't stop the blush from rising up Charity's cheeks.

"Yes. Well, I need to look over my first official Flora Day speech again, anyhow." He slipped his fingers through Charity's and squeezed. "And I must say, I am quite looking forward to seeing you in your peach silk gown again."

His raised eyebrows told her the rest of the words that remained unspoken: He was looking forward to seeing her *out* of the gown, as well. Her blush deepened; at least that's what she *hoped* he was thinking. "Then I shall wear it just for you."

She lifted their joined hands and brushed a kiss against the warm skin of his knuckles. All at once, gratitude swept over her, stealing her breath with its intensity. Here in this place, this tiny, perfect little corner of England, she had everything she ever dreamed of. A sister in Felicity, who had so joyfully welcomed Charity to Cadgwith. An adorable niece who brightened all their lives and for whom Charity hoped a cousin may soon be on its way. A grandmother who enriched her life every day. Dear friends who not only corresponded with impressive dedication, but who planned to reunite in Bath in less than two months for the second annual Summer Serenade in Somerset.

And, most of all, a husband who loved her the way she had always dreamed of being loved, and whom she loved every bit as much in return. A man who wasn't perfect, but who was absolutely perfect for her. A grin came to her lips as she remembered her thought last summer after their first meeting: *This, Lord Cadgwith, means war*.

No, she thought, giving him an impromptu hug.

This, Lord Cadgwith, means love.

Don't miss the next sensual romance
in Erin Knightley's Prelude to a Kiss series,

The Earl I Adore

Coming from Signet Eclipse
in January 2015!

Sophie Wembley had always prided herself on being able to find the bright side of any situation. When she was compelled to play the oboe, when all the other girls were learning violin or pianoforte, she'd chosen to embrace her mother's belief that the more unique the instrument, the more memorable the musician. Yes, in the beginning, the tricky little instrument had sounded more like a duck than a songbird, but in time she'd learned to play quite well.

When she'd discovered how embarrassingly modest her dowry would be, she'd brushed off any disappointment. At least she could be sure that no self-respecting fortune hunter would ever consider her prey. Any man wishing to marry her would do so because of his regard for her, not for her money.

Finding the silver lining today, however, was proving somewhat more elusive. But, then again, hearing the words "Your sister has eloped" did tend to drown out all other thoughts in one's head.

Without the slightest twinge of guilt, she reached for yet another shortbread biscuit. It was her fourth of the morning, but with news of the elopement sending her mother into such a dither, Sophie's indulgence was the least of their worries. Taking full advantage of Mama's distraction, Sophie bit into the crisp treat, savoring the buttery goodness. It was absolutely divine. So good, it *almost* made up for the minor issue of Penelope ruining the family's good name by running off to Gretna Green with the estate manager's son.

Sophie sighed, still unable to believe her sister could have done such a thing. If the missive hadn't been written in Papa's own hand, Sophie could have easily believed the whole thing was a cruel joke.

One look at her mother confirmed that this was no laughing matter.

"What could she possibly have been thinking, Sophie?" Her mother paced past the sofa table for perhaps the hundredth time, her hands red from hours of wringing. Tearstains marked the pale skin of her cheeks, though thankfully the tears themselves had finally abated. "Does she hate us so very much? Does she think herself above the lot of us?"

Swoosh. Her emerald skirts billowed out behind her as she turned for another circuit of the tidy little drawing room. "The *ton* will have a field day with this. I'll never be able to show my face in polite society again. And you," she said, shaking her head with the quick, jerky movements of one who had consumed entirely too much tea. "You and Pippa will never find husbands now. Thank God Sarah is safely wed."

Sarah's marriage last month was the only reason Mama had allowed Sophie to travel to the first annual Summer Serenade in Somerset to begin with. So far, the music festival had been everything she had hoped it would be, filled with musicians and music lovers from the world over, and with so many events and activities, there had yet to be a dull day in the whole first month. It was absolute heaven.

Her mother had claimed the trip was a special treat during which Sophie could relax after such a whirlwind spring, but Sophie knew better. The festival had drawn many an eligible bachelor, and where there was an unmarried gentleman, there was opportunity for matchmaking.

Or at least there had been.

She took another bite, willing the goodness of the biscuit to overwhelm the dreadfulness of the morning. Numbness had settled deep in her chest. In a few weeks' time, when news of the elopement got out, she'd be a pariah. All the things that she had taken for granted these two years since her debut—the grand balls, the lavish dinners, the friendly waves during rides at Hyde Park—all of it would be gone.

As she swallowed, a new thought occurred to her. What about the musical trio she had formed only a month ago, but which by now was as dear to her as family? And what about the recitals she was supposed to have with Penelope next spring? Sophie had actually been looking forward to them—the recorder was so much more complementary to her oboe than Sarah's bassoon had ever been.

Taking a deep breath, Sophie pushed back against the fear that threatened to dislodge the numbness. This wasn't the end of the world. They'd figure something out—hopefully *before* life as she knew it ceased to exist. Hadn't she spent the last two years wishing that Mama would stop pushing so hard for her to make a match? She almost laughed. *Be careful what you wish for.*

Setting down the uneaten portion of shortbread, she wrapped her icy hands around her still-steaming teacup. "At least we have a bit of time before the news becomes

known. We might even be able to make it to the end of
the festival! Since there is nothing we can do to change
what Penelope has done—though hopefully Papa will
come up with something—I say we make the most of the
time we have." She offered up a helpless little grin. "Why
walk the plank when we can waltz it instead?"

Mama blinked once, twice, then not at all, staring at
her as though she'd quite lost her mind. Perhaps she had.
Why else would she suggest they carry on as though
their family hadn't just been shaken by what was sure to
be the scandal of the summer? It was fanciful thinking,
born of desperation.

Sophie stuffed the rest of the biscuit in her mouth and
flopped back against the sofa. What were they going to
do? They'd undoubtedly be packing for home before the
day was out. For the first time, a spark of anger pushed
past the shock. Why did Penelope have to do something
like this now, just when things were going so well? This
had been the best summer of Sophie's life so far, and she
wasn't ready to give it up yet.

Blast it all. She wished her friends were here with her.
May would know exactly what to do. She was bold and
fearless and unswayed by such insignificant trifles as scandal and rumor. And Charity would know exactly what to
say to calm the emotions building in Sophie's heart like
steam in a teapot.

But Charity was away for a funeral until next week,
and May's aunt had decreed that Sundays were strictly
for worship and reflection, so Sophie was well and truly
on her own until tomorrow at the earliest.

"You are right."

Sophie looked up, startled by Mama's pronouncement. "I am?" she said around a mouthful of biscuit. It
was not a sentiment she was used to hearing from her

mother, particularly when Sophie herself wasn't sure if she was right or simply delusional.

Nodding with impressive confidence, Mama swept her skirts aside and sat for the first time since receiving Papa's letter. "Indeed you are. I imagine we'll have two, perhaps three weeks before the gossips catch wind of the scandal. That is more than enough time, if one is committed."

She leaned forward and poured herself yet another cup of tea, as though the entire issue had suddenly been resolved. Sophie eyed her mother suspiciously. *Is this what hysteria looks like?* Calm, rational words said with overbright eyes and the nervous tapping of one's foot? Should she ring for a footman just in case Mama suffered a fit of vapors from the stress of it all?

Brushing the crumbs from her lap, Sophie tried to work out what exactly her mother meant. After a minute, she finally gave up and asked, "Committed to what, exactly?"

Mama held up her index finger as she took a long sip of her tea. Soft morning sunlight filtered through the pretty white sheers on the windows overlooking the street, lending a much cheerier atmosphere to the room than the subject warranted.

"We must carry on as we have been. Parties, recitals, dances—we shall attend as many as possible for the next two weeks."

So they weren't going home after all? They were merely postponing the inevitable. "To what end? Do we pretend that all is well, laugh, dance, eat, and be merry until the moment someone points in our direction and brands us outcasts? No, thank you."

The determination tightening her mother's mouth was unmistakable. "No, my little magpie, *I* shall laugh, dance, eat, and be merry. *You* shall laugh, dance, eat, and catch yourself a husband."

Choking on her shock, Sophie reached for her tea and nearly knocked it over before getting a proper grip and downing the contents of the cup. "A husband?" she gasped. "You can't possibly be serious! If I haven't caught a suitor's attention in two years, what on earth makes you think I could catch one in two weeks?"

Her mind spun. It was absurd in the extreme. She wanted a husband she could adore and who could adore her in return. She was even mad enough to hope for a love match, despite what the *ton* thought of such a thing. Finding such a man took time and, well, more *time*. She put a hand over her suddenly rioting stomach, heartily wishing she had stopped at biscuit number three.

Mama's eyes changed in an instant, narrowing on Sophie with utter seriousness and disconcerting intensity. "You haven't a choice, my dear. I don't care how you go about it; I don't care who you choose. But by the end of a fortnight, you *will* be betrothed." She stood, smoothed her skirts, and smiled. "Now, if you will excuse me, I need to write your father. Be ready in an hour, if you please. The husband hunt begins today. I do hope you have someone in mind."

Sophie watched in openmouthed shock as her mother swept from the room, a vision of efficient determination. For a moment, she couldn't breathe, couldn't even think. Oh, dear heavens, what had just happened? She couldn't possibly be expected to woo a man in a fortnight. She wasn't beautiful or alluring or the least bit captivating. Though she normally talked entirely too much, she hadn't even been able to say two words to the man she'd—

She sat bolt upright, her heart nearly leaping from her chest. *To the man I've secretly admired for the past two years.* Actually, *admired* was much too tame a word. *Adored* was more apt. A *tendre* to end all *tendres.*

She pressed trembling fingers to her mouth, her pulse pounding wildly in her ears. He was here for the festival. She'd seen him twice now, and both times she had made a ninny of herself, grinning like an idiot and stammering her greeting. He was kind and jovial and terribly handsome as always, but with her stomach doing somersaults, she had been keen to escape.

Drawing in a long, deep breath, she dropped her hands to her belly. Desperate times called for desperate measures.

It was time to woo the earl.